MOSAIC

Caro Ramsay

This first world edition published 2019
in Great Britain and the USA by
SEVERN HOUSE PUBLISHERS LTD of
Eardley House, 4 Uxbridge Street, London W8 7SY.
Trade paperback edition first published
in Great Britain and the USA 2020 by
SEVERN HOUSE PUBLISHERS LTD.

British Library Cataloguing in Publication Data
A CIP catalogue record for this title is available from the British Library.

ISBN-13: 978-0-7278-8892-1 (cased)
ISBN-13: 978-1-78029-617-3 (trade paper)
ISBN-13: 978-1-4483-0239-0 (e-book)

This is a work of fiction. Names, characters, places and incidents
are either the product of the author's imagination or are used fictitiously.
Except where actual historical events and characters are being described
for the storyline of this novel, all situations in this publication are
fictitious and any resemblance to actual persons, living or dead,
business establishments, events or locales is purely coincidental.

All Severn House titles are printed on acid-free paper.

Severn House Publishers support the Forest Stewardship Council™ [FSC™],
the leading international forest certification organisation.
All our titles that are printed on FSC certified paper carry the FSC logo.

Typeset by Palimpsest Book Production Ltd.,
Falkirk, Stirlingshire, Scotland.
Printed and bound in Great Britain by
TJ International, Padstow, Cornwall.

PROLOGUE
1994

Four pink candles.

Burning for me.

The cake is blue with two cream-coloured ponies standing in a field of peppermint icing, fenced by strands of black liquorice. The flickering candles peg the corners of the field, and there is a golden fondant dog burying a white chocolate bone. That will be Oodie.

Melissa lit the candles as she's eleven and allowed to use matches. We sit about for a while, on the big settee, my feet swinging in mid-air, kicking up the blue-and-white lace on the skirt of my birthday dress. Melissa looks at the cake while I scan the pile of presents, all wrapped up in pretty paper. I can see a box, tied in a red bow. It might contain a new riding hat but I'm still hoping for a puppy, a wee playmate for Oodie.

We sit in silence.

Melissa gets bored and leaves the room without a word, I hear her footsteps running up the stairs.

Oodie sighs as I pat her on the head, watching the first candle fizzle out, sending fine wisps of black smoke to twirl and twist in the cool air of the drawing room. I'm not usually allowed in here on my own.

Half an hour ago Mum and Dad had been bringing in presents; Papa came in with a handful of cards, now fanned out neatly on the arm of the sofa. The plates, forks, rolled napkins, cups are all set for my birthday tea.

I'm waiting.

But Mum, Dad and Papa have gone somewhere else, they rushed out the door as if there could be something more important than my birthday.

I climb off the settee and look out the bay window to see Papa hurrying down the long drive, going somewhere exciting. Oodie jumps up, her front paws on the window ledge. She isn't allowed in the drawing room either.

I slide off the chair, ready to follow Papa, but Oodie pauses, reminding me to blow the rest of the candles out. Collies are very sensible.

Then we both scamper into the hall and erupt out the front door onto the gravel. Papa is almost out of sight, nearly at the bottom of the garden. Oodie and I try hard to keep up with him but he's walking quickly. I guess where he's going. Our favourite place, the Benbrae, the pond where the *Curlew* was moored. Papa is planning a wee surprise for my birthday.

But Papa doesn't turn off the drive, he walks towards the woods, not the sunny bit round the Benbrae but the dark bit where the faerie pools are. I'm not allowed in there either.

I can't see Papa at all now but Oodie's sniffing the air. It doesn't seem fair that I'm standing in my garden on the day of my fourth birthday with only my dog for company.

I call out for Papa, as loud as I can. There's no reply except for my echo rolling back across the water. The ponds look warm and welcoming but I know they are full of deep, black, cold water. If I fell in, I would never get out.

With my hand on Oodie's hairy shoulder, I set off after Papa, down to the narrow dark path. We go slowly, so that Papa can't hear us and then I can jump out and shout '*boo*'.

It takes me a while to get to the faerie pool where I see Papa at the overhanging trees on the bank at the far side. He's putting a necklace on, then he takes a step out over the water.

He drops.

There is a thump. Papa dances on the end of the thrumming rope, arms and legs and head all going, then he winds down until it's just his feet twitching, like his batteries have run out.

I see a shadow in the trees. Somebody is giving Papa a little push, just to keep him dancing.

ONE
Monday
2019

Megan

I had learned early that it was better to drown in silence than to swim in a world of noise. Noise is nothing but a painful distraction from the truth.

Noise is abhorrent.

So I hated to walk out of my beautiful soundless world and into the hot city street and a riot of rabble. Retreating to the quiet was not an option, I was heading out on a journey that I didn't want to start.

The keys to the Merc were in my hand; they were a symbol of the advantages of being a Melvick; the money, the name, the house; here is a car to take you anywhere. And the disadvantage of being me; here is a car so you can always come home and do your duty.

There's no excuse, Megan.

Not now.

At the traffic lights, a couple of kids were screaming on the pavement, their red angry little mouths opening and closing, throats tightened. Mums were laughing, talking, scrolling on phones. Three teenagers were losing themselves in their head-phones, bouncing on anxious heels as they wait to cross the road. As I joined them, I felt the constant boom of the bass beat, knowing that the delicate tympanic membranes in their youthful ears will thicken and scar, a revenge kept for later life when all their conversations will become half-heard and half-imagined.

My car was parked across the road, the door opened immediately as I pressed the fob, waiting for the traffic lights to change colour. Then the crowd and I moved, we didn't touch, didn't collide, we smiled and sidestepped in unison.

Glasgow was still that kind of city.

I felt the traffic vibrate the hot air as I jogged across the road, cutting the diagonal to get to my car. A delivery man, driving up the inside, didn't see me and his van juddered to a halt. I smelled his brakes and felt his fury as his passenger rolled down his window and his mouth moved, eyes angry and narrow. Did he realize how stupid he looked as I lip-read the words 'fucking, pavement, stupid, bitches'.

Glasgow is that kind of city as well.

We were warming up for another day in the low eighties, the air already stale and fetid, stinking of sweat and alcohol as if the city had not breathed since the weekend's drunken revelries.

Maybe going home is a good thing.

Home.

Strange word for the place, the sound of it was foreign on my tongue.

I got in the car and slung my handbag onto the passenger seat that had never seen a passenger, the laptop and my small travel bag on the floor.

The Merc was a birthday present. A gift the day I left the Benbrae Estate.

My dad thought the car was fitting only because he had already bought one for Melissa the day she left to go to university. It was the *right thing to do*.

The fact that I didn't want it, or need it, was neither here nor there.

My dad, Ivan Melvick, the Lord Lieutenant of the County, is like that.

By the time the ferry docked at Hunter's Quay, I was already queasy. The crossing from McEnroe's Point is only twenty minutes. It's a journey I have endured many times but never without that creeping uneasiness as the ground moved under my feet.

Usually, I sat in the coffee bar, concentrating on the horizon, ignoring the holidaymakers in their bright summer clothes, wrestling with wheeled cases and overexcited children. I kept them on the periphery of my vision, mindful of any sudden change in their behaviour, paranoid of an emergency siren that I won't hear. I glanced at the emergency exit. Closed. No flashing lights. Nobody was hurrying.

When they do move, there is a synchronized choreography to it; phones swiped off, newspapers folded, computer games ceased, tablets folded away, everybody rises leaving paper cups and crumpled napkins littering the tables.

Out on deck, the glare of the sun was matched by the ferocity of the chilling wind that raced in from the North Sea. From the top of the stairs, I could see the opening to the Holy Loch, the wide arm of water that ran northwards from the Clyde estuary to peter out onto an ever-changing beach near Kilmun and above that, the narrows that connected to the Benbrae and the faerie pools beyond; the boundary of the Benbrae Estate.

Home.

In the distance, I could see the light-green patchwork of the trees round the Benbrae, the darker fringe of the Tentor Wood beyond, the folly of the Water Tower on the hill. They had belonged to my family for five hundred years and some things never change.

Like I know the rooks, as always, are circling high in the sky, drifting and watching.

Waiting.

For me?

I can't see them but I know they are in there somewhere.

They are as unwelcome as my memories.

It took twenty minutes to drive from the ferry slipway to the intricate wrought-iron gate at the bottom of the Long Drive. My favourite part of the journey was always the sweep round the top of the Holy Loch and then over the narrow humpback bridge; here was the real sense of being home. Then a right turn skirting the waterside again before heading slightly inland. I'm sure the road, and the view, looks the same to me as it looked when horses carried my ancestors up to the grand gates.

I always slow slightly at this stretch of road, it's common for cars to U-turn here, pulling out from the innocuous looking lay-by with its neat recycling bin and small friendly sign indicating the pathway to the osprey viewing site. I am cognizant of that, but

much more of the fact that this was also where my mother decided
to leave us, driving off into the sunset with some secret lover.
My heart still misses a painful beat.

It's been three years. I left soon after her and haven't been
home much since; it's too painful. Every time I pass this point
I go back to the child I was, a wee girl, one hand on Oodie's
collar, my other hand safe in my mother's grasp, waiting to cross
the road.

Mum needs to come back now. I have no idea what I will say
to her, never mind what words will pass between my parents.

As I passed the lay-by, I saw a red Ford Fiesta parked, a young
man in his shirt sleeves, leaning on the roof, casually looking at
a map, or maybe checking what the sightings of the golden eagles
are today. His right arm was holding a mobile to his ear. His
strawberry blond hair glinted in the sunshine. I slow down as I
passed him, thinking that the phone signal must have been boosted
since my last visit. He raised his left arm when he saw me and
I felt that discomfort of stranger's eyes meeting mine, and holding
for a moment too long, questioning.

I return his wave. He knows me.

But then, everybody does.

The gates had been opened, especially for me, like the maw of
a snare trap, the key pad on its metal post stands idle, its sensor
unblinking. The land is protected now, not because of us, but
because of the eagles.

Many sensations floated through my body, through my mind,
but being welcomed was not one of them. It's more like walking
into jail to start a life sentence, although I'd never have to worry
about a roof over my head or what I am going to cook for my
tea. I might never have to think for myself ever again.

I drove the Merc in and then pulled over onto the lawn, rock
hard after six weeks of constant sunshine. The car would now
be visible to anybody watching from the house. To stay out of
sight I needed to be in the Tentor Wood behind the ten-feet-high
boundary wall, or down at the Benbrae, the beautiful pond created
by a skilful gardener and the roll of the landscape. The dip and
rise in the land had concealed many a mischief of the Melvick
family over the years. I bet Dad was upstairs at the paladin

window right now with his photographs and memories, pretending that he's not watching and waiting for me. That window was my favourite place in the house too, up on the first floor, the wide arc of glass that showcased the magnificent view. Many a picnic we had there as kids, Melissa and I, Mum and the dogs, sandwiches and lemonade on rainy summer days. Those reminiscences were now ruined, overwritten by the nightmare memory of Melissa and Jago speeding off in their Jag, the carousel at a standstill, the police cars strobing their lights over the water. I can still feel the throbbing of that helicopter landing close by.

Life spins like a carousel, moving on a spindle.

Like the rooks, still circling in the sky.

I got out the car to take a minute to myself, drinking in this view, this peaceful view. The still, deep water of the Benbrae pool, the weeping willows brushing their leaves on the surface, the small copse of trees that bordered the water on the far side before they merged into the darker, ancient trees of the Tentor Wood. The small path, Melissa's path, was overgrown and dry now. That seemed apposite.

A few steps up the rise of the lawn and the best view of the Italian House revealed itself to the eye. The building was stunningly beautiful, the weathered grey stone outlined against the backdrop of the brilliant azure sky. It was a work of incredible symmetry; the elegance of the first-floor balconies, the low wall around the ground floor, the two grass terraces below that and then the long stretch of verdant grass that ran towards me, and beyond to the banks of the Benbrae. Everything from this spot drew the eye upwards to the majesty of the house and that huge paladin window. It always took the breath away, designed to do exactly that by one of the lesser known Glasgow School architects. He had made an excellent job of it.

It's easy to forget the huge heating bills, the porous roof and the ever-present smell of damp.

One day, those bills and that roof, would be all mine.

Then I saw the boathouse, rebuilt and pristine, baskets of flowers swinging on the wall, the hooks neatly resting on their cradles. *Curlew 2* will be tied up at her pontoon, like her predecessor had been for a hundred years, like the ancestry of the cappuccino-coloured ponies pulling at the grass in the home field.

Deceitful memories of my youth came flooding back, portraying an idyllic childhood in this paradise; dragging the canvas trolley out the boathouse loaded with rugs, books, dogs and sandwiches. Heading off for a picnic, Oodie stealing the biscuits, swimming in the Benbrae, sunny, walking the ponies through the water, long, long balmy days when summers lasted forever.

I thought things would not change; kids don't. I expected permanence in my life; Dad, Mum, Melissa and Carla, but it looks like I was wrong on three counts, and hope for the fourth was fading. We still have the ponies, the dogs and the *Curlew*. They were here long before I was born and no doubt will be here long after I have died. The dogs are buried in the orchard in childish graves with painted stone cairns. Martha, Fern, and my own Oodie, the collie who ate my birthday cake the day Papa passed away. All my memories were trapped down here, like the leaves that tumble with the wind, trying to get free but inevitably getting caught, stuck at the bottom of the wall. They were as ensnared as my family were.

The *Curlew 2* sat low in the water, her varnished mahogany prow sticking beyond the end of the pontoon, her brass rowlocks glinting like she's winking at me. The water level has dropped since I was here last, no doubt an effect of the hot weather which has dried the earth and burned the grass.

I filled my lungs with the silence, taking time to settle myself, standing at the side of the water, watching the gurgle and slap of tiny waves against the bank. Timeless, comforting sights.

Running my eye along the north bank, I couldn't quite see the brightly coloured tiles of the sunflower mosaic, a memorial to friendship that lasted a lifetime; a short life, though. I can close my eyes and see Carla's elfin face, laughing, mischievous. She was always up to something.

This was a house of many beautiful views. Weird that none of them are happy.

Despite the heat, I felt the breath of a chill on my neck. The beauty of the Benbrae pond was always darkened by the danger of the faerie pools beyond. Were they called that when I was young? I don't think so. They were forbidden territory for Melissa and me after I nearly drowned in one when I was wee, but I can't recall it. The thick trees there were borne from Tolkien fantasy, as dark and dense as Mirkwood, isolated from the house and the road. It's very grown over now but I knew the faerie pools were still there. There used to be three of them, who knows how many there might be now. They appeared overnight as if by magic, hence the name but like much that was magical, the reality was mundane. They were merely the signs of tidal water eroding the subterranean soil. I preferred the faeries explanation, dark faeries who lurked in the flowers and the deep dank grass where no sunshine penetrated to warm their cold hearts, they waited there to drag children and adulterous wives into the murky depths. The police searched the pools after my mother disappeared, in case she had come to harm. Maybe while looking for a runaway dog, she had come across a pool sooner than she thought and tumbled in. They are impossible to climb out of, the banks roll in over the water, underwater branches and roots of surrounding trees catch on struggling feet, or strike the skull on the way down.

It wasn't true. Everybody knew that my mum, Beth, had left us for a man.

Just like that.

This place hasn't changed, not really. The grass was a little longer, the trees were bigger, the wood denser, allowed to grow as it wanted after Tom McEwan went to jail. How long would that be now? Four years? His actual incarceration would be short; I have no doubt that he would be a model prisoner. The prison garden would have impeccable lawns and well-trimmed trees.

My memory caught and stopped.

It's remarkable how easily the eye picks up the familiar figure of a loved one. I could see Dad leaning against the bonnet of his Land Rover, his hand raised, cupping his eyes from the glare of the sun. He was looking for me, scanning the land at the bottom of the drive. Then he waved, and jogged towards me, maybe not something a man of his age should do. It's a long way. And then the dogs were running down the drive to greet me. Molly, the retriever, was a golden, galloping streak. Mo and Midge, the two Russells yapping and tumbling behind her, stopping every few yards to take a snap at each other.

I waved back at him, slipping my hearing aids in before dropping to my knees to hug the dogs, readying myself to go through the routine of being the perfect daughter. Then Dad's arms were outstretched, lifting me and swinging me round, the dogs jumping and barking. I laughed and warned Dad to watch his back. He held my face in his hands and kissed me on the forehead in a rare show of emotion.

'Megan, it's so good to see you.'

I smiled at him. Every time I come home he's older, slightly leaner, his once sable hair is greyer and longer but his eyes were still the blue of the Caspian Sea and his smile as wide as the moon. He's a very handsome man. Melissa inherited her looks from him and is, was, a very beautiful woman. I took after my mother, kind-faced and pretty, so I have been told, but never beautiful, not in the heart-stopping way Melissa was.

The way Melissa used to be.

'Have you heard from Mum?'

I truly expected him to say yes but he shook his head. 'Not a word, Megan. Not a single word.'

Trying not to meet his eyes my line of vision drifted past my father, up to the house, to the far window upstairs on the left, where the curtains were closed. My sister was in there, dying.

Then I saw the other woman striding purposefully down the long drive.

Well, well, well.

So it wasn't only the rooks that were circling.

Carla

I can hardly wait for Megan to come back. After a year of speculation, there are rumours that it might be this week. That it might even be today.

It has been three years since Beth walked out, and then Megan, for her seventeenth, got her Mercedes. She doesn't think she's coming back for me, she thinks it's for Melissa.

All this homecoming is for Melissa.

That's what they think.

I think – I know – different.

I knew it when I saw the rooks swooping high above the Tentor Wood, squawking and cawing. They have been flying around the bay for the past few weeks, then the Benbrae, in the last few days and this morning they are right up at the house, black-winged demons. Soon they will be flying into the house, smashing their brains, smearing leaded glass with blood. I wonder if they know, if they can sense death and are preparing for what may come their way. There's talk Ivan will be out with the shotgun before the end of the week.

Their presence reminds me of Melissa's wedding day. The sun was very bright that morning too. Ivan Melvick said the rooks flew into the windows at this time of year, when the sun's rays hit the old window panes at a certain angle, and the rooks, stupid buggers, were attracted by the glint and the flare. On the morning of the wedding they battered into the paladin window, covering it with bloodied smears and black feathers. We'd be plunged into darkness for an instant with a sickening dull thud, and Megan thought they had died, bursting their brains, but rooks, like the upper classes, have very hard skulls. They bounced off, leaving us looking at a raspberry ripple sky.

That day my dad was in the middle of the Long Drive with a clipboard, overseeing the parking of two transporters, directing catering vans and the odd guest that was parking up at the house. He was an important man on the day Melissa, or Princess Frosty Pants, got married.

Today it's Megan's dad who has top billing. He has been pacing about downstairs, scared to go out and welcome his daughter back to the family home. When Megan sees Heather I think she'll realize how often Ivan has been mentioning her mum's best friend on the phone. Heather Kincaid is a bloodsucking, gold-digging little tick. With Beth gone, Ivan is now up for grabs and the bold Heather is right in there. I almost feel sorry for him.

Megan will pick up on that, she's sharp where her beloved daddy is concerned. My mum is keeping out the way, knowing her place as the hired help and all that. She'll be in the kitchen making tea and providing sandwiches, preparing to pick up the pieces once the prodigal one has passed away.

I've never liked Melissa.

And she's always hated me.

Strange how things pan out. I am scared that they will pull

Megan apart now she's back, just as they destroyed Melissa, just as they drove Beth away.

Megan is delicate and she'll not come to harm, not while I am here.

Over my dead body.

I have the same memories of the wedding day as Megan.

I remember the carousel starting up, slowly at first, with Jago and Melissa, the newlyweds, both on the same horse. The barrel organ music rolled out down the Long Drive, discordant in the night sky. It rolled over the water as the spinning rhythm wound up and the starey-eyed horses flashed past, their coloured lights dappling and dancing on the Benbrae. Then the carousel slowed, becoming more definite in form, horses and the bride and groom, those sweeping, magical lights changed to single bulbs covered in cheap plastic.

We all climbed on for the photographs, a battery of mobile phones. Melissa and Jago stayed on board, Beth and Ivan, Beth holding the reins properly. Megan and I hitched up our skirts and we posed on top of our mounted steeds, their painted bright eyes wide and red mouths open like they were out their faces on cocaine. Round and round we went, holding onto the poles with one hand and letting the wind whip through our hair; the flowers went flying through the air, the music ground on and on. The lights sprinkled over the land, brightly coloured, reds and blues and green, all flashing through the darkening air. Once it slowed, the guests lined up, ready for their turn. I had necked a few vodkas by then and I fell off, I lay on the ground and waited for my guts to stop churning and my head to stop hurting. I don't think anybody noticed.

Then I should have gone off looking for Megan as she hates fireworks but I didn't find her. She'd come to the Curlew *as soon as she had escaped from whichever boring relative had pinholed her. I had been stockpiling a few bottles for our own private party later. The Italian House would probably be open all night so nobody would care if Megan was there or not.*

I had planned a beautiful end to a beautiful day, out on the Curlew. *She was at the bank, bobbing, there was nobody else on the water, everybody was drinking around the carousel, waiting for their ride. The oldies were climbing aboard, getting legs up onto the horses, some of them sitting side saddle. Those old posh biddies were probably on a horse before they could walk. But the carousel was a social leveller, the duchess and barmaid, side by side, laughing. Minutes passed, the music went on and on, I was out on the* Curlew, *close to the bank, drinking my vodka, waiting. I remember feeling warm and cosy when the first firework rocketed into the sky, bursting again and again, flowering sparks of colour all over the heavens.*

Then the explosion happened.

TWO

Megan

All I ever wanted was a life filled with a million happy days. I would live out on the Benbrae, floating in the *Curlew*, my fingers turning blue in the cold water. It didn't even need to be summer, Carla and I could giggle at anything and our laughter would have kept us warm. As long as we were together, we were happy.

That was my vision of the life I wanted.

Instead, my life so far was best described as adequate, although it looked like it was going to take a turn for the worse.

The small figure dressed in black trousers topped by the bob of auburn hair bouncing on her head was engaging in a pincer manoeuvre. I noticed how puffy her eyes were, tears already spent. Her triangular face was grim with concentration as she strode down the Long Drive, struggling in high heels, her elbows pumping to give her short legs more momentum. Heather the Blether. My mum's best friend.

I took my father's hand, squeezed it. This was supposed to be a family moment. Heather Kincaid was not, and never would be, a Melvick.

'Are you OK?' he asked, which was Father Speak for 'you don't mind, do you?'.

Bar the odd quick visit, it was me who had not been home for the last three years, who was I to criticize him for the company he kept? But this woman, waving at me, smiling as she stuck her nose in, well, she was betraying my mother.

Nature abhors a vacuum, and now that Mum was off the scene, here was Heather, an heir apparent, no longer content to wait. My mind cast back to the phone calls of the last few months, Dad peppering Heather's name into the conversation. Here she was looking thinner, younger, dressed in linen casual chic and her hair cut into a soft, modern bob.

For my dad's benefit?

I shouldn't comment. I left Dad just as much as Mum had, as Melissa will in her turn. Again it struck me, looking up at the Italian House with the welcoming paladin window and the carvings on the balustrade, that it will be all mine one day, soon.

Dad had commissioned the rebuilding of the boathouse after the explosion, no doubt for future generations, although grand-children were now looking a rather remote possibility. He needed to believe that we were not the end of the Melvick family and I felt the doors of the Italian House closing on me on my twenty-first birthday. The day of my inheritance.

Then I will be trapped like the rest of them.

Heather got busy, she adored helping and being needed. She offered to drive my car up to the house, leaving Dad and I to walk up the Long Drive with the dogs. It was thoughtful offer, I wanted to enjoy the house and drink in the view as I walked, hand in hand with Dad. The Italian House never changes. The land has been in the family for over five hundred years, and this house, or variations of it, have stood on that site for 150 of them. It was carefully designed to take advantage of the view over the Holy Loch, with huge French windows from every room on the upper floor that opened onto a long veranda. My bedroom was up there, on the east side of the house above the front portico. It was three years since I had last slept here but I knew nothing would have changed. My sister is dying. We all ride the carousel of life and death but this house is a constant. All the good things in life have to be balanced with the bad. We Melvicks knew that, as a family we had a worse curse than the Kennedys.

I stood in the reception hall, a guest in my own home, looking up to the huge portrait of Agatha Emmaline Melvick staring down at me as if she had uttered the words, 'Where have you been, my dear?'. I was making the usual chit-chat with Dad about being well and the weather. At the bottom of the stairs, before the first turn, was the copy of the Munnings oil, *The White Horse*. The original, probably my dad's most treasured possession, was safe in his study in its protected case. If this all panned out the way it seemed to be going, I would be moving one rung up the ladder of inheritance. Melissa and I joked that we would never be as close to Dad's heart as the Munnings was. That and the Hornell we had in the dining room, the *Three Shell Seekers*. It was a picture of three girls, very typical of the artist's work, rosy-cheeked and round-faced, smiling girls, dancing. Dad thought two of them looked like Melissa and I and as a kid, I used to wonder who the third one was. If there was some dark secret that Dad hadn't told me, a third half-sibling somewhere. If there was, I hoped she had the good sense to keep away. Then, on the day I was lying on the pavement, bleeding and helpless, Carla came to save me. I felt the question of the third girl had been answered.

We were complete.

For a while.

As I looked upstairs, checking the house was all as it should be, I saw Deborah waiting behind the door like the hired help waiting to be summoned. We exchanged glances. If I was surprised that she was here, I hope I didn't show it. I sensed that she was asking me not to say anything, like she had crept into the house without anybody noticing.

'Megan?' She addressed me directly, rather formally. 'I've got your old bedroom ready. Is that OK?'

'Of course it will be,' said Dad. 'Megan's just happy to be home, aren't you?'

'Thanks,' I said, aware of the uneasiness of manners between the three of us standing at the bottom of the stairs, in this house of twenty rooms. A shadow fell over the floor, a clatter of heels broke the silence, heralding Heather's arrival from the kitchen.

'Deborah, can you take Megan's bags up for her?' suggested Heather, 'and put the keys on the rack so they don't get lost.' She had my car keys dangling from her forefinger on an outstretched arm, commanding the space in the way that only very short people can do. She then proceeded to usher the dogs out the front door, wafting the scent of Pomegranate Noir around the hall.

'She doesn't like the dogs in the house,' explained Dad, managing to look sheepish.

Then I noticed Debs had her hand out, ready to take my bag from me.

'No, I can manage,' I said. 'Honestly.' Few things are more embarrassing that your dad's girlfriend ordering your friend's mum around like a servant.

'Oh well, you're much younger than me, Megan, so fill your boots.' Debs was her usual unflappable cheery self as she turned towards me. 'I've opened the windows in your room but if it's too drafty be careful closing the top window. The hinges are very stiff.' With a nod she walked off back to the kitchen, her Ugg boots scuffling on the timber floor, muttering something I didn't catch but it probably involved putting the kettle on. For Debs, tea was a remedy for everything. A faint scent of nicotine drifted along behind her, sparking happy memories of Carla.

'Megan, would you like to see your sister now,' Dad said, his voice trailing off, not willing to say, 'before she slips away'.

My room was exactly as it had been. I sensed that the bed was freshly made, the glass on the photographs newly polished. Me at five years of age with Oodie. Dad and Papa at the pontoon, both in sailor's hats. Me, Melissa, Mum and Dad on the sofa downstairs with Anastasia, the Boston Terrier, as a pup, so that would have been taken just before Mum left. And one of the carousel pictures of Melissa's wedding, Carla and I flying round, our arms outstretched, not holding on, screaming with laughter. We were so secure in the certainty of our youth. We thought we had it all ahead of us. Now we were all back where we started. I unpacked my laptop, my books and candles, put a few clothes in a drawer and then had a very quick shower to remove the grime of the Glasgow streets, and any infection I might be carrying. I dressed in jeans and a T-shirt, and left my room to tread the squeaky floorboards of the corridor that ran the length of the upstairs of our home.

At the top of the stairway, the paladin window rose in a great arch from the floor on one side to the apex of the roof and then back again. Beneath it was a wingback chair and the old mariner desk covered with more family photographs. Pride of place was one of Mum, sitting on the sofa in her favourite spot with me and Melissa, Dad is perched on the end. Martha the yellow lab has pride of place. We are all laughing, especially the dog. I love that picture. It's the one I have on my own desk at work.

It's bittersweet, there are five beating hearts in that one picture, and by the end of today we could be down to three.

Maybe two.

Mum had taken one, of Melissa and I, with her when she left. The frame was still empty, as a reminder.

No curtains fettered the view. It was everybody's favourite part of the house; from here I could look right down the Long Drive to the Benbrae and to the woods beyond. Here you could look Agatha Emmaline straight in the eye. She was telling me to get on with what I was here for.

I felt the soft carpet runner beneath my feet as I paused at Dad's bedroom door, curious to see if it had changed in three years. I opened it, quietly. The bed didn't look slept in, the room didn't seem lived in. No scent of the shower being used or clothes in the basket, just rows of neat cushions where the pillows should be. My dad would have piled them up at the bottom of the bed. So he was sleeping elsewhere. With Heather? There were not many people Dad would let order the dogs around.

I wondered where Mum was. Downstairs Dad was waiting for her to come back. And she needed to be quick if she wanted to say goodbye to her eldest daughter.

The tension of that was almost unbearable, the idea that it's now or never.

I shook that thought from my mind, waiting a minute or two before I pushed the handle to Melissa's bedroom; the catch had been tightened and oiled so it was as deathly silent as the rest of the house. Inside the room was warm and dark but it smelled fresh. The curtains were closed over the open windows, giving the drapes an eerie undulation, wafting and waning on a breeze I couldn't feel.

Melissa was lying on the bed. What was left of her.

Her dog, Anastasia, the Boston terrier, was curled in a little black ball at the bottom of the bed, between Fred Bear and Winnie The Pooh. Her ears pricked as I slid in, but she didn't move. Dogs sense death very acutely.

Melissa did not react. Her room, like mine, had been frozen in time; pale yellow roses and antique cream lace, white cotton and cream rugs on the warm parquet floor. A white embroidered sheet was neatly folded over the bottom of the wrought iron frame. In the fireplace was an arrangement of fresh white flowers and greenery.

All very Melissa, flittery and feminine.

Except for the corner behind the door, where the Victorian washstand used to be, adorned with some porcelain figurines of Greek goddesses. That was her kind of thing. Now there was a lifting device, a commode, a machine with a screen surrounded by switches all parked neatly. They had been removed from her body at midnight according to Dad in his text earlier. He said the removal of the oxygen mask had been at dawn, witnessed by Dad and the doctor. And the doctor had then left, allowing nature to take its course. Whatever was keeping Melissa alive was running out. I had called Dad back with my hearing aids in, he had asked me to come home, his voice breaking, telling me the times of the ferries, no time to drive the long way round, get here now, or don't bother. Not that he said that, but having given so many excuses over the last three years, he was leaving me with no choice.

The Italian House had a habit of pulling back those that had been born there, driving them to insanity, or suicide by inherited melancholy.

And here we all were. Listening to the silence of history repeating itself.

It seems a heartless thought, but when on the phone that morning, I had looked at my desk, my work colleagues staring at their screens as I listened to him. Despite his pleas, his obvious desperation, I waited, thinking, was this really it? Or was it another act from the drama queen? Was Dad trying to lure me back to the house, the Benbrae and happier times?

I had no doubts now. The machines lay redundant, her life slipping away by increments, like the ever-slowing ticking of an anniversary clock.

On the bed, she was a stick-thin figure, covered to the chin by a duvet, her body impervious to the heat of the room. From the look of her, she might have passed already, except for the faint flicker of a translucent eyelid. Round her neck, lying flat on the nacreous flesh throat was the family heirloom, a necklace with silver unicorn and lion intertwined. I reached out and repositioned it, in case the chain was annoying her, then pulling up the quilted chair, I sat at the side of the bed, watching her. She's like a delicate rose wilting in a drought. Something so pretty, disintegrating. Her dark hair looked like dried seaweed spread on white sand, her eyes were closed. Her face unrecognizable, narrow, pinched, the cheekbones that had wowed audiences as Cleopatra were now knife-blade sharp, a couple of white cliffs falling into the dark hollows of her cheeks. For her final act she was wearing a chiaroscuro mask.

I placed the back of my hand on the skin of her face and was rewarded with a flicker of a smile. I was content to hold her hand, she knew I was here.

My eyes drifted along the mantelpiece. A photograph of Jago and Melissa on their wedding day, an award for her portrayal of Ophelia, a pair of antique statues, a gold anniversary clock spinning, and another version of the carousel photograph. Mum and Dad were in this one, standing. Melissa and Jago are on a horse. I'm standing at the back, there is no Carla. Her absence makes it bittersweet. We were so happy in that moment, with no idea the disaster that was going to befall us in the next few hours.

If Carla was here, now, what would she make of this? Me watching my sister, measuring time by her slow, shallow breathing, seeing her skin drift from pink and warm, to blue and chilled, then purple and cold?

Carla would see something funny in it, she always pricked at Melissa's pretension.

I sat there for hours. Debs came in with a coffee and a cheese sandwich for me at five o'clock, gave me a hug and left. Heather appeared and sat with me for a while, Dad joined us for a few short conversations, before they both left me alone to say my own goodbyes. At one point, maybe in the early evening, Melissa's cold, blue fingers crawled over the surface of the daffodil duvet towards mine, little more than cold clammy sticks covered in human flesh, her nails merely purple picks on the end.

Her lips pulled and contorted, trying to form a word. I checked my hearing aid, leaning forward to catch it. She breathed out, the sound formed on her lips and would have died there if I had not been able to lip-read.

'Megs?'

I recognized that.

I leaned down, my mouth close to her ear. 'Yes, it's Megan.'
I looked again at her lips, they struggled to move.

Watching carefully, I thought they were going to form a smile, ask for Jago, maybe ask for Dad or Mum. Or say goodbye.

None of these things. A five letter word, a soft word, formed by a pliant tongue, leaving the roof of her mouth, her lips kissing it to life.

I saw it.

There was a change after that, a subtle relaxation of tension.

Her eyes sank back into her head, her eyelids stopped flickering. I looked at the clock, half past seven. I sat beside her, numb. There was a slight reaction, a twitch of her mouth when Deborah knocked quietly on the door just after eleven, and came in, offering me another cup of tea. She hesitated a moment, looking at Melissa, fighting back the tears, then retreated back out the door.

Ten minutes later, Dad came in, carrying a malt. There was no reaction from Melissa at all. He cleared his throat, trying to be brave as he closed the door behind him. He stood at the bottom of the bed, straight backed and strong, no doubt wondering why his child was dying before him. There is something erroneous about that in the scheme of nature.

If he said anything, I didn't catch it. When I glanced round to see him, his eyes were not on Melissa or on me, but they were looking around. Was he recalling the day Melissa was born, in this very room, twenty-eight years before? Fred Bear and Winnie The Pooh have been here since then with the odd trip to the nursery and the laundry.

Melissa's eyelids had not flickered since that one slight blink at the back of nine. I did check, placing my clumsy little thumbs on the translucent skin and gently peeling it back only to see and reveal opal white, her eyes had rolled upwards looking to heaven, her destination if there is any justice in the world.

By midnight, I knew, sensed, that the real Melissa had gone, the process of decay that had started five, six years ago had destroyed the previous twenty-two of wonderment. It had finally come to a close, and how can that be? Do we both have a different expression of the same condition? The same curse more like. There is something malevolent in this house.

The Melvick curse.

Melissa had lost her beauty now. The face of Ophelia lying in the water surrounded by flowers, plus her rosemary for remembrance was gone. She had been a passionate, bitter Ophelia that audiences had applauded, an empowered Ophelia as some feminist wrote in a cheap paper. Melissa had hated that review.

The actress had gone. Her final curtain call.

Suddenly I was aware Dad was looking at me, having said something I had missed.

'Has she gone?'

'I think so.'

We sat for another twenty minutes gazing at her.

Dad stood up and walked round the bed to stand behind me, tapping me on the shoulder so I'd look at him.

'Did she say anything?' He leaned forward, gently pulling the chain from her neck, easing the catch to the front and opening it.

'She said my name,' I said, as he lifted the necklace and turned away.

He nodded as if this was the way it should have been. 'Nothing else?'

I turned my head back to look at her face, as still as marble. Dad had expected her to say something. 'No,' I lied.

Her last word on this earth, spoken with such intense effort to ensure clarity?

Sorry.

Carla

It's sad when somebody dies but it was only Melissa and she was a pain in the bum. We didn't call her Princess Frosty Pants for nothing.

I had known of them, Melissa and Megan, Mel and Megs, all my life, of course. We called them M and M, because they were both nuts. Growing up, Melissa was an ethereal creature of great beauty who had been on the telly. Gran said Melissa had been a corpse on Midsummer Murders *and had been 'quite good'. I guess that is ironic, she's playing that part for real now.*

Everything was about Melissa though. My dad, who worked up at the Italian House, had to tell me that Melissa was not the only daughter. There was a younger one, Megan, who was my age and perfect and not an 'ungrateful little shit' like me. Megan Melvick didn't answer back, didn't steal money and didn't bite people.

If I had lived with Dad all the time, rather than only when Mum was in the pokey, I would have got a chance to know both the Melvick girls because of Dad's job. He said he actually spoke to Ivan Melvick sometimes, like the guy was God.

The family were loaded though.

Where did it get them, all that money? I might have been the result of a good curry and a fumble in Morrison's car park but from humble beginnings great things can happen. The mighty have fallen further as my gran would say. The Melvicks were a case in point, they had a daughter who couldn't manage the simple act of eating, yet they have a protective glass panel on a painting to save it from air pollution. So work that out. And it was a picture of a horse. Just a horse. And not even a very convincing horse, his head was too long and the neck too bendy, his eyes were too high up. I could do better.

And even weirder, in the home field of the Italian House were pedigree Highland ponies all with normal heads and necks, both eyes in the right place. So the dad, Ivan, likes pictures of horses more than horses whereas the mum, Beth, liked her horses more than her she liked her kids, Mel and Megs.

So I considered myself lucky that I had my mum's drunken attention and a dad who always kept an eye out for me. Even Gran felt moved to give me a slap with the back of her hand in an attempt to keep me on the straight and narrow. We might be a dysfunctional family but at least my parents knew my name, unlike up at the Italian House where the nannies were employed to look after the dogs and the girls just tagged along.

Or did I make that up.

So the Melvicks were always on my radar. Looking back, it seemed there was something predetermined about it all but maybe that's just so those involved can ease their guilt.

In the summer, when I had run away from Mum after a fight in the pub, I was back up north and, in an attempt to appease

Gran, Dad got me a paper round. I had to walk from the far side of Kilaird back through Kilmun. After a week of a Land Rover driving past me at the same point in the road after Kilmun, I, being clever, decided to start a little earlier. Dad was pleased that I was keen, thinking that I was proud to be earning some money for myself, but I was early so that Ivan Melvick would be driving away from the Italian House just as I was walking that long stretch of the road where the lay-by was. I knew he'd stop and give me a lift as far as Sandbank and I'd deliver the papers on the way back.

I loved sitting in that car, high off the road, pretending I was his third daughter. I fantasized about having a car like his, with automatic gears and leather seats that didn't smell of dog shit.

Dad found out of course and went ballistic. He said I had to stop taking advantage of his boss's good nature in case it affected his job. Mum said I was to say that Ivan Melvick touched me and we'd do him for money. But I knew Ivan Melvick was a true gentleman. And there was a long game to be played here. I could sense that. I asked Ivan about the golden eagles, the powan and the otters. He explained things to me, like how the powan were rare and he was breeding them in the pond in the garden. I looked things up and came back with more questions. He was impressed.

Gran took me to church and I remember the three Melvicks all had something to say as they came out from the service; a hello and goodbye and chat about the weather and whatever, the way that posh folk can afford to do, they had that easy confidence. Ivan spoke to me and shook me by the hand, asking me how the paper round was going. I asked him about the powan.

I say three, Ivan, Beth and Melissa, but I mean four. Megan was invisible amongst them, if she wasn't as rich as she was, she would have got bullied rotten. Maybe I shouldn't say that, given what happened later.

Both girls were barking mad. Maybe Melissa's problem was that she was so startlingly beautiful, much more so than Megan. Melissa was tall, willowy, slim, raven-haired and with ivory silken skin.

Gran had told me that they once wanted to make Melissa the Queen of the Kilmun and Kilaird fete, even though that would be important for who exactly? About eight hundred people? The Melvick family politely declined quoting a fear of favouritism as the fete was held in the Tentor field of the Italian House but in reality the Melvicks thought the lovely Melissa should never steep so low. In the end the fete queen was Fatty Sally McGuire, a spotty girl who worked in the Greggs in Dunoon. Sally had two great loves in her life: the pies in Greggs and the cakes in Greggs.

The queen was supposed to arrive on the back of a pony, provided by the Melvicks of course, a small white pretty thing called Marple. I don't think the pony that carried Fatty McGuire ever recovered. Afterwards Beth took it away for a good feed. Maybe she should have tried a bit of that with Melissa.

Gran knew a lot of the goss. Melissa was studying business with languages and then, on a trip to Paris, she started doing a little modelling. That led to her giving up her course and trans-ferring to acting. Her love affair with Paris and a hedge fund manager Jago Harrington Hyphenated, all started from there. She got the part of Ophelia in some small production and smashed it, then the part of Cleopatra and with her looks, and the fact she was really bossy, I guess that was the part she was born to play. She loved all that Shakespearean stuff, all that strutting, dying and talking to yourself.

She was not impressed when she was wittering on about Dame Eileen Atkins and Caesar, and all I could think of was Carry On Cleo *and the 'Infamy, Infamy' joke. Weirdly, Megan gave me one of her quizzical looks. Nobody ever told her jokes, nobody. Imagine living in a world where you have never pissed yourself laughing at a Carry On film because you can't hear it.*

So Melissa's trajectory was very much on the up. After a couple of years of modelling in very posh magazines with shiny pages, her academic stuff was forgotten, much to her dad's disappointment. The bright lights of London and Jago were a permanent fixture by then, and Jago had money.

But was it the fact that her career relied so much on appear-ance that made her start to unravel? I can be excused for not noticing as I was not around much and I always thought Melissa should get a grip on herself.

However after her wedding, the radiant Melissa slowly faded

*in front of the eyes of the Melvick family and once that train had
left the station, there was no way of bringing it back.*

*Nobody in the village was surprised. There was a sense that
a permanent winter had settled over the family, nothing would
be right for them.*

*And now Megan is saying goodbye to the brightest bauble
from their family tree.*

*I do wonder how many Melvicks actually died of old age;
there can't be that many families that have their own hanging
tree at the bottom of the garden.*

While Melissa was a right cow, Megan was just a wee bit odd.
We first met the year after I had seen her in church. Mum had
got out of jail and taken me to Brighton where she had a new
man with long arms and a short fuse. He had me back in Kilaird
before the end of term nursing a badly broken arm, and I was
still gunning for my revenge on Wullie Campbell after the school
disco incident the previous summer so I was happy to be back
north, although it could be boring and I had to suffer Gran's
cockaleekie soup. I already had a difficult relationship with the
forces of law and order, Constable Harry Murray, or Hairy
Monkey as we called him. He knew I wasn't a bad kid, just
bored with a dad who worked long hard hours and whose wife
hated me, and living with a gran who never knew where I was
plus a mum who was either drunk or staying at her majesty's
pleasure.

Over that summer I was constantly pursued by a gang of tossers
from the estate. Such things are important at that age. Some kind
of tribalism kicks in while growing up on the streets, in bedsit land
and refuges, even drifting out to a small village like Kilaird, or a
town like Dunoon. Humanity is the same the world over. The
Kilmun kids fought the Kilaird kids. The village kids joined forces
to fight the Sandbank kids and we all tore into the Dunoon kids
whenever we could. It's very easy to pick your allies when you
know who your enemies are.

But my big memory is me, on my own. I was the outsider.

Then, on that last day of term, the usual chilled wind was
absent, making the air strangely tense. At school, the kids were
restless, their energy was high, looking forward to the long

summer holidays of illicit drinking. They were tired of school, tired of being poor and they were in a pack.

And they had their eye on their prey.

One day, walking home from school in a bad mood because my arm was aching from the weight of the stookie. They had plastered it from thumb to elbow and it was annoying me. I was swinging it about, testing how good a weapon it could be. That's the sort of thing I like to know. I was keeping to the backstreets away from the coastal road. I was in primary six but this was the first time I was going to be around the Holy Loch for any length of time. I had visited Dad before but this seemed it might be for keeps. Mum was in jail at the time for grievous bodily or something. It might have been the fight when she hit a bloke on the head with a stone and blinded him in one eye. All he'd said was he thought she had nice tits.

She always had a tendency to overreact.

I might rethink my use of the stookie as a weapon.

Then I heard the noise of the gang in full pursuit; their victim was making no noise at all. She was on the ground, her blazer was torn, her school bag had been flung into the hedge, some boys from the high school were on her, pretending or not pretending, to kick her, showing off to the younger kids. Then I saw her body jolt, so one foot must have made contact. It was Wullie Campbell's big brother. He was a bit mental. He always had snotters and he stank of cheese.

I don't really remember the next bit. I ran at him, shouting, head down and rammed him right in his stomach, they never expect that. He didn't expect me to bite him on the wrist either. Or the backhand in the face with the stookie.

He collapsed, hitting the ground with a resounding smack. I stood back, and looked at the girl lying on the road, blood pouring from her forehead. Then I noticed the blazer was not from our school. I could hear the crowd behind me shuffle, so I stood waiting for them to turn on me, or walk away. There was a sense of something else. A fear, a fear they had gone too far.

I thought they might have killed her, she wasn't moving. She was curled up, her school bag had spilled its contents and there was something on the road beside her, like crushed plastic shells with bits of wire. Now I know they were her hearing aids.

The police appeared very quickly and I was huckled into the police car and driven back to the school. The girl was put in an ambulance. She didn't look at me. I was taken to the head-mistress's office by the Hairy Monkey and an even thicker cop. The headie appeared, then Dad was sent for. He was somewhere out on the estate so my gran turned up. And all hell broke loose. What was I thinking attacking a defenceless girl? But I had no voice, there is no point in talking if nobody listens, I had learned that lesson early.

I was grounded, confined to my bedroom at Gran's and not allowed any ice cream. Gran wasn't allowed to go out in case I escaped. Dad put a lock on the bedroom window so I couldn't get down the drainpipe, my normal route for nipping out for a cider at the beach. There was talk of being detained in a home somewhere, the usual parade of social workers was about to appear. Mum would blame Dad, everybody would blame Mum, nobody ever blamed me.

Snottery Campbell wasn't even mentioned.

I can recall sitting at the bottom of the stairs looking at the lock on the door, no keys hanging there. Gran was talking to somebody on the phone, one of her wee gossipy friends. There was a feeling that the village was holding its breath. Were charges being pressed? Reports to the procurator fiscal? The children's panel?

I was a disgrace.

Everybody was sorry for my gran and dad, nice people who had lived a good life until THAT dreadful woman got herself pregnant and spawned the devil. They were talking about me, of course, saying I had led the attack on Megan only because she was different and on her own.

Even I saw the irony in that.

Next morning, my gran brought me my breakfast without a word, and shut the bedroom door on me, locking it behind her, leaving me to eat my sugar puffs alone in my bed. This summer was turning out to be great fucking fun.

By half eleven, I was really bored, so bored I was thinking about reading a book. I heard voices downstairs, the front door opening, feet on the stairs. My bedroom door opened and my dad came in. He couldn't look at me, he just opened the door of the tiny bedroom and waved his arm, indicating that I was to go downstairs. I thought this is it, I am about to get arrested properly. His eyes said I was on my own and there was nothing more he could do.

But the front door of the house was open, a Volvo was idling in the street. I saw the neighbour's curtains twitch and I just managed to avoid flicking her the finger. Next door called out to my dad, 'Is everything all right, Tommy?' like I was going to be put against a wall and shot. Dad raised his hand, saying that everything was OK.

The door of the car opened and Beth Melvick was sitting there, all quilted jackets and a lovely coloured scarf. I thought my gran was going to curtsy. I wiped my nose on my sleeve, thinking I was going to get toasted but she just smiled and said that Megan wanted a wee word with me but she wasn't feeling so great so would it be OK if we went up to the house? Her voice was kind and crystal clear.

So I climbed in to the front seat and Mrs Melvick helped me with my seatbelt.

When we turned into the Benbrae Estate and saw the house, I thought it was a hotel, even when we opened the double front door, and all the dogs came running out, I didn't believe that this was all one house.

I was taken into a room – the Drawing Room – which was the size of the gym at school. It had no proper carpet, just old floorboards. The walls were covered by paintings of dead guys who all looked like Ivan Melvick in various hats and haircuts plus a huge picture of a woman in a white frock. She looked like Ivan in drag. Megan was in the drawing room, sitting on the settee with a bandage round her head. The cop, Harry, was there too, just in case I stole anything. Melissa was all very lovely and attentive to her wee sister. She was even more beautiful close up. Some other woman came in with the sandwiches and jelly and ice cream and lemonade that hurt my mouth. I was given a cushion to rest my plaster on. The other woman was a nanny or a maid or something and wasn't allowed to speak. The dogs were great, lying around, farting. I was introduced to an old yellow hairy thing called Oodie. I gave him the sandwiches I didn't like. Then Ivan came in and gave a speech, asked me about the paper round and went out again. I didn't say much, I was too busy cramming food in my mouth with my good hand, everybody else spoke and thanked me for looking after Megan. Then I was taken home again.

And never invited back.

The scar on her forehead was still there the day Melissa got married. As a bridesmaid, Megan's fringe was side swept to hide the scar, just as we borrowed her mother's make-up to hide my bruises. We decided on that style the day we sneaked off to Glasgow to get our hair cut identically. The day of the haircuts was the day our friendship started to end; it had started with her lying on the ground bleeding, and me having a sore neck from driving my head into a brammer's guts.

But I wasn't finished with Wullie Campbell or his snotty brother.

I wasn't finished with the Italian House

Or Megan.

A bond was made that day. A connection so strong, not even death could break it.

THREE

Tuesday

Megan

A death in the early hours of the morning leaves a lot of the day to be tolerated. Everything seems inappropriate.

I had remained at Melissa's bedside while the doctor appeared, made a few notes and signed his certificates. Then we all paused, none of us wanting to leave the room. Was this the final goodbye? Dad hung around the side of the bed with his arm slightly outstretched, wanting to touch Melissa one last time but not quite able to bridge the gap between life and death. I had kept hold of her hand as the doctor left. Heather had appeared a few minutes prior to the doctor, and was now teary and white-faced, holding onto Dad's arm. I'm not sure who was supporting who. Dad eventually left with one final look over his shoulder at me. A single tear fell as he left the room. Deborah ghosted after them like a silent blue shadow, her eyes on my father's back.

Eventually, I decided to go downstairs, and get something to eat, leaving Anastasia shivering, mourning on Melissa's bed. My sister lay with her daffodil yellow sheet pulled high to her chin. She was sleeping her endless sleep. I looked up at the ceiling, wondering if that was the last view she saw.

A pale yellow sky.

A Melissa sky.

And a Heather sky. They both had a passion for delicate blues and lemons. I wondered how much of this house Heather had redecorated. She would probably be pointing out what looked a bit shabby, then followed up with, 'Ivan, you have far too much on your plate, and you are not much use at that kind of thing.' She's an expert, used to have an interior design business and I suspected that she had steadfastly gone about transforming Mum's

vibrant reds, purples and golds that so resembled a Turkish
brothel, but hid a lot of dog hair, to a pastel palette of duck egg
blue and gentle yellows. The house now resembled a nursery for
silent children.

My mother was a dogs-all-over-the-sofa and wellies-at-the-door
type of woman. Heather was always plumping cushions and moving
ornaments one millimetre to the left. Her shoes matched her skirts
exactly. Her trousers skimmed over neat hips that had been lipo-
suctioned to the bone, her tinted hair was trimmed every four
weeks so it accentuated the triangularity of her face.

And there was something there, an echo in their slimness;
Melissa and Heather, two of a kind. Controlled. I wonder how
close they had become. I didn't really know Heather, except as
a friend of my mother, as a friend of the family. Now she seemed
to know my house better than I did. She comforted my father
over the death of his oldest daughter while I waited for them to
get out the kitchen so I could make a cup of tea and some toast.
Instead of being overwhelmed with grief, I was overwhelmed
with hunger. Maybe watching someone die of anorexia has that
effect on you.

Mum would have made me something. Scrambled eggs on
soggy toast was her panacea for everything, whereas I could see
Heather Kincaid designing a special cupcake to celebrate a
judicial hanging. Now nobody knows where my mother is and
Heather has her feet well under my dad's table.

The twenty-sixth of May. Three years ago. A Thursday. I was
seventeen. My mum woke up, decided she had had enough and
walked out. I had expected her to come back. Dad seemed to
suspect she would not, probably because she left her wedding
ring behind. I missed her, but I wasn't angry at her going, more
angry that she had left without me. She had turned her back on
us. For the next couple of months, I thought every phone call
would be from her, so I just took my hearing aids out to stop
the constant disappointment.

As I walked along the main hall, my feet were silent on the new
runner. It was light blue, of course, and useless in a house with
Molly and the Russels, dogs who ran free in the mud at the
Benbrae. The watchful eye of Lady Agatha Emmaline Melvick

was upon me, in command in death as she was in life, her portrait suspended, in its heavy gilt frame. She looked as though she might step out of the painting and walk away, disgusted at having to be in the same room as the proles who gawped at her.

The smell of fresh coffee drifted from the kitchen door. There was still somebody in there so I passed the door, heading for the drawing room thinking of the last time I walked this way. I was born in this house, it felt reassuring to me that it was the same house; time had moved on and we have all moved on with it. In some ways the house had not. Walking across the floor, floorboards sanded as they always had been but now covered by a Persian rug, grey and lemon of course, to the big bay window where I could look down to the Benbrae, the woods, the freshly striped lawn cut by the new gardener, employed after Tom was sent to jail. How many years had passed? Four? Nearly five? He would have been out for ages but could, and would, never come back here. He had nothing to come back for now. His wife had left him when he was convicted, taking the baby with her, and his ex-partner is now working for my dad, his ex-boss. And Carla . . . well . . .

Deborah had changed and re-invented herself as people do after tragedy. She was a stroppy, wild Deborah, the one who chased us with a pitchfork when Carla and I had climbed a neighbour's apple tree, threatening to run us through. She was only partly joking.

It was all snakes and ladders, swings and carousels. When the music stopped, somebody died.

From the window, I could just about see the mosaic at the water's edge, a colourful and permanent memorial to the murder that had happened on that balmy summer night, the night of Melissa's wedding. And it was murder. I don't care what anybody says.

The early morning sun was catching the yellow of the tiles, but the full picture, the beauty of the sunflower pattern, remained hidden from view. Carla always had a thing for sunflowers, they live short and beautiful lives, colourful and vibrant then they die. Her dad taught us both to grow them, on the sunny wall at the back of the stables. We named them, Carla's idea. A childish silly thing, but I regretted that I can't recall what they were.

Beyoncé and Jayzee. Ant and Dec. Flip in Hell. Something like
that.

The house was cold, like the people who lived here, and it
remained chilly, even on a sunny day like this. I glanced at my
watch; still early. I lived in a mausoleum where nobody laughed,
the windows remained closed and the curtains stay neatly pleated
and folded into their brass brackets. The bay window was wide,
six panels of glass and I could see for miles. I knew the floorboard behind me was the creaky one, although I have never heard
it, but I remember how that floorboard, that little Judas, betrayed
me so many times as kid when I crept out my bed and down to
the kitchen at midnight to steal a bit of cheesecake, or when
Melissa, Carla and I would sneak down when Mum and Dad
were having a party, just to look at the clothes (Melissa), the
food (me), the drink (Carla) or the men (Melissa and Carla).

But I did sense, a heavy foot, a shadow reflected in the glass.
It's often the way; I think I hear things that I can't, but I can
sense a presence. I turned. It was a young man, *the* young
man. The one whose Fiesta had been parked in the lay-by
yesterday. His titian hair falling in his eyes and a fine film of
sweat glistened his already shiny face. He looked ill. Or at least
very tired. And he didn't fit in this house. He was not expensively
enough dressed to be one of Melissa's friends although he looked
closer to her age than mine. He looked as if he was here out of
duty and wanted to be elsewhere. I pinned him as a junior doctor
or an undertaker's assistant, maybe a young lawyer, though if he
was any of these things he'd soon find out the Melvicks didn't
do underlings.

His voice wavered a little when he spoke. Definitely a
subordinate having suffered short shrift from my father. He was
nervous.

I smiled encouragingly.

'Megan? So sorry about Melissa, how are you?'

That was unexpected. 'I am fine, thank you.'

He looked at my face closely, looking for tears. He found
nothing. He had a rather soft kind face and blue eyes the colour
of the Holy Loch in mid-winter sun.

'I am sorry but you have me at a disadvantage, I have no idea
who you are.'

'Andrew Murray. Not the tennis one. Call me Drew,' he said automatically. 'I came to see your father, it's a very testing time for families, losing a loved one.'

His words were not exactly trite but said as if he was used to saying them, and I did notice he had not introduced himself, not really. He was a bit young to be a friend of Dad's.

'The doctor has given Heather something to help calm her. She's very upset,' he said as he tilted his head, indicating upstairs. 'She's gone for a lie down.'

He stood, wanting a response, so I said, 'Heather will be taking it harder than me, she has been here all along dealing with Melissa. I only got back yesterday, as you probably know.'

'The entire village knows. Your dad has been so looking forward to it.' His response was quick. 'I didn't know Melissa well.'

'Did anybody?'

He stood there like a schoolboy, waiting for permission to sit down. Did he want me to offer him a seat on the pristine duck blue sofa with its beautifully plumped-up lemon and grey cushions? I noticed the tassels were all lying in a straight line like dead soldiers, as if each thread has been combed through. He followed the path of my gaze.

'My house doesn't look like this.' He sighed.

'Not many do.'

'You are OK though?' His eyebrow rose.

There was a kindness in those soft blue eyes, something questioning. Or did he know about my condition? Or was I reading too much into a simple statement of concern for the recently bereaved.

'I'm fine, I think I'll get something to eat and then take the dogs out.'

'That sounds a great idea, get some fresh air. Molly is down at the stables.'

He went up in my estimation.

'Good, I'll collect her on the way past. Hopefully the exercise will tire me enough that I get some sleep, you know, good restful sleep.'

'Yes, time and sleep are great healers. A cup of tea very rarely misses either.'

I thought he was about to add: *And you have been through a lot.* But he didn't. Was it just paranoia? What did he know? Had they been talking about me?

Of course they had.

With Melissa, Carla and Mum gone, there was only me to talk about.

The kitchen was empty, a lot of cups and mugs were piled up ready to go into the dishwasher. A few plates with crumbs on were stacked at the side. I think other people had been and gone, maybe in the hours of darkness, it was a big enough house to hide in, if you know where to go.

I placed my hand against the kettle, lukewarm. I put it on to reboil and opened a few cupboards looking to make a sandwich. Debs wasn't a cook, she did the shopping, the washing and cleaned the house. Since Mum left, we cooked for ourselves. I took some cheese out the fridge and a packet of oatcakes, feeling an absence of something. Dog bowls. No food bowls, water bowls, toys, baskets, twigs or clumps of mud. This wasn't the kitchen I grew up in. Looking out the window, the sun had now reached the roof of the stables, the triangle of light worked its way across the yard. I saw Molly, lying on the grass verge, in the sunshine. The two Russells were trotting around, going to the stables, looking as though they needed to be about some business. Molly raised her head, ears up, her instinct telling her that I was looking. Then she was on her feet, at the other side of the back door before I could reach it, up on her hind legs, pawing, tail wagging, squeaking with delight. She was all over me, jumping and licking my face. I hugged her tight, it had been too long.

I was rubbing her ears when I saw Deborah, still in her pyjamas, wrapped in a jacket that looked like the one my mum used to wear to bring the ponies in. Debs was outside the door of the Nether Lodge, smoking, leaning, one hip hitched up on the garden wall. Did she live there now? Had I been told that? It would explain why she was still here so late last night.

It was easy to think of her as my father's generation but she was only thirty-seven now, maybe thirty-eight. A single woman, she'd had Carla when she was sixteen. I had noticed when she spoke to my dad, her blue eyes opened wide. When she had walked past him when filing out Melissa's bedroom, her hand had reached up to touch him, no doubt it was a gesture of comfort but I wouldn't be surprised if she had fallen for his charm a little. Heather Kincaid had. The only woman who was totally immune to his charm was my mother.

I couldn't see any of Carla in her mother, nothing at all. Carla had rather pinched and elfin type features. Her mum, Deborah, was round-faced and pleasant looking, there was a calmness about her that belied the life she had led before she came to the Italian House.

I was glad she had a home here. I felt partly responsible for the death of her daughter. I raised my hand to wave at her. She waved back, and stubbed out her cigarette and walked across the back court to the lodge.

Molly and I retreated to the kitchen and I gave her some cheese before sticking bread in the toaster, a slice for her, a slice for me. I liked sitting down here, in the bright sunny kitchen, the weight of the dog on my feet. She had already scoffed her toast and now had her eyes on mine except I had covered it in Marmite so she was on a holding pattern at the moment, still hopeful of negotiating a crust.

I jumped at the sight of Heather standing at the open door, I had no idea how long she had been there for, listening to me talking to the dog.

And I did feel, as I scrabbled about in my pocket for my hearing aids, that I was slightly unwelcome in my own home. That I was the guest, the stranger, the one who should have asked before making the toast or bringing the dog in.

Heather walked into the kitchen, shaking her head ruefully at the pile of cups, but I noticed she was not doing anything to put them away. 'Deborah will need to see to this.'

'She was up all night, she went for a nap. I thought you had too.'

She shook her head. 'Your dad was too upset.'

'I've just boiled the kettle,' I said, watching her lift it up and assess the weight.

'Your dad went back to the study, I think he wants some time to himself.'

'Who was that he was talking to?' I asked.

'Drew.' She didn't expand.

I saw my mobile flash, that would be a colleague wanting to know what was going on and how I was. I had a very short list of people to inform of Melissa's passing but they can wait, today is for me.

'Do you want anything else, Megan?' Heather slid into the seat opposite me at the kitchen table. I was holding a cup of tea, feeling drained and tired, gritty-eyed and that worn out non-hunger of being deprived of sleep. I had to pay attention while Heather was blethering, and she didn't make it easy for me. She turned away, I didn't catch what she said but she got up and walked towards the back door, opening it, I thought she was letting in some fresh air. '. . . better to be outside, don't you think.' She pointed at Molly and then out the door. The dog didn't move, she just looked up at me.

'She's OK,' I said, 'here.'

'Oh, but so much better outside, in the fresh air, not in the kitchen.'

'No, she's fine.' I went back to my toast. The dog stayed where she was. Bloody useless conversation.

Heather sat back down, moving things around the table top, straightening up some cutlery, the salt and pepper, putting the cover over the butter. She smiled at me. 'Do you want anything else?'

'No, I am fine. I was just talking to Drew in the front room.'

She didn't blink an eye.

'Who is he exactly?'

'Drew? Andrew Murray. His uncle died recently, he knew Ivan quite well.'

'He did seem very well informed of what goes on in this family.' Not adding, '*More than I do*' as I knew she would just say, '*Well whose bloody fault is that*'. She wasn't a Melvick so she would point a finger, whereas we were far too well brought up. We just let these things simmer and then we run away, like Mum. Or commit suicide.

'Yes, he's very nice, came over as soon as he heard. Your dad likes to talk to him, they were in the study for more than an hour. Did he mention what they were talking about?'

She's fishing now. 'I think he was very careful not to say anything,' I replied

Her lips pursed at that so she changed tack. 'How do you think your dad is doing?'

'He's just seen his eldest daughter die.' I have no wish to make it easy for Heather. If she wants to join this family then she had better learn how bloody hard it can be.

'I'm sorry, it must be so hard for you too. But I meant, how do you think he is coping with all this? And where is Beth? Why is she not here?'

Silence. 'No idea.' I let my eyes drift to the clock on the wall; it had only been hours.

'I was so glad you came home, somebody he can share it with. I don't understand why Beth didn't make it.'

Silence.

Carla

Megan will clock Heather straight away. I knew the minute Heather Kincaid set her L K Bennetts on the Turkish rugs in the Italian House that she'd have her eyes on Ivan. I could smell the hormones off her.

The fact he was still married to her best friend was incidental.

It takes some balls to sniff after your best friend's husband while standing in her kitchen, drinking her gin and ignoring her children. Then of course Beth left with a secret lover, died in a faerie pool or was eaten by a kelpie, depending on what the rumour mill was saying at the time.

Heather claims she had no idea why Beth left. I didn't buy that for a moment, women talk all the time and bored rich women like Beth and Heather rabbit constantly over bridge hands while sipping gin and tonic.

She did take a photograph of her kids with her. But not one of her beloved Ivan, so that spoke volumes.

*   *   *

*I can see why a woman would do that. Men really don't
stick around and any that do are the ones you wish would go
away and bother somebody else. My mum went through loads
of men and still didn't get a decent one, although I believe she's
working on that now.*

*There was one good one, a real gentleman, a dead old guy
that Mum befriended. We were in temporary housing on the
sixteenth floor in the east end of Glasgow. Bernie was very fat
and had an oxygen mask on his face and red scales on his legs
like a diseased fish. He puffed his way through sentences,
watched the racing on the tele and gave me a few quid to run
to the bookies. He had two grandsons about the same age as
me, both of them in Australia. There was always a nurse coming
or going.*

*They were good times. We'd go in in the mornings and open
the windows in Bernie's flat, he'd howl and protest at all that
fresh air. Mum would make him breakfast, I'd boil water and
stick it in a bowl for his feet to steep in. I'd stick a clothes peg
on my nose, he thought it was a joke but it wasn't, he was rank
rotten. Bernie encouraged me to read and so I sat in his house,
reading books on the sofa, reading out the* Daily Record *when
we were at the table.*

*Mum made a point of answering the phone when Bernie's
daughter called from Adelaide. Mum was chatty, everybody liked
her. Life was going good, I had somewhere to go when I came
home from school.*

*Then Bernie died. Mum had been in to check on him the
previous night, making sure that he was OK. I went in the next
morning and he wasn't sitting in front of the TV. The flat was
very quiet and you can't help have a sense about these things.
I didn't shout and open the windows or boil the kettle, I went
back into the hall and pushed open the door to his bedroom. I
could smell something not quite right. The oxygen tank was still
there, but it was quiet, the little sizzle sizzle sound had stopped.
I put my hand out and touched him on his big toe. He was
propped up against the headboard, eyes open, his glasses squint
on his nose.*

He was cold.

Megan

I could sense Heather was here to say something but she was taking her time working up to it. Her fingers reached out towards mine, crawling across the table. 'I do worry about your dad, you know. I care for him very much. I just wonder what is going through his mind.' Then she realized what she had said and looked away.

'Why? Why do you worry about him? Because of me?'

She backtracked. 'No, no. Just the family history. What happened to his father, your Papa? It makes you wonder if, well, if it's all starting again. He's under so much stress.' Her brown eyes are creased a little in thought. She's looking at the floor, I see a shiver going down her back. She's starting to second guess herself. The Melvick curse. And she knew my mum very well, they were friends for many years when Mum first came here, but Dad always thought that people like Heather should be kept at a little distance. Dad might have her in his bed, but he will not allow her into the family. I bet Melissa said the same before adding *'over my dead body'*, which is, sadly, now the case.

'Deborah mentioned that your dad has started misplacing things. She found his mobile in the fridge last week, then she came in and he'd left the gas on. I'm sure it's just stress but, well, I hope it's not the family trouble rearing its head.' She frowns, looking at the floor. 'And you, well . . .'

'I have Dissociative Identity Disorder. I am not mad, Heather.'

'Well, I hope all this doesn't upset you. Melissa's mental health was so fragile.' She looks at me, her expression alternating between sympathy and curiosity.

'It's a different generation. Different times and different people. If you think Dad's heading that way, ask him to go to the doctor. He trusts you enough that if you expressed your concern, he would go. If he asks me what I think, I will back you up.'

Heather smiled as if I have given her some comfort, some place of influence in our family. It wasn't really my intention, I was just stating a fact while wondering who Drew Murray was and what was he doing talking to my father in the study, a father who is forgetting things.

I took another sip of tea, content not to talk. Heather pulled herself up, sitting straight.

'If you resent me being here, Megan, then I will go.' She looked me straight in the eye. I'm surprised to find that I believe she means what she says.

'Heather, this is not my house, my dad can invite who he wants to stay here.'

'I am not staying here . . .' She had the decency to get a little embarrassed. 'Your father and I . . .' She splutters to a halt.

It's the first time I have seen her in discomfort. It's quite amusing.

'I don't expect my dad to live like a monk.'

She smiled, raising her shoulders like a teenager in love. 'I guess the gossip is all over the village.' She put her hand out to cover mine again, I don't pull mine away. I knew where my dad's responsibilities and loyalties lay.

'I wouldn't know. I'm never in the village,' I replied coolly just to see her response.

She sailed on undaunted now, her hand up at her hair. 'But yes, I am very fond of your father.'

I fully expected her next line to be, 'Does he ever talk about me?'

'I mean as a friend, I am fond of him as a friend.' She's backtracking now. 'And I am trying to help him through this. I was pleased to be able to do that last night. He was Beth's husband and she was a good friend to me when Peter died, that was pancreatic cancer, so quick I didn't know what had hit me. In fact she introduced me to Colin, but that didn't work out.'

'Are you divorced now?'

'Yes, we split up.' She looked around her, up at the old pulleys hanging from the ceiling. 'I think of your dad as very alone, trapped in this huge house.'

Not quite as insensitive as her silly shoes may suggest then. 'It can be a very lonely place this house.'

'Only while there were no other members of his family here, but now that you are back, just say if I am getting in the way.'

'You are not getting in the way, Heather,' I reassured her. 'Not at all.'

She smiled again.

'Like you say, it's a big house.'

'You are very precious to him, Megan, he thinks such a lot of you.'

'When did you get so close to Dad? It seems only yesterday that Mum was still here.'

Heather sat back as if I had slapped her, then shrugged. 'Beth was a very close friend of mine, I miss her very much. I don't know why she'd leave your dad.'

'She had another man. She told you that, not any of us. I've often wondered why she texted you to say goodbye, not any of us. Not a word, not a phone call. Nothing. Yet she kept in touch with you for a while.'

'Just a few days. I did ask her to come back, but she said she couldn't. That I was to look after you and your sister.'

I couldn't imagine my mum putting that in a text while walking out of our lives. I looked at my phone, a few text messages and emails from people, some little more than strangers, asking after Melissa, wanting to know how I was doing yet my own mother hadn't bothered to say goodbye to me. 'I guess she had her reasons.'

'Maybe she thought you would talk her out of it.' For the first time, Heather looked upset, or maybe guilty.

'Maybe it was all too much for her.'

'There were a few messages, all wanting to know about her girls. I think it broke her heart leaving you behind.'

'Good. Maybe she shouldn't have gone.'

Heather smoothed the tablecloth with the palms of her hands, slowly, carefully. 'And I really do like your dad, you know, but I don't want to cause him any distress or embarrassment.'

'Good.'

She smiled, still not looking up. 'You are a tough young lady, Megan Melvick.'

'My dad taught me well.'

'Maybe he is not as tough as you think. This last year has taken its toll and I'd like to think that I, in some way, have helped him with that. And you have not. You were very content to leave him to cope. Well, if you don't mind me saying, you have been very self-absorbed, looking after number one, so yes, I do think I have a right to stay here and help him through this in any way

I can.' Her mouth slammed shut, little lips pursing again like she had more to say but was stopping himself from saying it. Her speech sounded rehearsed, memorized from a self-help magazine. Then she sighed, her head tilted, her hand rubbed her upper arm, caressing herself as a smile played on her lips, bending them to a smile. 'Does he ever talk about me?'

'No,' I said.

Carla

So Melissa is gone. Out of reach. The Italian House is now actually quiet, rather than quiet because Megan's entire world is quiet. But the sun is splitting the sky, so all is not bad. Megan is no longer alone in the house, she has Molly with her now, and they will soon be walking down the Long Drive to the Benbrae, to the water's edge where she will sit on the bank and throw sticks and stones in the water. Molly will run after the first one. Maybe Anastasia, Melissa's stupid wee Boston Terrier will trot after them. The Russells will please themselves.

I'm glad Megan is not on her own but I don't really think of Heather as a friend, she's a wee parasite. Megan needs a friend and that Drew bloke was a bit tasty. I hope she noticed. No wedding ring. I clocked that, no wedding ring and no baby seat in the car. The car was a year old, so he's earning. Yeah, defo a bit tasty with his nice hair, a gentle golden red colour, shame it's cut short like he's a cop.

And then it clicked. Andrew Murray. And PC Harry Murray, the Hairy Monkey. So he's passed away. There was a likeness. I hope he's good to her. Megan didn't realize she needed friends until she met me.

Maybe I sensed that, which is why I had to push it after I wasn't invited back to the Italian House. I bet the Hairy Monkey had told them what I was like so I had to take my chance when it came one miserable rainy day, later that summer holiday. Gran had taken to her bed with a really bad cold and Dad was out working at the Italian House. He had popped in to see me and brought a pint of milk, a loaf and a box of Lemsips and I was laughing as he had his suit on instead of his gardening clothes so I guessed he was going up, actually into the house for some kind of meeting. I asked if I could go with him as Gran was in her bed. He looked shocked and, bless him, tried to explain why I would not be welcome.

Gran must have been feeling pretty ill as she had left her handbag down the side of the sofa. I had cabin fever so I pulled on my anorak and, taking what I could out Gran's purse, I started to walk. Six miles to Kilaird, a long way for my short legs, but I was on my own and therefore safe. Weird that nobody stopped to ask a child what they were doing walking the long road that skirted the top of the loch.

They probably knew it was me. More likely to run me over than stop and offer me a ride. Mr Melvick would have stopped, of course, that would be one of his 'do the right thing' activities. Maybe Mrs Melvick would have stopped as well, now that I had saved her daughter, and been rewarded with a sandwich. But nobody did so I was bloody soaked by the time I got to the big black gates, ten feet tall. They were closed as usual. To the side was a wee box on a metal post with a light and buttons, I guess that opened the gates. I didn't know where my dad would be, like I said, today he had his suit on.

I got over the fence easy peasy, my feet were narrow enough to use the ornate cross struts as footholds and once over, I scuttled round the small path that followed the inside of the wall, between the dark wood and the outer limits of the estate. Much later I found out that this was a track made by Melissa's feet as she ran to burn off every calorie she had eaten, silly bitch. It became my secret route when I was sneaking out to meet Megan at the Benbrae unseen. It was totally hidden with the high wall on one side, the dense trees of the Tentor Wood on the other. Nobody ever went in there, not when the rest of the estate was so beautiful. At the gate the path was little more than a gap in the trees. At the other side, where the water of the Benbrae thinned the trees out, the path was a meandering strip of flattened grass, the water on one side, the field on the far side with the Holy Loch beyond.

The path was a bit spooky, within a mile of all that luxury up at the house but so secluded. Down here anything could happen and you were on your own. If I hid here, nobody would ever find me.

Nobody ever did.

On that first excursion, I did come across the old gnarled tree with the huge branches that grew out over the water, the wide twisted trunk itself sprouting from a raised part of the bank. I might even have sat on it and worked my way out over the water. I found some rope attached to a high branch, thinking what a good swing that would make, one push and you would be flying over the water, only a little momentum needed to bring you back safely onto the bank and dry land.

Now I know that was the Melvick hanging tree.

I had no real idea what I was doing there, being nosey, maybe thinking about stealing something, patting the ponies, curiosity about where my dad worked. Or was I just really lonely. Did instinct tell me that Megan didn't have any friends either?

Who needed friends when they had money?

I had been listening to Gran who, although she never talks to me, is a terrible gossip. The reasons for Megan being on her own so much? It started with a rumour from Mrs Thompson in the dairy who said that the Melvicks had forgotten to put Megan's name down at the same school that Melissa and her mum had gone to. There was another rumour that they had remembered that Megan wasn't bright enough to pass the entrance exam. Another rumour was that there was something wrong with her, like she wasn't all there in the head, and what a shame that with all their money they couldn't do anything for their kids. The village liked this last theory as it meant, despite appearances, the Melvicks did not have it all. And that rumour gained some truth when Melissa went doolally.

Oh yes, Megan was very much the lonely girl, the little chubby one, a second-rate version of her beautiful sister in those days. Megan didn't give a shit, couldn't hear, couldn't care. Seemingly, she used to chatter like a chimp, then something happened and she went deaf and then quiet. But Gran said that was a nasty rumour to cover up the nastier fact that Megan had always been deaf and her parents were too busy to notice, and the succession of nannies didn't think to mention it.

Shame on them.

I couldn't stop myself, crawling around the woods at the far end of the Melvick estate, thinking about the way Snottery Campbell had beaten up Megan. There was one thing I had a great instinct for. Trouble.

Megan's problem was she didn't react. If she had, Snottery Campbell would have got some satisfaction from her reaction, but there was nothing. She had walked on, her head up in silent defiance. So she got thumped and I got taken away in a police car for putting an end to it.

Then I was invited down here.

And now here I was uninvited.

From my vantage point I looked round and fell in love for the first time. At the end of the drive, beyond the gates was a pond and a boathouse, weeping willows over the still and reeded water, it was like a painting. How lucky was she to live in the house with that at the bottom of the garden. I had never seen anything so beautiful, I didn't know why I was so excited, but the time I looked back to the drive my heart gave a little jump. I climbed up on the fence as high as I could go, determined to drink in every last minute of that view and I think I might have made myself a strange little promise that day. That I would never ever let Megan out of my sight again.

I had made my way back down to the boundary fence and waited. I had nothing to do, I could wait all day if I needed to.

But ten minutes later, I saw the Land Rover coming slowly down the drive. It drove past me, right past me. I was in the trees, watching like an assassin. Megan was sitting in the back, alone, then she turned her head. I don't know how she could have seen me but I got the sense she knew she was being watched. I wasn't bothered who was driving, I didn't really have any interest in that but I was curious to know where they were going. What way would they turn – left towards Sandbank and the ferry, so they were heading to the city maybe?

I slid through the gates before they shut after the vehicle exited, keeping close to the side of the wall. I took out my phone, looked at the time, then jogged down to the bus stop with a new idea of how I might spend my day: spying on Megan.

The first bus stopped, and took me back to Hunter's Quay.

He was one of the drivers that I knew – he liked to be on the school run so he could chat up the senior girls – so he stopped to let me on, and I stood right beside him, chatting and rolling my eyes at him. Men are such arseholes.

At the ferry, I sat near the traffic barrier not wanting to go into the waiting room until I knew there was a point in getting a ticket. The Land Rover was not in the traffic queue but the incoming passenger ferry was still doing its manoeuvre out in the bay. Where had they gone? We didn't see the family around the village much, only when they were at the fete or at the church but never in the chemist buying deodorant.

So I waited, watching the ferry dock; everybody does, no matter how many times you see it; left a bit, right a bit . . . Then I saw them, on foot, waiting in the queue.

I too joined the line.

And waited. At least the rain had eased off.

I didn't know where they went once on the ferry. There was no sign of them up at the cafe or in the lounge with the old ladies and the day trippers. I carried on my search and found them eventually. Beth was with Megan out on the deck. Megan looking rather unwell as she holds onto the barrier, suffering from sea sickness. That never bothered me, but all the money in the world wasn't going to turn that face from green back to its normal tawny olive tone.

So what now? I didn't have a plan, the danger of being a spur of the moment kind of person. Shadow them, like a spy? People were streaming off the boat, Megan still looking unwell, a bit green round the gills. They then set off towards the station slowly, maybe for the Glasgow bound train.

I jogged along sometimes right behind them, sometimes on the opposite side of the road, paying detective, then watched them buy a ticket, paying with a credit card. I bought my ticket with the grubby fiver I'd nicked from Gran.

And I was on the train, going through the quiet carriages, sitting on the same side as them but about five seats away. I'm sure Megan's eye flickered up and saw me, then turned away. Probably a quick flash of recognition – somebody that she knew but nobody worth acknowledging, although I had been in their bloody front room just a few days before.

But I had her in my sights. They sat in silence as it would be difficult to talk to Megan over the noise of the Scotrail train soundtrack, all that rumbling and clanking would have meant Beth raising her voice. I could hear nothing, so I guess they didn't speak for the entire journey.

They didn't get off until the train terminated in Glasgow and I am already on the other side of the barrier when they emerge.

FOUR

Megan

I suppose it was natural that memories should come flooding back. I had not slept in my room for over three years, and now the house was talking to me. I recalled the chill of its words, the sense of death and tragedy that pervaded these beautiful walls. I paused at the front door thinking how many times I had run in and out here, after a dog, after my sister, after Papa. Always trying to keep up. The house was quiet. Deborah would be tied to the sink in the kitchen, I had no idea where Heather was, or Dad. Or my mother. I knew exactly where Melissa was.

Melissa who had come down this hall on her wedding day like the Queen of Sheba, so full of expectation, of certainty of the life that lay ahead of her.

Sorry.

Sorry?

What for?

When did it all go wrong? Was it the day of Melissa's wedding? Melissa? Had the guilt eaten away at her? Her health had certainly declined since then, a five-year slow spiral downward.

I have never seen anybody as beautiful as my sister on that day. It all came together for her when she walked down these stairs under the proud eye of Agatha Emmaline. Dad, looking very handsome in his morning suit, was waiting for her right where I was standing now. Carla and I were outside, as we were going down to the church first. Carla was staring at Melissa, I have never seen anybody's mouth actually fall open before but hers did. I wasn't so taken aback; I was fed up hearing about the dress, this dress, that dress, the dress that nearly was, the perfect dress that got away.

I had no idea what she would have looked like in the perfect one but this one, well this one made Dad cry when he first caught sight of her, as she rounded the half landing under Agatha, the sunlight behind her making her veil glow like a halo.

Melissa held a simple bouquet with flowers from the garden that matched the ones Carla and I had in our hair. The long veil was the one Mum got married to my dad in, and the one that my granddad had married my grandmother in all the way back to Agatha. The dress though, was incredible. A soft silk with a loose neckline that gathered in soft folds. A tight, seeded pearl, structured waist showed off her curves in a way that managed to be both sexy and discreet, and Melissa could pull that look off very well. The bottom of the dress was a flowing mass of white silk. The movement made the sheer wings of the skirt billow out behind her, it seemed as though her feet never touched the ground.

She looked like an angel.

Which she probably was now.

I could see it so clearly, Melissa, with her huge sense of drama, pausing right at the top of the stairs, just long enough to draw the eye. Dad gave her a tearful nod, and she continued her descent, her head bowed slightly because it looked suitably demure and chaste, knowing that we were all looking at her anyway. Her dark hair was neatly pinned at the back of her head, the veil falling from the French pleat like a comet. Two spiralling curls fell to either side of her cheeks, framing her face, stopping just short of her ears and the diamonds that hung there had been picked up from the bank earlier that week.

But what a palaver it all was. My dad, in a rare moment of candour, said how quickly Napoleon could mass an army and march it across Europe, so why was this bloody wedding taking forever? I didn't hear him say it, I lip-read that he said it. Sometimes he was so used to me not hearing that he forgot and spoke his mind.

I think he was as fed up with the wedding as everybody else by then. Mum and Melissa going off to Glasgow for The Dress every weekend for about a year. And once to Edinburgh, twice to London, and then Melissa and her friends had gone off to New York for a quick look round Kleinfields as she had seen it on the telly. And that was just The Dress. We had to go through the same

rigmarole with the flowers and the food and the wine and
the band and the bridesmaids and the flower girls and the . . .

I wonder how quickly Napoleon got married.

In the end Melissa had decided on one of the first dresses
she had seen in a couture boutique in Glasgow but by the time
she decided on it, it had been sold. She went mental. I went to
bed early. Dad made one of his biannual outings to the pub. I
lay in bed and vowed that I'd never get married. I couldn't hear
my sister's screeching, of course, but I could feel it on the back
of my neck. The pipistrelles didn't come out that night, it was
too noisy.

But in the end, as Melissa stood on the stairs, she was the
picture of perfection. It was easy to like Melissa as long as you
didn't know her.

She had insisted our dresses were Royal Tea-green, covered
with seed pearls and Grecian folded necklines. We were told to
wear our hair scraped up in braids that wound round our heads
so as I walked down the aisle behind her, everybody would see
my hearing aids. I had protested but Melissa wouldn't change
her mind. I looked at Mum for support; she shrugged in sympathy
but uttered that it was just for this once and it was your sister's
wedding.

At that moment I could have happily killed both of them.

If, at that time, Melissa was aware of anything going on
between Jago and I, she showed no sign of it. She said nothing
at the reception. In fact, she said very little to me all day so
maybe she did know, but was so much in demand, so much the
centre of attention, that she decided to let it go.

'For now.'

Melissa never forgot a slight.

Funny that I don't really remember Melissa being around me
during the meal or the dancing. I wasn't really aware of her, not
the way I was aware of Jago and the way I knew he was aware
of me.

Just before the wedding, he had said, the way men do, that this
would be the end of it. That is what he said, when we were both
lying in the *Curlew* on the Benbrae. Five minutes later he was
talking about the flat in Cambridge and how often they were
coming up to stay with my parents, and was I going to be staying

at the house or going away to university. He said it kind of hope-fully, as if it wasn't really the end of it.

Shagging him had only been a bet between Carla and I. He really was a grade A arsehole.

The thought of him brought me back to the here and now, and unconsciously, I was walking the path of the wedding car down the Long Drive, thinking about that day. After the meal, I remember Jago making a show of trying to get me to dance to the jazz band. It looked as though he was helping me, and holding on to me as if the deaf can't dance because we don't hear music. The audience, and there was an audience, smiled. The groom looking after the bride's little sister. Over my shoulder I saw Carla, her fist making wanking gestures. My snort of laughter was misinterpreted by Jago as a sign of joy. He always thought everything was about him.

I walked past the lawn where the marquee had stood for the wedding. Jago must have seen me go into the house, and he followed me up to my bedroom. I was fixing my hair, and adjusting the folds in the neckline of my dress, tightening the flowers. No doubt I took my hearing aids out to give my ears a rest. But as I saw him in the mirror, he didn't make me jump when he came up behind me.

It was only a bet, but I got my thirty quid off Carla.

Half an hour later he was back down on the step, dancing around with the best of them, glass in one hand, bottle in the other, filling glasses. He had that drunkenness that upper-class men do so well, when they have sex with their teddy bears, or bridesmaids, or fall off balconies in ski resorts, all in good spirits.

I look up to my bedroom window. I had been watching him from there, from behind that same curtain. My bedroom has French doors that open out onto the stone terrace that runs the length of the building. It does make us feel like the Royal family, waving down at the little people, those who have warmer houses than ours, bigger TV screens and faster Wi-Fi. But on the day of the wedding, I was in there looking at Jago, at my dad in his backless waistcoat, at Mum on the temporary dance floor surrounded by the village children doing the hokey cokey. Now I remember the kids waving; I had looked across to see what they were waving at. Melissa standing in her beautiful white gown, alone at her own wedding, staring up at the window, staring right at me. Looking at me like she wanted to kill me.

Looking back, I think she knew.

But on her death bed, she had said sorry.

For what?

The mosaic at the Benbrae bears witness that somebody died a tortured death, burned alive, surrounded by water. There are men in Kilaird today bearing the scars of the fire, brave men who waded into the water to try and help. My mum screaming, my dad on the bank, his arms outstretched. The air full of smoke and the stench of burned flesh, the endless, endless noise of a human being burned alive.

Such was my sister's wedding day.

Carla

It doesn't take me long to find them. Megan and her mother are acting like spies themselves, standing in the huge concourse of the station, under Victorian glass. Beth looks at her watch and gesticulates so even I can understand it from behind my hiding place of the newspaper stand at John Menzies. They are deciding on a time to meet back underneath the clock.

Megan leaves to walk onto Renfield Street. Beth watches her go, a studied look of concern on her face. I don't think I have ever seen that look in my mum's eyes. I watch Beth for a few moments, debating whether to go after Megan just to make sure she is OK, a vulnerable child in this big noisy world, but she merely checks the time, comes to a decision and then walks away to the taxi rank. When I get to the exit at Renfield Street Megan is nowhere to be seen. She had been swallowed by the crowd and vanished into the network of back alleys, shopping malls and department stores that make up any modern city centre no matter where in the world.

She's gone.

I jog across the road and stand up on the bin at the bus stop with some woman shouting at me in Russian, thinking I'm jumping the queue. I tell her to bugger off. She's fearful of the slightly mad look I've been told I have in my eyes and backs down.

I spend the next hour or so wandering round T K Maxx, buying myself a mega expensive iced coffee in Starbucks where I pay for one ginger biscuit and nick another two. The stookie is off my arm now but I'm out of practice with my style of shoplifting. I sit at the window watching the big city go by. It makes me think that everybody has something or someone, whereas I am here with nothing but a few quid nicked from my gran.

People going about their business, I'm not even allowed in school.

I wonder where mum is.

After that I go into Frasers, the easiest place to shoplift cosmetics. With my little weasely face, I look about eight. My pockmarked skin looks awful. Junky pallor like my mum. I look at their make-up, checking stuff. I have a few bits and bobs of course, black eyeliner and bright orange lipstick that goes with my blue hair and thousand-mile stare. Melissa doesn't wear make-up like that. I'm sure she wears tons of it but it would all be soft-toned and natural looking, classy.

This is the look I am after.

I am looking at Estée Lauder and then at Chanel, where it costs more for a lipstick than my mum spends in Lidl for a week's shopping. I see a lipstick called nude. What's the point of that? But it's very Melissa. I think it will do me fine so I lift up the tester and hold it against my lips, looking obviously at the mirror while looking like somebody that hadn't had a decent meal in weeks. There's a range of eye shadow called neutrals 'to enhance your natural beauty'. The assistant's watching me carefully and the big sign above my head that says 'poor'.

I make a play of looking at two eye shadow pallets, holding them against my skin. Then a couple of lipstick testers having picked up a third brand-new tube without being seen, I mess about putting one on the back of my hand and peering at it as I palm a mascara with the other. I put two back and pretend to flick through the selection of small palettes appearing to be looking for something that would be exactly what I wanted. When I look up the counter girl is right in front of me, staring at me, hands on hips. Her black-rimmed Cleopatra eyes drift over my shoulder, I don't need to be told that the security guard is fast approaching. I don't give a shit, I have my trainers on, I can out run that fat, old bastard any day of the week.

'*Young lady, you are in big trouble.*'

She has no idea of the truth that comes out her puckered mouth, bright red like it was inflamed. She looks like a diseased trout ready for a surgical procedure in her immaculate white uniform. While I am sure I can run, I can also hear the crack of a radio. So they would be gathering at the doors, which makes escape difficult. I'd make for the emergency exit. If caught, they'd prosecute and I could be detained in young offenders, actually detained and locked up. Again. Bloody social workers trying to find my mother, curfews and locked doors, secrets and being abused by those that were paid to look after me. I clench my fist, narrow my eyes, I'd take them both down if needed.

The trout's moving its big gob again. '*Big, big trouble. If you'd just like to . . .*' The next words were bound to be '*accompany this gentleman to the office*'. I sense the security guard bristling behind me, some code that means we have caught a right little tyke this time so watch the exits. There's a stalemate, they can't really do anything as I have not attempted to leave the store with the booty in my pocket but I can't exactly take it out and put it back while I am in this trout security guard sandwich.

There's a stand-off while I consider my lack of options.

'*Carla?*' It was a question, not a summons. I don't recognize the voice but I do know the ease of confidence that glides up beside me. '*Did you get it? Sorry I got held up, the doctor was running late.*' Then Megan Melvick only goes and picks up the eye shadow pallet I had been looking at. '*Was this the one you thought was best?*' She holds it up and peers at it.

That I can answer. '*Yes, but it's a fifty-fifty between that and that.*' My grubby little fingernail points at the first one sitting back in its shining black slot.

Megan then points at the lipstick. She had been watching me. What a fucking double act we are.

'*That one is Nude but I didn't know if that's what you were after?*' I shrug. '*Sometimes it's more of a pink than a beige.*'

Megan, I notice, is totally ignoring both the assistant and the security guard who are silently wrong-footed by this turn of events. The appearance of somebody my age wearing cashmere and speaking posh is confusing them.

'*To be on the safe side, let's take both.*' She selects the palette

I had been looking at, and one that was slightly darker. 'And yes to the Nude lipstick' – she shows it to the assistant – 'do you have this in the long lasting matt? The gloss finish always looks so cheap, don't you think.' Megan says this with a straight face as the diseased trout nods, blissfully unaware of the insult to her huge shiny scarlet gob.

'Well, we have a shade very close.'

'Pardon?' says Megan, twisting her head towards the till.

'She's deaf, she has to lip-read,' I say, having no idea if it was true but if it was, Megan isn't going to hear anyway. I repeat what the diseased trout had said to Megan.

'That's would be great, thanks.' Then Megan says with a straight face, 'And a mascara, Carla, what do you think? It will be a long time before we are back on the mainland.'

'What about this?' I point at the gap in the display. I had already lifted it. They will know one is missing.

'I think blue black rather than just black,' Megan tells the assistant, forcing her to lean forward towards us and pick one up, the long scarlet talons scrubbling around as Megan opens her handbag, Burberry of course, opens a leather purse and pulls out three crisp twenties.

'Yes, well you know her better than me,' which is totally truthful as I have no idea what fictional person has employed us as their personal shoppers. The one I had nicked might have been green for all that I knew, I had just lifted the closest one.

The assistant makes a nice little bundle of our purchases, firing her scanner over the barcodes, smiling. The tables have turned. It's all about the nonchalance as Megan hands over the cash without looking at the assistant; the red-mouthed trout is an irrelevance now. 'Where have you been?'

'I lost track of time,' I say, playing along. 'I went for a coffee in Starbucks.'

'Sorry, you must have been bored.' She turns as the assistant hands her the change. 'That's lovely.' A smile and a nod, a hand takes the small paper bag that's almost handed over but then retracted.

My heart misses a beat, shit. Shit shit shit shit.

'Would you like a few samples?' Trout opens the bag again, looking right at Megan.

'No, thank you,' says Megan, reaching for the bag and my arm. 'We need to go upstairs and collect Mummy at Jaeger.' She says thanks, goodbye then marches me round the shop to find the central stairs.

Then she whispers in my ear. 'That mascara in your pocket? Dump it before we leave the store, will you?'

Like I said, what a fucking double act we were.

Megan

There was an idyllic perfection about the Benbrae, so at odds with the traumatic memories, which made it seem like paradise had been defiled. I knew I should have been trying to confront these memories, I had been running for too long. I was being a coward. Carla was so much braver than me, the heart of a lion. And the teeth of a tenacious ferret.

I wished Mum was here. Dad was in his study making phone calls. Just putting the news about Melissa out on the grapevine so that Mum might pick it up. Somebody had to know where she was.

Molly bounded behind me, Anastasia trotting along, keeping up as we set off to the Benbrae, knowing that more memories needed to be dealt with and this seemed as good a time as any. The sun was splitting the sky, the heavens above a cornflower blue. I wanted to say hello to the few remaining ponies we had left.

I sought out the dogs, the birds, the ponies and the colours of the summer flowers to calm my soul.

Melissa had gone. It kept hitting me in the stomach. As much as it was difficult for me, I'm glad that I came back to say goodbye. We'd never had much in common to talk about, but she knew I was there at the end.

Sorry.

I stood at the fence, watching the ponies. Lorimer, the stallion lifted his head and strolled over to me, immediately, ears pricked, slowly lifting hoof after hoof. He was an old boy now. He nuzzled my hand, I pulled some grass for him and stroked his grey hairy face. Dad had texted me when Lorimer nearly died the year before, I think it was an attempt to get me to come home. The pony had taken ill during the winter, some nasty infection in his lungs, the vet had gone far and beyond to save him. He was cream coloured, like all the Benbrae ponies. He was my favourite type of Highland pony, a light brown dorsal line along his cappuccino back. Apart from his arthritic walk and a slight roll in his hip, there was little evidence of his age. He knew me and seemed glad to see me. I was always the one to give him sugar lumps and gingernuts. Mum and Melissa were too strict. The two mares were out on the far field, both of them up at the fence, ears up, rubbing their necks on the upper strand of wire, wondering when I was going to go over and see them. Marple and Tuppence. We started with Poirot, of course, the first champion colt that mum bred, and he put her on the map as a breeder of some expertise. Then we had Queste and Pascoe. Pascoe grew too tall and became a pet for Melissa at her pony club events; I inherited him when Melissa gave up ponies for boys. But Poirot's good blood, fine looks and friendly nature were all carried down the Benbrae bloodline and Queste was sold as a breeding stallion for a small fortune. I never viewed them as good or bad ponies, they were just the ponies. It broke my heart when one was sold because they were too tall or too small, their back was too curved or their coat was not the desirable shade of cream.

Being rejected for an imperfection was a bit of a sore point with me.

And I liked animals, especially dogs and horses with their pointy ears that perked, then swivelled like a satellite dish. Animal's ears can act as an early-warning system for the deaf, their hearing was my hearing. I do believe in my heart that the family dogs of my childhood, especially Oodie, knew that I couldn't hear as well as they did. They'd stare at me until I looked at them, then they'd turn away, ears pricked in the direction that they wanted me to look in. In a world where sound could be uncertain, they were my other sense.

Molly and I, then Anastasia, set off towards our boating pond, the Benbrae. The boathouse has been rebuilt, now only for boats. Tom McEwan's – Carla's dad – old shed and the adjoining hut where he kept all his gardening stuff including the picnic trolley and the ride-on lawnmower, had been blown to bits. The

Curlew 2 was out on the water, tied up onto the pontoon, but on a loose rope. The charred remains of the *Curlew* lie at the bottom of the pond, in a leafy dark grave. There was no wind or movement on the water. I stood for a minute looking across the surface which is the colour of polished almonds, kaleidoscoping in the bright sunshine. It had lost depth. No surprise, there had been solid sunshine for the last six weeks, the water table was dropping. We were lucky to be so close to the top of the sea loch, and the rain belt of the west coast.

Past the boathouse, past the pontoon and the *Curlew 2* sat the mosaic.

Carla's mosaic.

It featured a sunflower, *sunflowers*, I corrected myself. Tiny fragments of coloured tiles fixed to a thick webbing. As individuals, they meant nothing, just fragments of tile and porcelain, a square of one colour here, a triangle of another there. But put it all together and it becomes a field of sunflowers against an azure sky. Had some debate about it at the time. Which way round it should go on the ground, facing the house or facing the water? The sort of thing that people argue about to avoid the bigger issue. In the end, I suggested that it should be circular and that the sunflowers should spread out from the middle.

Everything else may be hidden and covert, but the mosaic was a constant and painful reminder of all that had gone bad for us. It's difficult to recall exactly when that was. The wedding? The day we built the mosaic? The day Mum left? Now Melissa had died. Not bad for one little life.

Molly trotted over the top of the mosaic, busy investigating the scent of something small and furry that had run over the tiles during the dark hours. The colours, the beautiful bright colours that remained so vivid despite the passing years. Carla should have got that chance. That hurt me more than the passing of Melissa. My sister drifted into her illness, by her own warped sense of self-worth.

But Carla?

There are times I think the suspicion runs deep and is eating away at each and every one of us like metastases.

Molly turned and looked up the Long Drive, tail wagging, ears pricked, tongue out and looking keenly. Then I caught the scent of a Penhaligon's aftershave, carried by a breeze I hadn't even realized was there.

I turned to wave to my father.

'Are you OK, Megan?'

'Yes.'

'What are you doing down here?'

'Getting some fresh air.' I tried not to snap back.

'I've been in touch with Jago and the family. He's driving up straight away. I said they could stay at the house. Are you OK with that?'

Sometimes I wondered if he knew. 'Of course, you have to do what you need to do. He's still Melissa's husband.'

'It's all just a bit difficult, with the way things were between them at the end.'

'That was only because she was ill and not herself, Dad, if she had been OK they would still be together. I'm sure they loved each other really.' My dad liked to use phrases such as love; love, commitment and duty. 'How was Jago? With you, I mean?'

Dad shrugged, we began to stroll along the bank, the dogs scampering around our feet. 'He was upset, of course. But he had been expecting it. I've asked Deborah to get the rooms prepared.'

'It might help us all, having a house full. I think it's what Melissa would want, her friends and family all together.' It was the very last thing that I wanted. Did Dad have any sense that Jago and I had history? If he thought Melissa's death would smooth that over, he was very wrong. 'Did he say what his plans are?' I asked lightly.

'He'll be here for the funeral. It's looking like Friday. He was saying that all the old gang will want to come. So he's phoning round them.'

'Of course. Any word from Mum?'

'No. Not, yet.' He rubbed his hands together, his tic of discomfort.

I know I looked down at the mosaic at that point, I'm sure Dad's eyes followed, both of us thinking exactly the same thing. Five years on and everybody will be here again, just as they were at Melissa's wedding. Mum must come back. Those memories are painful, and I backhanded a tear from my cheek.

Dad had walked up behind me, his hand rested on my upper back, in silent support.

I was still looking at the sunflowers as I talked, my eyes following the stalks at the centre out to the bright yellow petals against the blue sky on the outside. 'Dad, all this is about Melissa and Jago, and what you two want to do for her. I imagine a lot of her friends will want to stay here. Like the old days.'

'Hardly.' His voice was heavy with grief, that intense grief when it could have all been so different, there was nothing inevitable about all this.

'Don't you worry about the guests, Deborah and I will see to them.'

Dad laughed a little, surprised at himself. 'She is so good at that kind of thing, surprisingly.'

'She does makes me smile, she reminds me of Carla so much. She sees no point in calling it a spade when it's a fucking shovel, quote unquote.'

'Megan!' he remonstrated, a broad smile on his face.

We both stood and looked over the quiet, silken water, the water boatmen, billowing clouds of early midges. Leave it until twilight falls and then the bats would come out for their midge buffet. *Curlew 2* was starting to bob a little, the breeze disturbing the water. Overhead the rooks started to gather in the trees, noisy and unforgiving. They freaked me out.

Dad looked up. 'We will have to do something about them. I have no idea what gets into them when they start attacking the house. We'll organize some shooting. We need to protect the eagles on the hill.' For a moment, he was caught in profile, in shadow against the sky. A handsome man. He watched the rooks spinning in the sky, heading towards the house and then my eyes dropped to the Tentor Wood, thick and dark, no light penetrated there. The air immediately chilled.

'You're getting cold, Megan. Go back to the house, put a jumper on.'

He talked to me like I was twelve and couldn't think for myself. He put his arm round my shoulder. 'I swear the Long Drive is getting longer,' he said as we walked off the grass onto the gravel of the drive, 'or maybe it's just me getting older.'

'Aren't we all?'

Carla

So here's Megan, aged twenty, with her father's arms around her as they walk back from the Benbrae. I think a lot about the way they interact, the way his arm floats round her shoulder. At first, I found it really odd the way he touched her, like she was a girlfriend, or a possession.

And there was Megan smothered by her family, to the extent she needed to get away from them but instead they left her one by one.

Her dad, Ivan, was eminently shaggable, even though he was a bit of a coffin dodger. A handsome man with a handsome wallet, but he was rather formal, distant even if he was in the same room. Or close enough to look him in the eye. I wonder if he ever noticed that his wife was gone, or did the hired help tell him.

That was three years ago. The wedding was two years before that, the engagement the year before. The village went into quiet hysteria when that was announced, and that the wedding was at Kilaird Kirk. And that the locals were invited.

The wedding itself was piss funny. In the small, packed church, it was tense, silent except for the low droning voice of the minister. The sun had been baking the church all day, the service being in the late afternoon so the congregation was hot and uncomfortable in new shoes, borrowed kilts, hired suits and hats bought from charity shops. The tension knotted tighter as the hymns went on, then the ceremony started and everybody in the church had a quiet giggle as the minister read out Jago's full name. It sounded like the football commentator reciting the entire line up. Plus subs.

His first name was actually William, as in Bill or Willie. Megan and I were standing a little behind the couple, dressed in our bridesmaid gowns in a colour that had some high falutin name but meant light green. We had the same ring of garden flowers in our hair, the style being adjusted after we had mutinied by haircut. Megan spent most of the ceremony looking straight ahead so she wouldn't laugh. But when the minister read out the name Montague, we happened to catch each other's eye and I had to bite my lip so that I didn't laugh out loud and add to the general snorting from the congregation.

It was a beautiful day, and as was tradition after the wedding the family had invited everybody in the village to a celebration on the parkland of the Italian House. It was the traditional thing and it happened for christenings and weddings, basically it was an invite for the villagers to drink themselves under the table.

After the ceremony, the bride and groom drove off in an ancient Rolls-Royce up to the Italian House to their private reception in a marquee on the flat ground at the terrace. A route master bus then appeared to take everybody else up the road from the church, a three-mile journey. By late afternoon, the sun was still cracking the sky, softening the tarmac at the edge of the road and the bus itself was bedecked in flowers and branches as it ferried the guests in a strict order: bridesmaids, the parents, close family and friends, then the rest of them. We were categorized by class and bank account, folk the family liked and folk the family tolerated. The wankers were last. Debs and Tom, my mum and dad, separately, were high up in the food chain at that point as Dad worked for the Melvicks and Mum was the mother of the bridesmaid. I heard a few mutterings about her getting her foot in the door at last. Mum wasn't really tolerated in the village as my dad was popular and Mum was seen to have dumped him and run off with the baby in search of a better life in the big city. If only they knew. The unlikely friendship between Megan and I was explained by the facts that my dad was a good guy and that Megan needed a companion to help her through life.

But like I say, the invitation was open but restricted, numbers were given back for the catering and nobody in the village dared to abuse the family's generosity. There was a huge marquee for us and long tables outside for the others. A buffet with all kinds of dead birds at the top and two bars on either side for the constant flow of chilled beer and wine. It was a beautiful sight, the Long Drive and the fence were covered in white and flowing ribbons with flowers that matched those in our hair and the bridal bouquet.

On the lower part, near the fence that ran the length of the home meadow, was a large 'thing' covered in hoardings. It was very big, as if her dad had bought her a house for her wedding day and had popped it halfway down the drive so they could decide later where they wanted to put it. For now, it was under wraps.

I had an inkling what it might be, Megan had once told me that they had both told their dad what they wanted on their wedding day and Megan said, looking at the juggernaut that towed the first of the three trailers, it looked as though Melissa had got her wish. Then she added, rather pointedly, that was what happened when daughters were divine and sweet. And perfect. It might have been different now Melissa was twenty-six and was about to marry a complete tosser, but Ivan Melvick was a man of his word, a man who always did 'The Right Thing.'

Megan wouldn't tell me what she had asked for as her wedding present from her dad, probably something soppy like world peace or getting her hearing back. I'd like to see Ivan trying to sort those out with his Coutts bank account.

The meal in the marquee was accompanied by some boring tinkling music from a sour-faced string quartet. We could still hear the folk outside, laughing and joking and having fun, while we had to act like grown-ups and use cutlery.

I was allowed in the house to use the toilets but the rest of the guests had to make do with the portaloos in the hedgerows, and a long separate table for the children with chicken burgers and chips while an ice cream van dispensed cones and ninety-nines.

Then a swing jazz band took over at eight o'clock or so. People, slightly drunk, dancing in a Glen Miller style. The kids had discarded any appearance of being dressed for the occasion; they were rolling down the slope close to the water. This was also a tradition, it could even get competitive at the summer fete, and at Christmas midnight mass if it snowed. Or sometimes, they would roll down in the mud. Like I say there was not a lot to do in Kilaird.

The real guests then drifted back to the house for gin and a comfy seat, from where they could watch the fireworks from the paladin window. There they would enjoy unspoiled views right out over the Holy Loch in the distance and the Benbrae, easing their swollen ankles out from tight-fitting shoes and slipping on a cashmere shawl as the evening air chilled.

Agatha, hanging behind them, would have the best view of all.

I first saw the haze over the water at nine or so, people were still lying around drinking, eating sandwiches, picking at the remains of the hog roast. A few of the boats were out on the Benbrae, some brave souls had disrobed and swum out. My dad was on the bank watching, hanging around the water aware that drink and water do not mix. He later said he had actually been more worried about stuff getting nicked out of the boathouse.

My favourite boat, the panama called the Curlew, *was far out under the weeping willow, deep in the shade. An arm was hanging out, a finger dropping through the water, getting covered in wisps of green algae. The wedding guests were relaxing, things were winding down. Anybody who was going to be offended by anything was now up at the house behind a closed door, all the guests had to do to was keep out of sight and they could misbehave as they liked.*

Once the jazz band had played their set and everybody was buggered with the dancing, the big present was unveiled. I couldn't make it out at first, or maybe I could but I didn't believe it. One by one the plain brown hoarding boards dropped off the side like the leaves of a musical box, to reveal a series of red brightly painted scenes. And then the music started and I realized what it was. Ivan Melvick had only gone and got his daughter a bloody merry-go-round.

A fucking full-sized carousel all to herself.

Every guest gasped, then clapped or shrieked, even the posh ones were impressed. I saw the doors of the Italian House open, seats were repositioned around the twirling horses and the oldies, gins held tight in arthritic fingers, tottered down the length of the Long Drive to have a closer look.

And we all know how that ended.

FIVE

Megan

I t seemed just like the old days when I pulled my feet out of my ancient boots, dusty and dry as there was no mud out there in the parched soil. The dogs were scampering around me, thinking why were their beds outside in the stables and not lying in a smelly heap in the back hall or in the corner of the kitchen. Anastasia ran off, her paws pitter-pattering on the wooden floor, Molly lay under the kitchen table, the long walk and heat tiring her out. Dad had drifted back to the darkness of the study like a bear in search of hibernation. It's difficult to mourn in sunshine.

I walked through the house barefoot. Everybody seemed to be somewhere else, a feeling that was very familiar when rattling around in this great old mansion. It was a very silent house, especially for me, a home of rolling emptiness. The portraits of older generations peered down from the walls and inhabited the place in death, as they did in life. I suppose they had first dabs. The paintings were worth a fortune because of the artists that painted them. And the last few generations had added to the collection. Ivan Hendry Reginald Melvick had had four sons, two were killed in the First World War, the other two, including my great great grandad, both committed suicide when they came home. The last portrait, towards the rear hall on the way to the walled garden was of my grandfather, John Ivan Reginald Melvick, 21st October 1924 – 12th June 1994, a small reminder that he'd died on my fourth birthday. Like I was going to forget.

Money, just money, hanging on the walls.

Just pictures.

Daubs of coloured pigment stuck on a canvas.

I did think about how much they were worth. That started me wondering if there was a cure out there for Melissa somewhere.

But at what cost? Had Dad decided that he loved his art too much, the Hornell, the Dali, the Munnings? The family had started the collection as an investment for a rainy day. One wonders how much rain had to fall before he'd part with his paintings.

It didn't make him sound like a good father, or even a good person, but he just answered to a different calling. He wouldn't sell any of it just to benefit one of us, it was there for future generations.

My ancestors were all the way down the stairs for twenty generations or more. One of them, can't recall which one, had lost a title over a game of cards and a sly ace kept up a sleeve. All the portraits that hung along the corridor sat at eye level, watching as we walked past, giving us the once over. Not so with the Lady Agatha, we needed to be on the top landing to look her in the eye. Her portrait was the showstopper, full-length, painted in 1910 by some Dutchman who was quite famous at the time. Agatha ruled the roost, the portrait was the biggest and grandest in the entire house and I have no doubt that it nearly broke the bank when it was commissioned. In life, Lady Agatha looked a good laugh. She was young, tall, slim, dark-haired and mischievous-eyed, at least I hope she was. It was how the artist caught her. She had been painted against a dark, leafy backdrop, maybe an image from the Tentor Wood out beyond the Benbrae, out at the faerie pools, her long silk dress falling in delicate cream folds, her angel sleeves falling almost to the leaves underfoot. Her hair was piled up, loosely, strands drafting over her forehead as if the merest drift of air from our front door would brush it against her skin. She was incredibly beautiful. She'd died young. I was eighteen when I realized the painting was done posthumously. She too had committed suicide, hanged herself over the faerie pools. I felt a weird connection with her, she had wanted to escape as well.

Did Melissa have that same madness, in a different form? Did I? Melissa was the dead spit of Agatha, those knife-edge cheekbones and huge eyes that spoke of some kind of Italian ancestry. They could have been twins; I was more like the little sister. And then all Dad's ancestors round the walls all over the house, you could see the likeness of Dad in every one of them, gradually changing over the generations for sure, but it was all there.

Then there was Carla, she had as much ancestry as the Melvicks, biologically speaking, but somehow she seemed more like an end point. The result of years of bad breeding, the sort of thing that Mum was eager to breed out of the ponies; bad blood. And genetically, Carla became a full stop.

I knew her dad, Tom, of course, a quiet, rather steady man that my mum had liked. He was a turn-his-hand-to-anything kind of man, good with machines, good with the mares when they were in foal with his low voice and endless patience. Carla's mother hated him.

'Yes, he's a good guy,' said Carla once, lying on the bottom of the boat, her arms up and out, her fingers curling round the rowlocks, her eyes closed. Her hair that day was bright green with banana yellow streaks at the front, like a sunflower in summer time. The sun was shining on her forehead. Relaxed though she was, there was a wariness about her urchin looks, around her thin, feral features, the tip of her nose was upturned, her ears a little pinched at the top. She could never have been a Melvick, she would have been found out by the cheekbones. 'My dad has one big problem,' said Carla, her finger up in the air, drifting to point at the sky, indicating a number one, 'one big problem'.

'Gay?' I hazarded.

'Nope.'

'Can't be infertile, or impotent, because of you.'

'That's true is that. All his tadpoles are fit and well.'

'I know.' I had a flash of tabloid inspiration. 'He sleeps with his mother.'

Carla opened her hazel eyes and rolled them in mock shock. 'Does he? I never knew that!'

'I was only guessing, but you do get a sense of these things.'

'No, he's never shagged Gran, she's not his type.'

'So what put your mum off him?'

'My dad was' – she opened her mouth, yawning with the effort of staying awake – 'just so bloody boring. Boring. Boring. Boring.'

'Oh,' I said, 'is that a crime?'

'Oh God, yes. You can be many things, Megan, you are rich,

you are pretty, you are clever, you can't hear the starting pistol
in the hundred metres, but at least you are never ever boring.'

'I think I'm boring. I never have anything to say. Nobody has
ever told me a joke. What does that tell you?'

'No, you are not boring. The Melvicks can't be boring, your
bank account alone will always be of huge interest to me.'

'Not boring?' This was a new version of me I wasn't familiar
with.

'Well, even if you were boring, Megan, nobody would ever
have the balls to tell you in case you stuck them in a dungeon
or got them deported.'

When we hear what others think of us, it's often so different
to how we perceive ourselves.

There was movement in the front drive, looking out the window
I saw a black van reversing up to the front door. Maybe this was
what Dad wanted to get back to the house for. Two men got out,
dressed in black, they didn't pause so somebody had opened the
front door for them. Molly pricked her ears but wasn't really
listening, her head moved, watching the sound as it moved up
the stairs. Then Melissa would be brought down and out, taken
away to be prepared for the funeral. I wasn't sure what happens,
would they wrap her up in something? Put the body in a box?
Or just remove the body?

My eyes passed over the photographs of Melissa doing Ophelia,
then Mum and Dad on their wedding day, then Melissa dressed
in white. Behind her, standing to the side, were Carla and I. I
had forgotten that we would be there, in eternity in all these
pictures. Melissa looked so tall and elegant, Carla and I looked
like twins in our Royal Tea dresses and our hair piled up on top
of our heads. At the time I thought the flowers in the hair were
ridiculous, but now, looking at them, it was just perfect.

So alike, Carla and I.

So very, very alike.

The photograph gave credence to the rumour that the wrong
girl had been killed.

I ignored the men coming and going through the hall, seeing my
father pass the door, Deborah followed close behind. I lifted up the
photograph, heavy in its antique silver frame. Questioning it.

The whole farce of interminable discussions, debates, tears and tantrums of the previous three years. The bridesmaids' hairstyles had been a huge point of tension. No matter what I said, Melissa, with that air that might at best be dismissive, and at worst might be cruel, shook her head and said, 'No, scraped back, nothing untidy.' At that point my mother looked at me with some sympathy, I stopped biting my lip so I could pretend that I didn't care. But I hated her for that, and was so grateful when Carla came up with her sneaky plan. She smirked and whispered, 'They can't stick it back on, can they?'

Clever Carla.

Maybe too clever for her own good, trying to outwit a Melvick?

I placed the picture back, noticing the top of the sideboard was free of dust, Debs was doing a good job. Molly's ears pricked up again, she was on her feet, looking out the window, I glanced at the time.

Was Jago coming back? I looked hard at the horizon, and yes, something caught my eye in the far distance, the slow imperceptible movement of the big gates opening. From here I couldn't see what, or who, was about to come through. I'd see the car when it emerged from the dip in the land.

I remember hearing that car one time I was down at the pond, Jago and his E-Type turning to climb the gentle hill of the long drive. What a tosser. Dad had had a word with him about it once, saying it's OK to have such things but don't flaunt them. Dad had bought me the Merc for use in the city but I wasn't really allowed to drive it around the village. That would be drawing attention to yourself and was frowned upon. *People like us*, another one of Dad's phrases, drove Land Rovers covered in dog hair, bits of pony with the dried blood of dead animals in the back.

I watched Jago park, leaving his car on the gravel at the front, the car abandoned. He got out and looked at the private ambulance, shocked. He stood for a moment, looking much older, thinner than when I had last seen him, shock on his face, wary of what he was walking in to. It was suddenly going to be very real for him.

I'd like to say I felt sorry for him but I didn't.

I'd like to say I went out to greet him but I didn't.

I had nothing to say to him at all.

Different people, different lives.

He walked behind the ambulance and into full view, his well-cut jeans, and his beautiful leather handmade shoes. He moved across the gravel, not looking at the black transit now. I had never really wondered what happened to them and their marriage. Was Melissa's illness driven in part by her neurosis and constant need for attention and approval? Was it the fact he worked somewhere in the City, she toured with plays and he would stay over in London. Two people, with two separate lives that collided on a Monday night.

Shame it didn't work out for them but I didn't think any marriage could hold up to having that many egos or Jago's sexual predilections. But I was being unfair, we are different people now than who we were then. Carla and I were little more than kids and while Jago had no doubt met many girls like me before, he had never encountered anybody quite like Carla.

Or was there something else they couldn't live with?

The guilt?

I had very vague memories of them leaving the Italian House on the day they married. They left in a haze of smoke and the stink of burning flesh, as they drove off into the sunset leaving devastation behind them.

I had harboured vague suspicions that Melissa had caused it for years, a little non-specific idea at the back of my head. Was that what Melissa had been apologizing for? That fleeting look on my dad's face, as if the last thing she needed to say was something that could be taken as a death bed confession.

But had she killed the wrong girl or the right girl?

I thought, as the door opened and Jago came in, that I wasn't sure which Melissa would find more difficult to live with.

Carla

I know who the car belongs to, bloody Jago. Some men you meet and they blow you away, others you meet and you want to blow them away – with a sawn-off shot gun. Jago was one of the latter.

He was good looking for sure, any boyfriend of Melissa's was.

Megan and I used to hang around casually waiting to catch a glimpse of any new man Melissa brought home. Then we'd give him marks out of ten for all the things that were important – looks, wallet, car, personality and shaggability, but not necessarily in that order. Sometimes they were such pompous braying arsepieces we just considered how good we would feel if we threw them off a cliff.

Jago, as his name might suggest, was a total wanker, and a bit on the plump side. But he was incredibly rich, not quietly rich like Megan's dad, but good cars and expensive presents kind of rich. He was good fun in small doses and easy to take the piss out of as he was so stupid. His money, though, was awesome.

We had looked at him, in one of our slightly drunken hazes and had a bet that one of us was going to shag him as this thing between him and Melissa wasn't going to last. We had a short window of opportunity and we had to make the most of it.

I knew the minute that I caught him looking at us, he was the kind of man who liked young flesh.

I had known men like him, too many of them.

If Ivan Melvick was a good guy, then Andy Pandy McColl was way down at the other end of the spectrum and then some. He was a stick-thin, waster, heroin addict and he lived slumped in the corner of the living room, between the fire and the tele, in a house share Mum had dragged me into when I was twelve or so.

Andy was always pissing himself, his head lolling from side to side, slobbering. On the day he died, I had noticed Mum had left her bag on the fag burned sofa. I reached out to get it as I thought he was in his normal stupor, but I was wrong. He struck like a cobra. Pulling the purse out the bag, his nose in the zip, helping himself. Propping himself up on his elbow, he focussed on me and said if I told Mum, he'd kill me. I didn't believe him so I kicked him in the face.

Then I did believe him and kicked him in the balls as well.

He went out like a light, his head hit off the wall and ricocheted, leaving a red smear and spatter. It took him ages to slide down the wall, back to his corner.

SIX

Megan

I sat down on the settee, Molly flopping at my feet, I could sense the thump. Dad would be annoyed that I had not come out to greet Jago, but I could always claim that I never heard him. Nobody could argue with that.

I looked up at the beautiful ceiling. It used to be white, the delicate cornicing pattern of cherubim, seraphim and grapes was left to speak for itself, now it had been picked out in white and duck egg blue. Heather again. How much did that cost? How much chaos did that cause, all that scaffolding? The whole works. Another part of my mother's simplicity had been eroded. Weirdly, my mind then turned to how quickly I would put it back the way it should be as soon as I inherited. And that thought did not make me feel guilty, it should have been my decision not Heather's.

But for now I lay back, in between the cushions of the big sofa. Molly, sensing my disquiet, jumped up and lay beside me. This sofa, this room, a different dog. My fourth birthday. How did it all come to this? The five years between the wedding and this, all that happiness and expectation of all those lives on that carousel has come down to me lying on the sofa of this big house, dreading seeing my dead sister's estranged husband.

The garden had looked so beautiful that day, the wedding was in full flow, it was getting dark, the garden looked like a fairyland covered in nightlights. The water of the Benbrae looked alive, glistening with fairy lights, flower candles drifting. I was intending to go down there, meet Carla, have a float around in the water, escape from everybody else and have a good bitch.

But everybody wanted a photograph taken. It was then that it became clear to me that Melissa considered Carla was an add-on to the wedding, and in the pics she wanted it to look like one bride and one bridesmaid; subtly, Carla had been sidelined.

And Carla was not the person to take that lying down.

I had been walking down to see Carla, desperate for a drink and a fag and to get away from Melissa's lovely friends who kept saying, I paraphrase, 'Oh you are the deaf sister, how awful,' to which I would reply, 'Pardon?'

If I recall correctly, that was one of the first times I actually spoke to Deborah. She grabbed me on the way past. At that time, I hadn't known her, she was Carla's mum, and had never been in Carla's life while she was up north. Carla had told me what Debs was capable of and my first instinct was to ignore her. After a brief chat I realized that maybe Carla had her own internal narrative of what was going on in her life. Children rarely truly understand why their parents make the decisions they have to make. A few words and, even at age fifteen, I knew she was fiercely protective of her daughter in her own way. She was then and still is now . . . Whereas my own mother . . . Well, when the going got tough she went.

Deborah wanted to ask if I was OK, if I had seen Carla, was she OK which I took as meaning, was she still sober? We were only fifteen but Carla liked a good bevvy and there was lots of alcohol about. Debs was complaining about her feet being sore, blisters on her heels and moaning about posh folk having no seats at their weddings. If I remember right, my feet were also hurting and we ended up strolling barefoot in the soft grass down to the Benbrae where Tom would be, us looking for Carla. Maybe Debs wanted a little company before she walked into the father of their troublesome offspring. Most of the guests were still up at the carousel, the noise of it was starting to hurt my ears. The fireworks had not begun at that point.

We stopped to have a quick puff and bitch about the guests. We were walking down by the fence, she said that spinning on a carousel always made her feel sick, I agreed. We watched it from a distance, she lit my cigarette with her DuPont monogrammed lighter, not monogrammed with her initials though. She told me she nicked it when she worked in a pub in London. It was worth more than her week's wages, so she pocketed it and left. We shared a few laughs at the expense of some drunken guests. I realized that I liked her, I really liked her, she had all Carla's endearing qualities, a straight honesty, unlike our family's stiff upper lipped duplicity.

I said I was going off to find Carla, and she hugged me and told me to watch my ears with the fireworks, she would come out and say that, in a way my family would pussyfoot around the situation. The carousel was slowing down to a stop, people dismounting. I said that the fireworks must be about ready and looked up at the sky, I know that my ears were hurting and I wanted to take out my hearing aids. The plan was to go down to the water and get on the *Curlew* which either Carla or I was going to bag, whoever got there first.

The sky was a deep indigo blue and crystal clear, it was getting a little chilly.

Deborah asked me if I was warm enough as we were walking down the slight slope to the water. I said I was, the words just out my mouth when she fell, right over on her ankle. I remember putting my hand out and nearly catching her.

She jammed a fist in her mouth to stop her screaming. 'Oh shit! Shit. Shit.'

I asked her if she needed any help. There were at least three doctors at the wedding. I could have called on any of them.

Debs, by then, was laughing. She shook her head. 'Oh, don't disturb anybody, just give me a hand back up to the fence, will you? I've done this before, five minutes it will be fine,'

'Will I get you some ice? If it swells in those shoes?'

And I hurried away, holding my long dress up, to the long table, now strewn with empty bottles, glasses and scrunched-up napkins, and watery ice buckets.

The fireworks started in fine style, high in the sky, sparks and explosions and stars of colour bouncing around, all truly marvellous. I continued to walk up from the Benbrae, keeping my head down, avoiding all eye contact, looking like I was going somewhere with purpose.

Then there was a flash of flame close to the ground, a bigger bang, a huge noise, then a ball of white and blue fire. Some people clapped, some screamed in delight and then there was another sound, a collective gasp, a shuffling of uncertainty. The crowd, whether they had been close or not, all moved slightly away. There was a hum of realization that something had gone terribly wrong.

Then there was the loudest noise I have ever heard. I felt my ears explode. I fumbled to pull my hearing aids out, screaming, clawing at my hair and my face. I saw flames and in the flames was flesh, a hand came out, it looked as though it was grasping for air, for freedom, for life itself.

It was a small hand, a small, fine-fingered hand.

The smell of burning flesh.

The screaming, agonizing screaming that rolled around my stomach.

The stench of acrid smoke and flesh worming its way up my nose.

Screaming, awful endless primal screaming.

Then it stopped.

Abruptly. Like it had never happened.

And the world was silent.

When the screaming had started, I thought it was the worse noise ever, until I heard the chilling silence.

How did I get through that? Well, I did.

I was on the ground, somebody picked me up, thinking I was hurt. I thought my ears were bleeding and that was where the noise had come from, but I think I knew, deep inside, it had been Carla.

They wouldn't let me go near the fire. I wanted to go down there to help, but I was held back. Guests, shocked and stunned, had drifted into little groups. Disparate, lost. The catering staff were tidying up in the way that people do when they feel the need to keep busy. Some were talking to police, I saw Carla's dad talking to two officers and then they put him in the back of a car and drove away. Debs was sitting on the ground, at an ambulance, ankle strapped, a silver blanket round her shoulders. She looked as though she was sobbing. Dad had his arms round Mum, Melissa was with Jago, both in shock.

Me? I was alone. Deep inside I think I knew that Carla was gone. It was that sense of loneliness that did it. If she could have been with me at that moment, she would have walked through hell to do so.

What did I think? Well, I had no real idea what had happened, but I suspected even then, that it was no accident. I even suspected, that I was supposed to have died in that inferno, or is that a false memory?

At that point, it is considered that I suffered my first blackout. My brain did not want to know and shut down.

I was taken upstairs by some friend of my mother's. I lay down in my bed staring at the ceiling, suddenly feeling very alone. Jago's parents were still staying in our house, as were many of his closest friends. They had gone from merrily drunk, or extremely drunk, to sober in that huge flash of flame.

All the fun had gone, it was all over and all I could think of was that there was a sense of inevitability about it all. Even then I thought that death and the Melvicks went hand in hand. Agatha was on the stairs looking down as I went past, staring at me with that smirk on her face. She knew that we weren't going to get away with it, the family had been on the brink of happiness, and that was never going to go unpunished.

All I recall was thinking that Papa had gone, Melissa had driven away with her new husband, no longer part of this family. And Carla? Where was she?

Carla was eaten up by flame and smoke.

I had never considered that she would leave me.

I had never felt so lonely, I watched the blue lights strobing across the ceiling, I made my loneliness absolute.

Always felt lonely living in that house.

Even afterwards nobody ever spoke to me about it. I was irrelevant, as if, because I didn't hear I also didn't see or notice anything, I was so easily forgotten about.

The dry wood of the *Curlew* was burned to cinders, her charred oak husk sank to the bottom of the Benbrae where I suppose it lies to this day. They didn't drain it or anything. But the boat was burned to a crisp, and so was Carla. The post-mortems, both of them, concluded she had not drowned. The small brain bleed from the fall off the carousel might have contributed to her slow reaction, as might her alcohol consumption. She was already dead when she went in the water, the flames intruding into the lungs and burning them out. It happened in explosions. They called it something like butterfly lung.

Somehow that was fitting; sunflowers and butterflies.

I often think of that. The way they blamed her for her own death. I had nightmares about it all until Dr Scobie, the psychologist, increased the medication with a diagnosis of PTSD and then deeper issues came to surface. My mental health began to deteriorate after that. I admit I became obsessed by fire and flames and what it would be like to die like that, in some dream-like state. I did used to burn myself with matches. Just a wee bit, just to get an idea of how much that would hurt. I wanted to feel a little of Carla's pain. I felt I owed her that.

And then, in one of those moments of loneliness when I was thinking about Carla, I was playing with matches, smoking in bed, dropped one, and the mattress went up and my boyfriend was asleep beside me.

The rumour mill said I had tried to set him on fire and the suspicion of the Benbrae fire turned back round to me, whereas I was still suspicious of everybody else.

What was it like floating out on a burning boat like a Viking sacrifice? Floating across the Benbrae, seeing the flames rolling across the water heading right for the *Curlew*. How frightening must that have been, out in the dark, on ebony water? The only thing lightening the sky above was the flash and shower of rainbow sparks of fireworks, when a tsunami of golden flame comes cascading across the surface. Straight at the boat, there was no escape. It was moving so fast it would have engulfed the boat before anybody had the chance to get out.

Tom jumped in. My dad ran down. Many men closer jumped in. Billy Williams, a farmer's son from Kilaird, waded right in, so did his dad, both got badly burned. The petrol had been poured onto the surface of the water so after the initial rush, it burned as a widespread fine film, the flames as hot as any other flame and just as capable of burning clothes and human flesh.

It was the beginning and the end of me.

Carla

I don't really remember much of all that. Probably just as well, the rocking of the boat, the flames going overhead, a wall of fire

coming close, then too close. As Megan said, it was the begin-
ning and the end of me.

I think I had a whole list of suspects, but those stupid buggers
didn't think it was deliberate, not at first, not until the rumours
started. I would have liked to have been at my funeral and looked
a few people straight in the eye. I wanted Megan to be there and
do that for me. She fought her corner hard and despite that
Scobie bloke and her darling dad trying an emotional armlock,
Megan came back for my funeral, a silent, black creature,
tearless and composed.

My memory is crystal clear. I had looked out the side of the
boat, hearing voices, I saw who was there and who wasn't.
Nobody who should or shouldn't. It was a wedding, people had
a right to be anywhere they wanted to go. I know that somebody
had tampered with the boat, the water. I don't know much about
combustion, but I know how fiercely that flame burned. I know
because I was on the receiving end of it.

I had smoked many cigarettes on the Benbrae out on the
Curlew, flicking fag ends and matches in the water where they
would fizzle out with a psst. That did not happen on the evening
of the wedding; there was a wall of fire.

There was a list of suspects because of my exceptional talent
for pissing people off. And maybe I forgot that the Melvicks did
not get all that wealth and power by being nice. And I had
freaked them out just before the wedding. We chatted about
pretending that Megan had done one of those ancestry dot com
things and then we'd bound in over breakfast and tell Ivan
Melvick, Lord Lieutenant of the County, that he was actually a
Muslim. He would have had a coronary right over his Eggs
Benedict while he decided what was the right thing to do.

Megan was quite funny, she whispered out the corner of her
mouth, 'As they load Dad into the ambulance, I can hear him
saying, "It could be soo soooo much worse, we could be
Catholics".'

But we didn't do that. To derail Melissa's plans for the
bridesmaids' hair, we went in to Glasgow to get a haircut. It was
strategic, ten days before the wedding, too late for it to grow
out.

We couldn't use anywhere local as they would know who

Megan was, for all the right reasons, and who I was, for all the wrong reasons, and some well-meaning and tattooed hairdresser would call Beth. And that would be the end of that.

I tended to forget that Megan always had money. To give her her due, she was never a mean person when it was something she wanted, although she'd never lend me a tenner for twenty Bensons. So, we went into Glasgow on the ferry and then the train. The city centre brought back memories for us. Megan's memories were of Christmas shopping in the darkness of a winter afternoon, tea in the Willow Tea Room, visiting the Museum of Modern Art. Mine were searching for a fiver in Mum's purse, finding a tenner, shoplifting some vodka, drinking it on the train home, homeless hostel hopping, me and Mum, here and there, bus shelters in the dark waiting for the first bus out, sitting with the drunks, make that with the other drunks, as Mum would be as bad as the rest of them. I'd be stone cold sober, especially the cold. I'd sit huddled up, hanging onto the rail, wanting it all to go away. Memories that were best forgotten, the kind that sneak up like a thundercloud covering the sun. Life was sunny and then the world went dark, and all I could think of was pain and blood, and being hungry on a midnight bus with no idea where we were going, being scared of the rain that spiked on the windows, stabbing my reflection. That afternoon in Glasgow I gazed at Megan as she looked in Hobbs' window, grey trousers and a cream shirt that never seemed to crease. A satchel swung across her shoulders in a way that looked cool, and not as if she had stolen it. That easy grace, the world was a safe place and she had it sussed. I think I actually did put my hand out and touch her shirt tail, mentally admitting how much I hung onto it. It reinforced how comfortable I had been back in Kilaird, round the Holy Loch. How calm. How safe now I had Megan.

Once I had put the haircut idea in her head, Megan had an idea of somewhere she wanted to go so she was already heading up to Buchanan Galleries and onto escalators, to some hairdresser up there that she knew but her family didn't. As I say, this was days before the wedding, certainly too late to grow back a full head of hair that had been shaved off. Not that we were going to get a number one buzz cut but that was our fallback position to appease the fury that would follow. It was Megan's 'it could have been worse' theory, like having one leg amputated is good news when the option was to have both legs off. The Melvicks had to capitulate – see the big words do rub off on me – and approve of our hair including Princess Frosty Pants. They had agreed that I should be bridesmaid. They made it a magnanimous gesture but Megan had told me the first two choices, some distant cousin of Jago's and one of Beth's goddaughters, were unavailable; one was single and pregnant – by a Muslim I would dare to hope – the other was in Australia on a gap year. It was explained to me, by Ivan, looking quite hunky and authoritarian in his study, that it was for Megan. I couldn't take my eyes off the Munnings on the wall, in its glass case. It was for Megan, he repeated, she could find herself on her own for much of the day. The attention would be on Jago and Melissa in her big white frock. So I was there as a companion and as a bridesmaid. And he added, taking my hand in a way that would have been creepy if he wasn't so rich, 'as her friend'.

I said, I actually said, I wouldn't let her down. So next thing, I am letting her down and leading her astray. We had talked about getting our heads shaved while drunk out on the Curlew. It was funny after a bottle of Thunderbird but Megan was worried she'd be disinherited and wouldn't be allowed to see the dog again.

We knew what the wedding hairdresser had said about the headpieces we were to wear, like a wreath of flowers, intertwined bits of twigs and flowers and leaves so that we'd look a bit like Nero's transvestite brother. Megan told the hairdresser what she wanted; a fringe side swept to cover the scar on her forehead and long enough at the sides so it covered her hearing aids. And then my hair cut and coloured to match exactly. The stylist had a long time poking and prodding at mine and then said how much it would be. I was glad I was sitting down, it was only a bloody haircut, but Megan, who was facing the mirror, did that thing that rich people do of looking stern and producing the dosh as if she had been slightly insulted at the suggestion she couldn't afford it. The sight of the money got us attention, especially when the pictures of the headdress came out, with the name of the dress designer on the bit of paper.

By the time we went home on the train, my peroxide and purple hair had been treated and dyed then re-dyed to an exact match to Megan's natural dark, dark colour, so densely dark it was almost black, but not dyed black. She said that looked so cheap. Megan's words not mine.

And the bridesmaid of a Melvick could never look cheap.

They might have been frugal, bonkers, inbred, sectarian and racist but they were never, ever cheap.

Back home, my mum just about pissed herself when she saw the two of us. Then she stopped and nodded appreciatively. She stood us side by side, shoulder to shoulder, and did a weird thing. She caressed our faces, comparing us. I swore she had a tear in her eye. I think she thought there might be some hope for me yet.

Ivan Melvick was a little puzzled, but on the basis my hair was no longer the colour of wet straw with mould he thought it was 'very pleasant looking'. Those were the words out his mouth but his eyes narrowed, the corners of his mouth tightened slightly. He looked right at me, challenging me. I stared him down. I guess we were fighting over control of Megan.

Well, I won that one, Ivan. And I still am.

Beth just said it was very neat and the style would take the headdress beautifully. She took her husband's arm and hugged him, looking at us as if we were her two daughters. I was the third girl in the Hornell painting, the third shell seeker.

Melissa, however, went absolutely fucking nuts. Full toto benny mental. She glided down the stairs and slowly halted, holding onto the handrail for support. She really was a great actress. Standing in the hall, side by side, in front of the grand piano, looking like two peas in a pod were two fifteen-year-old girls, both slim, both brunettes with exactly the same haircut. One her sister, the other her gardener's daughter.

Melissa raged. She was calling the wedding off. Again.

Beth tried to calm her down.

I couldn't stop laughing.

Megan kept asking her politely, and innocently, what the problem was. Wouldn't it look nicer in the photographs if we were both the same, we were wearing the same dresses after all. And surely all the attention would be on the bride. I'm bloody sure Ivan Melvick's mouth twitched at that, he could see the point

*we were trying to make. And Melissa couldn't exactly say, Yes
but for God's sake one of them is working class. What if Jago's
family think she's related to us? But she couldn't say that in front
of me. She was too well brought up for that. She'd wait until I
had left the room.*

*'But that's the problem, they look the bloody same, nobody
will be able to tell one from the other.'*

*'Who cares, we are only the bridesmaids, and nobody will be
looking at us.'*

*'No! I mean' – she was nearly foaming at the mouth by
now – 'nobody will know which one is my sister.'*

*'The deaf one,' Megan replied, 'they can say what they want.
I won't hear them.'*

'No, I mean . . .'

*But she couldn't bring herself to say what she meant, could
she? She didn't really want anybody mistaking me for a Melvick
and maybe, looking back, we shouldn't have pushed her that far.
She was already close to the edge, only holding on to her sanity
with her beautifully manicured fingertips.*

*She always had, as Megan once said tapping the side of her
head, a wee touch of the Ophelias.*

SEVEN

Carla

*I*t seemed to me that people always want to have control over other people. Or are some people incapable of living a life unless they are controlled by another as it absolves them of making any decisions about anything and it gives them an instant blame hound when it all goes wrong?

One of the social workers used to blather on about co-dependency and issues like that, talking about my mother and how she was drawn to a certain type of man.

Losers mostly, drunken, abusive losers.

And young people are vulnerable to bad adults, men or women. I don't think evil has a gender bias. And social workers can talk with very little awareness of the reality behind what they are saying: the pain, the bruises, broken bones, visits to casualty.

Even I could work that one out. Bad people hurt children. There was one guy who seemed OK, Chris the car mechanic. He had a tattoo of a Cadillac on his arm and when he rippled his muscles, it looked like the wheels were going round. He had a small modern boxy house that was warm and dry and a spare room that was slightly bigger than the average dog kennel. He offered to clean it out for me so I could have my own room. Chris kept his motorbike in there, I told him to leave it and that I'd look after it for him, and I did. It was like having a pet, I think I even gave it a name.

And we had neighbours, they had two boys, one a lot older than me, one a bit younger, and they let me walk to school with them and didn't laugh at me the way the other kids did because my uniform wasn't the right colour and my shoes were in such a mess.

That went on for a year, I think, maybe less, but then Mum

*got pregnant and Chris changed. He came home less, he got
short tempered. He wouldn't let me see the tattoo any more. His
eyes grew dark, he was pissed more. As our fridge stopped having
food in it, the neighbour started asking me if I had eaten anything.
She was a kind woman. I think the fighting between Chris and
Mum must have kept them up most of the night as it was a
terraced house and the walls were thin. And Eddie, the older
boy, asked me if the police had turned up as his mum had called
them out. Again.*

*As soon as Mum came home with Paul, the baby, all hell broke
loose. Paul screamed twenty-four hours a day, nobody got any
sleep. Then I was told to get my stuff packed. Chris had bought
me new clothes so they wouldn't fit into my wee rucksack anymore.
Mum came flying up the stairs, covered in baby sick and emptied
all the stuff Chris had bought me out the bag and set about
slashing my really nice clothes with a pair of scissors.*

And I left with what I had arrived in.

Plus a wee brother.

Megan

I felt slightly nauseous, I was worrying about this, but why
should I? It was my sister who had died but I was too scared to
go outside my room in case I walked into Jago. Outside my
window there were more cars parked, the private ambulance was
still there; what could be taking them so long? I could only think
that Jago's parents, or some of Melissa's close friends, had turned
up to say their private goodbye. Or it might have been the minister,
doing something. Maybe they were all along in Melissa's
bedroom, kneeling round her bed in silent prayer. I could imagine
me being there, praying with one eye open, seeing Jago doing
exactly the same.

I decided to stay in my room. But I was hungry. It was getting
late, but I didn't want to run into Jago unless Dad was there, I
didn't want to be in the hall with some toast, walking past
Melissa's body in a bag going in the opposite direction. Debs
would be down there somewhere, working her way through a
list of rooms to be prepared, linen to dig out, the dining table to

be set. I should have been helping her. I doubted that Heather would offer to lend a hand. Mum would have. She'd rather be busy than ceremonial.

And that's the rub, isn't it?

Would she come back now? I wasn't sure it would reach her ears; her eldest daughter had passed away. Or did she already know, having seen it on some social media somewhere and kept to her decision to stay away? Maybe she would come today. I was certain she wouldn't leave it until the funeral; she wouldn't do anything that would spoil the solemnity of the occasion. She might come afterwards though, quietly away from the eyes and ears of gossip in the village, up to the cemetery, carrying flowers for Melissa, and adding to the pile already there.

That would be more like it.

I told myself I shouldn't be lying here, Molly at my side softly snoring, and go and do something. Dad would want to talk about the order of service. Then something caught my eye, somebody leaving the house. I stood up thinking that this might be Melissa's final journey, but it was not her, it was Drew. He was walking slowly, over to the left of the house; he didn't turn to go down the Long Drive to the Benbrae and the way out. He kept going left, round to the side of the house to the sunflower garden, to the lodge and the very private gardens that belong strictly to the family. He walked freely around, looking for something and I guessed he might be a wildlife protection officer with the police. The Benbrae estate now has high protection status due to the golden eagles. There might need to be an official here, to oversee the shooting of the rooks. He'd have a lot of paperwork to do and my dad would force him to do it in triplicate.

I wished he'd come up to talk to me. He seemed to be on my wavelength, maybe because he knew what my family were like; his uncle knew us well enough.

What would Heather do if Mum showed up right now? What would Debs do? Heather had a life outside the Melvicks, I'm not sure Debs did. Sometimes when she was waiting for the kettle to boil, I saw a look on her face that was difficult to fathom. She was wary, as if somebody was going to walk up the Long Drive and take her away from all this. But she was a woman who had never had any permanence in her earlier life, she was

inconstant and peripatetic. Her eyes had a way of narrowing
when I spoke, as if she was trying to see the lies in the truth
coming out the mouth.

She had no reason to be like that now.

I saw movement out in the garden, and watched Drew walk
all the way round the fields with the horses to the boathouse then
round and back.

Measuring something, intently working something out in his
head, calculating.

I watched him for some time, rather intrigued by what he was
doing, when I noticed my bedroom door had opened.

'Megan?' Deborah accompanied this with a soft, apologetic
knock on the door.

Her floral perfume wafted in a few feet ahead of her. It
reminded me of Mum so much, not the same scent but close
enough to evoke memories that only the sense of smell can. 'I
don't want to disturb you if you are resting. But I thought you'd
like a sandwich and some tea. Even brought your favourite mug.'

'Thanks, you are a lifesaver. Deborah? Come and see this.'

She stood beside me at the French window, then we opened them
up and walked onto the terrace to get a better view. 'What the hell
is he doing?'

'He looks as if he is doing something important.'

'Well, even the most stupid of men do something, Megan,
although breathing can take up most of their brain cells.'

'I mean he's doing something in particular, what is he up to?
Wildlife cop?'

'Doubt it. Who knows? Who cares? He's fucking mad, he's
up to something that one, don't you trust him.'

'Really?' I looked at her.

'He's a cop, he's using this as part of his promotion, you know.
They have to be able to show that they can do stuff nowadays,
he's taking advantage of his uncle's ties with the family.'

'That's a bit harsh, how do you know that?'

'Because it's what I would do. Well I did, if I hadn't been
Carla's mum, I wouldn't have got my foot in the door here.'

'I can't argue with you there, Debs. Any idea what's
going on?'

'Nobody tells me anything. Your dad and Jago went out for a

long walk, I think his parents are going into Glasgow for the evening. They are staying until Melissa is taken away.'

'The funeral?'

'Friday, noon. I think that's what your dad and Jago are talking about, I've to get some help from the village to get the beds ready. I think there are a few folk going to be staying over.'

'Oh good,' I said, thinking that I'd stay here in my room and read. 'Or can I give you a hand. I have nothing else to do.'

'Thanks. Are you bringing over anybody, you know, for the church?'

I hadn't thought of that. Who would I ask? My ex-boyfriend Dan, who would have had me sectioned if Dad's money hadn't intervened? 'No. No friends of mine even knew Melissa.'

I was trying not to say that I didn't have any true friends anymore. I think Deborah knew that. Deborah looked out the window, a slight wistful look on her face; I guess she was thinking how different it all could have been. I walked back over to sit on my bed.

'You can't just be on your own.'

'I prefer it.'

'It wasn't always that way. Thick as thieves, you and Carla. The dynamic duo. Well, drink up your tea, get something to eat and get some sleep.'

I picked up my sandwich, egg mayo with a fine smear of mustard. That was something about Deborah, you could depend on her to remember the details. 'What perfume is that you are wearing?'

She grinned. 'It's Heather's. I had a squirt when I was . . .'

'Cleaning?'

'Maybe.'

'Cleaning where?' I ask, taking a sip from my Snoopy mug. 'Dad doesn't sleep in the master bedroom, does he? It looks just as Mum left it.'

'The big bedroom over the kitchen, the one with the view down the loch.' She looked away.

'He's always liked that room, that view. He used to sleep there when Melissa was a baby screaming the place down. Is that where the perfume is?'

'Yes.'

'So sometimes Heather stays over?'

Deborah nodded, looking out the window.

'Are you sure?'

'Sometimes the shower is adjusted too low for your dad; I have been cleaning that en suite for years. Your dad is tall and Heather is a smout. He is always up first. She leaves everything at her arse. How do you feel about that, kiddo?'

'I'm fine.' I shifted my legs over on the bed, inviting her to sit down, glad of somebody to talk to. She smoothed out the duvet cover before she sat, a tense smile on her face. 'But how are you coping with all this?' I asked her, sitting up slightly to rub her shoulder, just to say that she wasn't alone.

'If truth be told it's a relief. I know she was your sister but it's been a long slow process, hasn't it? And every turn has been a turn for the worse. Your dad has been beside himself for months now, taking her here and there, trying to get some help for her. Nothing worked. As you know.'

'I guess,' I wriggled my toes a little, thinking, 'I guess it's a disease like all other fatal diseases. I'm not sure I believe she has finally gone, she seems to have been teetering on the brink for so long now.'

'It's early days, I don't think it has really sunk in with any of us. I doubt that your dad will ever get over it.'

'I think he will, it's not as though he has lost something he really cared for, like the Dali or one of his dogs.'

'Megan, you do say the most awful things.' She tilted her head, it made her look very like Carla, a twist of the lip that belied a cheeky thought. 'But probably true.'

'Do you think she was ever happy?'

'She was designed not to be happy, that girl. Maybe she is better off out of it.' She sighed and glanced around the room. 'It's been a long time since I have been up here in this room for any length of time, it's nice.' Deborah resettled herself on the end of the bed. 'I think he's going to ask you to go in the main mourning car with him, so if he does, please say yes. If you don't then Heather will and her wee face will fracture with trying to not smile.'

'God if anybody should be in the car, it should be Mum, not her.'

'Megan . . . try not to build your hopes up.'

'Why does nobody want her back? It seems I am the only one who gives her a minute's thought.'

'Of course we all want her back, it's just, people move on, they change, times are different.'

'Why? Why don't you sit in the main car?' I asked, knowing the answer. 'You nursed Melissa through so much of this.'

'It wouldn't be the done thing, it wouldn't be the right thing either. Me being staff and all that.' She seemed very reluctant to go. 'Just wanted to make sure you knew what was going on downstairs. There's only you left now, of the three shell seekers, only you.' She pats the back of my hand, and stood up.

'Wait, what could be so important that it'd help that cop's career?'

'The rumour in the village is he's trying to discover who killed Carla.'

'Oh,' I say, nothing more to add.

'So you take care.' She smiles the way she always smiles at me, as if she is a little scared of me, she thinks she has something to be fearful of. As if I might have killed her daughter.

Carla

Yes, take care Megan, somebody is investigating the incident again. That's rather telling.

While nobody can dispute that Megan was lovely. She was as substantial as a Thunderbird puppet in a hurricane; I mean she really was useless at times. And more than a bit thick. She could speak Latin but then got into trouble crossing the road. I mean she honestly thought that all that palaver about Princess Frosty Pant's wedding dress was . . . about her wedding dress.

Nope.

It was all round the village and common knowledge to anybody who would listen, that those visits to Glasgow, Edinburgh, London and beyond were more about Melissa chucking her dinner down the toilet five minutes after she had eaten it.

I have always been far too greedy to be anorexic. But with Megan you never knew, it might have been what she was told,

*what she had understood or what she had presumed. She did
like to live in her isolated world. I had learned early that Megan
spent her life assuming things and making up the end of sentences
after only hearing the first part. Anybody with the faintest
modicum of sense would question why Melissa had been looking
for a wedding dress years before she was engaged.*

*Megan has always lived her life in a bubble, she sees every-
thing then makes up a soundtrack. She had very little idea of all
the private clinics for Melissa while the village was ripe with
rumours, some of them started by me. Some said that Melissa
was pregnant, that Beth was pregnant, OK that one was ridiculous
but they all enjoyed a good gossip and a laugh down the pub.
They said that the family was so inbred that the baby had three
heads and was walled up in one of the forgotten rooms at the
back of the Italian House.*

Then the weight loss became really obvious.

*And then we changed tack to cancer or AIDS as Beth and
Melissa were flying round the world. The weekends away became
weeks. Beth would come back without Melissa, then Beth would
go away again and come back with Melissa, thinner and weaker
than before. All the time Ivan was standing in the front row at
church with Megan standing beside him, trying to sing, trying to
keep up.*

*The family were trying to get a cure somewhere but as my
gran always said, the cure for that kind of thing exists within
four walls, there was no point in looking outside when the problem
lay inside. Gran wanted to know what they were doing about
that poor Megan one as everybody could see she wasn't right
in the head either.*

*Our family, such as it was, had different issues. I was back in
Dunoon. I think Mum and Dad might have been speaking to each
other rather than shouting abuse, so Gran stopped talking to
Dad and threatened to put him out the house if he got involved
with 'that tart' again. She always referred to Mum as 'that tart',
except when she'd had a few then it was 'whore'.*

I think it's fair to say that they didn't get on.

*But they had my best interest at heart, although I used to hear
them, Mum and Dad, Dad and Gran, and later Dad and Fishface
Norma, arguing about not wanting me. It wasn't that they didn't*

want to help me, every time I turned up at the door somewhere with no more than the clothes I stood up in and a pocket of money that I had stolen from somewhere, they opened the door to me, sat me down, gave me something to eat, usually toast and a cup of tea before phoning somebody to come take me off their hands.

They couldn't get rid of me quick enough.

It was just difficult for them to fit me into their life, Gran and Dad both worked, Mum did casual work and left me wherever was convenient. But whatever they had, I had my share. I used to think that I spent a lot of my life moving around, being wet and hungry, being cold and sleeping in strange beds, but Mum was doing the same. We were in it together, what she had, I had half of, except when I nicked it from her.

At some point, we were living above a pub, it was just before my twelfth birthday. Mum was having an affair with two of the customers at the same time. Then one of the wives found out and came into the pub. I was upstairs watching TV and eating peanut butter out the jar with my finger, I heard the sudden crescendo of squeals that sounded like excitement at first, and then it got violent. I heard crashing furniture, doors banging, voices raised, 'bitch' and 'whore', more doors banging, glass breaking, and that's never a good sign. I crawled off the settee and over to the window where I squashed in behind the table, it was dark and cold outside, my breath steamed up the glass as I cupped my hand to see better, letting the curtains close behind me. They were rolling on the ground. The traffic had stopped. My mum was being held down by her hair. Some woman, wearing a neat suit of skirt, jacket and heels like she worked in a bank some-where, was trying to kick my mum in the face. I was on the side of Team Mum of course. Some guy grabbed The Suit round the waist lifting her up off the ground so her legs flailed in mid-air, well short of their target i.e. my mum's head. The crowd started to clap, egging them on, maybe if someone had got hold of Mum, it might have ended there but as the other woman turned her attention to the guy who had grabbed her, so my mum went on the attack, head down and rammed the other woman, hands up like claws. At that point an onlooker realized that somebody was

*going to get very hurt, they were dragged apart, the crowd scat-
tered and the police arrived. It all happened very quickly, Mum
was handcuffed and huckled forcibly into the back of the van,
people came and went, and the pub door was opened and closed.*

Nobody remembered I was there.

Soon the street was empty.

*I took the money out of Mum's hidey-hole, a roll of tenners
at the bottom of one of her boots and scarpered.*

*It's easy when you are invisible, I slipped through the cracks
as easy as I slipped through the door.*

*I made my way to the train station, there were reasons I didn't
want to go back to the pub. I didn't like the way they talked or
the way they looked at me. I had a sense I needed to get out of
there before I got any older.*

*I spent the night in a few cafes round the station, kept looking
at my watch as if I was waiting for somebody to come and get
me. That stopped any busybody from calling the police. From
there, train to Glasgow Central then to Greenock and out to
the ferry, it was not a difficult thing to do.*

I walked to the house I once lived in, but Dad was not there.

*Fishface told me where to go at first, then looked at my face
and decided to take me to casualty. I told her it was nothing, but
the police were called when the fractures appeared on the X-ray.
So much for me being nice to my mum's boyfriends.*

Megan

In the end I didn't go downstairs. Dad would be annoyed that I
wasn't treating our guests properly and acting as the Lady Of
The House. I could leave that safely in Heather's hands. I could
rely on Deborah to spread the word that I wasn't up to it, and
being who they were, they would respect that.

I drank my tea, and lay down, waiting for sleep.

It came quickly and noisily.

Of all the noises I often heard in my sleep the loudest was
always Carla screaming. Now I am dreaming of Melissa's funeral.
The coffin opens and inside is my mother, smiling at me and
telling me not to bother.

But usually, it's Carla screaming and the flames crackling across the water. I think I am running to hold them back, I need to get there to save somebody but I can never quite do it, pulled back by the bedclothes or by the bedroom door being stuck. I try to move quickly while my feet are stuck in the mud. Dad, Mum, Melissa, Deborah and Heather. I cannot get any closer – every time I reach the water they move further away. They are talking and laughing at her, ignoring me. No, not ignoring me. They cannot hear me, they are deaf. Carla has taken my place in their lives and I am left on my own abandoned. In the dream I can't get out of the house. I am left to walk in and out of every room with only Agatha for company. I can see the sky out the paladin window, down to the Benbrae. There are people in the courtyard, drinking champagne and chatting, all laughing and drinking. Jago is there, in the centre of it all. As I move from window to window, so do they. I batter at the glass, but they do not hear me, and Carla has her arm round my mother. Carla then turns around, and looks right through me as if I am not here.

EIGHT

Wednesday

Carla

*B*loody hell the house is getting full of pretentious wankers. Megan is keeping out the way, I think we will be down at the Benbrae today. Not even Ivan would have the balls to be seen to disrupt his youngest daughter in her mourning, no matter how much he thinks that she should be putting a brave face on it. People do think that the deaf are simple, that because they can't hear, they don't understand.

Some of Melissa's friends have been popping in. The funeral is not for a couple of days, these are Glasgow, Edinburgh friends coming over, paying respects, then leaving. Jago is acting as host, like he owns the house. That will not happen now, Jago, will it? You have effectively just been disinherited. But if Megan had died first . . .

The Italian House is very beautiful, grand and stylized, but it's just as weird as the people who live in it. It's very big, built round a central courtyard, spacious and not located as you might think, on the plot of land that would give the best views to the loch and down the Clyde. It's built looking inwards. I think that says everything about the Melvick family.

The house is huge, so spacious you could get lost wandering around inside, except that some bugger will always come and find you. In the old days that would have been the butler. Even in the teeny totiest weest bedsit or the grubbiest hostel there was a big outside where I could escape; wandering around a market, being in a greasy spoon making a cup of tea last as long as it possibly could because there I was warm and lost, amongst people, so I felt safe. There's always a safety in numbers.

The Italian House is not like that. Big it may be, but it's a house of overheard conversations, staff going through your *drawers and reading private diaries, and you can be heard all over, the dogs always know where you are. You are lonely but never alone, and never really allowed to be yourself. The family were always a Melvick and the staff were always the staff. Megan felt that far more than anybody else.*

So Jago's parents, the Harringtons, his brother Jeremy and his incredibly vacuous wife called Cecily or Cecelia or some stupid name like that have arrived. If Cecily stands against magnolia wallpaper she disappears. His mother is a rotund woman who likes art and says 'jolly' a lot. I thought she was a painter but she buys art, invests in art, talks about art but couldn't draw a shit in the dust. She owns a small gallery in London and is always on the lookout for 'pieces' . . . not the Glasgow kind with jam on them.

They are supposedly here for the funeral on Friday, wanting a day of rest, going out for lunch. Some acting types are arriving, sad times but they manage to make the best of it. Sometimes, in my little working-class head, I think they get pretty close to partying. Like the Irish except they tend to include the dead in the party. Melissa is being forgotten already.

We are all gathering again. There was a wrong done at the Benbrae on the day that Melissa got married, a murder was committed. As far as I'm concerned nobody noticed apart from Megan, and now maybe Drew Murray. Though I doubt my murder is important enough to get him promoted, I was investigated and written off as, well, not worth bothering about. It might be interesting to find out what Mr Murray thinks might be worth investigating. This house hides a shit load of secrets, and I bet Mr Murray Senior knew a lot of them.

Interesting. Megan hasn't made that connection. Hairy Monkey sitting on the sofa, me with my lemonade and my stookie. Megan with her head bandaged and her pinkie sticking out. Oodie eating the sandwiches. Ten years ago. I bet young Mr Murray knows a lot.

Maybe Mr Ivan Melvick realizes that soon the same people who were there at the wedding will be here for the funeral, five years later, almost to the day. Yes, maybe now is the time for the hens to come home to roost, for the cost to be counted and the guilty to have the finger pointed at them. The past may have gone cold but that only fuels a desire for revenge.

Maybe Drew thinks he can take on the previous investigation and revisit it, maybe Ivan gives him a little more clout. There's something going on between these two . . .

But for now, I am keeping well out of sight down at the Benbrae, hidden but capable of seeing and hearing everything and everyone that goes past. I think the rooks know, I think that's why they have been so close to the house recently. The rooks and the family have been a permanent fixture for hundreds of years. A shotgun will not get rid of them.

And that was a difficult thing for me to get my head round, me having been in sixteen different houses by the time I was eleven. I couldn't imagine being in the same house for four hundred years, or at least living in the same bit of the garden, building and rebuilding the same house to make it bigger, smaller, easier to defend, easier to house a growing family, a stable of ponies, then a garage of cars. Nurseries being added, separate rooms for the grannies and nannies built on the ground floor.

Family, that's what it was all about, keeping the clan together. The Melvicks had got that really sussed since 1600, then I came on the scene ten years ago and it all started to unravel for them, such is my power for bad luck but their power for self-delusion is amazing.

I started to wonder if there was something wrong with me. Like a two-leafed clover, bringing sorrow in my shadow.

Still, they had years of The Family keeping them safe, giving them all some backbone and structure – something that they could all come home to no matter what little corner of the world they had decided to invade and occupy.

I think Mum just looked for corners of the world to hide in, then had to move on when they – whoever they were – found her. Or Mum's behaviour got so bad, it was get out or else.

There were times I felt safe. But not often.

And it could flare from nothing, the violence.

I'm not sure what sparked it the night Mum and Chris had gone to the pub, leaving me in charge of Baby Paul. They came back, rowing as usual. The noise of bone hitting flesh always woke me up. I'd listen for the footsteps coming up the stairs to have a go at me but I'd make sure that I looked as if I was sleeping. You learn to get these things right when it's bloody sore to get them wrong.

That night was different. I heard the usual shouting, the swearing, a bang. Then it all went quiet. Nothing. The baby must have sensed something and lay still, regarding me with big round blue eyes, wide with shock.

Silence.

I was wide awake by now, some spidery sense telling me that Mum was in deep trouble and I had to go rescue her. Or hope that Eddie's mum had heard through the wall and had called the police again.

There were footsteps on the stairs, running. Paul started screaming, a loud piercing scream, not a cry, and my door opened. I was told to get dressed, Mum hit me for not moving fast enough, before she took the scissors to my clothes. Then we were in the back of a taxi away to yet another refuge that would smell of cheap perfume and other folks' burned cooking.

We were installed in a tiny room, with walls the colour of a public toilet. It was ten feet by eight, made smaller by the cot in the corner for Paul, all his stuff and a pull down for me. Within a week I was in another school with a stookie on my other arm, my mum was the life and the soul of the whole refuge. I couldn't blame them. The refuge was too small to live in and they took their chances to go out and enjoy themselves, six of them, all female, feeling safe and secure in each other's company. One, a young girl called Mary, was left in charge of the kids who should have been asleep in their makeshift beds and boxes in the three stories above.

I heard them go out, clattering down the stairs in high heels, some shrieking in excitement as they opened cheap vodka and swapped clothes, some of which had been shoplifted that morning especially for the event. They would be cutting off the security tags now. Mum came up to kiss me goodnight and say goodbye to Paul lying in the corner cot. I didn't know what Mary was supposed to be doing, looking after me but I didn't hear anybody come up to our floor. I woke up, my arm sore, a little scared at first as I couldn't recognize where I was, the unfamiliar ceiling Artex and the single night light in the corner. I rolled onto the floor, pulled my sleeping bag around me and waddled off down the hall to the shared loo on the half landing, picking up our roll of toilet paper and remembering that I had to jam a brick in the gap so the door of our room wouldn't close and lock behind me.

I walked back to bed, dragging my sleeping bag. I saw Paul, eyes closed in his cot. I felt his cheek as I passed and pulled his cotton blanket up a little and tucked it round his neck as I thought he felt cold, very cold.

Megan

I had been up for a while, trying to retreat into what should have been the blissful quiet of my bedroom but I unable to concentrate on anything due to the constant pop pop of the shotguns outside. I didn't like the rooks but I didn't want them dead, too much death about this house. I slipped my hearing aids out, letting my mind tumble over thoughts of Mum, the fact I would be seeing her soon. What was the mysterious Drew after? I thought he and I had a connection but according to Deborah he was just using me to get a viewpoint on the death of Carla.

He certainly picked his time well, all the suspects were gathering. And there was Melissa's dying words. It took her a lot of effort to say that.

Who could I talk to about that? Everybody had an agenda.

I fell back into a strange and thankfully dreamless sleep, that left me cold and nervous about the days ahead. The heat outside, even at that time in the morning, was starting to build. The weather forecast was warning people to avoid the heat of the midday, to drink plenty of water, wear a hat, don't leave dogs in the car. All the big shops had run out of fans. The weather was becoming oppressive, there was a sense of danger in the air, the world was not the friendly damp place that Scotland usually was, it was parched and deadly.

Dad had been up and out on the estate already, overseeing the shooting, asking the tenant farmers to watch out for the wildlife, they would be suffering in the drought and for trespassers who might be after the eagles and their young.

I was going downstairs for a drink when I saw Debs walking, quickly, down the hall, her Ugg boots scuffing on the polished wooden floor. Something furtive about her movement made me stop, the way she cast a glance both up and down the hall. I sidestepped into the doorway of the dining room, immediately noticing the mess of the place, bottles and glasses strewn on the table. When I stepped out again, Debs had gone into my dad's study, emerging with a set of keys wrapped in her fingers, and what looked like a rash on her face.

And the keys looked like those of the gun cabinet.

I waited until I saw her leave the kitchen, going across the yard to the lodge.

There could be a few explanations for that but not one that made sense to me.

I took a bottle of water from the fridge then took the dogs down to the Benbrae; they could swim in the cool water. Molly was her usual happy self, Anastasia seemed a little confused. There was usually a slight breeze down here, so it was not too hot for them. They could run around and then spend the rest of the day dozing in the coolness of the house.

It was very hot down at the bank. The grass was burning in the harsh unsettling heat, the water was starting to look low, the clouds appearing on the horizon. There was going to be a high tide on the Clyde and the parched earth would soak up the excess. I saw Dad drive past on his way back up to the house, he'd been out since six. Whatever was happening in his bed it wasn't long lie-ins. I wondered when he had planned the shoot, he'd need access to the guns for that.

Another stress to worry about, I wanted to board *Curlew 2*, and think about nothing. I wanted the next few days to be over, I wanted to . . . well, where did I want to be? There had been no talk of me going back to work. I was now expected to be here in this non-life. I hoped Mum would turn up at the funeral. That was the unspoken question on everybody's lips. Would she, wouldn't she? Nobody had heard anything, even Heather was keeping quiet. She was around but keeping out of my way, I was sure her car hadn't moved from the back parking area and there were two glasses on the coffee table in the front room, evidence of a wee late-night warmer. A bottle of Grey Goose and a bottle of Glenfiddich, though from memory, Heather was more fond of designer gin. I sat there for a long time, looking over at the dark part of the pond, where the trees overhung the surface. It buzzed with flies and always smelled as if something was rotting in there. Dad had explained that there was an under-water connection there out to the faerie pools beyond, the current eddied there, causing the water to be stagnant. Evil and magical creatures of the night lived down there, I was terrified of the place. Melissa had known that and it had given her no end of amusement. She could be cruel. Instead of being my ears, the way Oodie, Molly and Carla used to be, Melissa used my deafness to terrify me. Because it was funny. More than once she had blindfolded me and marched me down to the Tentor Wood, claiming we were playing Blind Man's Bluff or she was walking me to a surprise and didn't want it spoiled. If I hadn't been so young, I wouldn't have fallen for it. Once I did fall, into a faerie pool. And I couldn't get out.

I nearly drowned.

She should have said sorry for that. It was a memory, uncovered in a session with Dr Scobie. I wish he had left it where it was, as it opened up something, the sense of another memory behind it. The vision I have in my mind is of the faerie pool at the Tentor Wood, then it goes out of focus and I am being carried up the Long Drive by Dad. Later Dad takes Melissa into the library for a 'talk'.

My memory never hangs around at the faerie pool, and I don't know why. And Dr Scobie never pushes on that the way he concentrates on other issues. I wonder if he knows.

I do have some memories of the place. No matter how much sun shone over the Benbrae, what time of year or how high the sun was in the sky, that part of the pond was always dark and dense. Jago and his mates, up one weekend, had got very drunk and dared each other, foolish young men, drunk, city boys, running through the thick undergrowth. One of them, Roddie, dived into a faerie pool, and couldn't get out, a fatal mix of drink and overconfidence. A sober friend ran out of the Tentor Wood and picked up the lifebuoy that hung on the wall of the boathouse. That kept Roddie afloat until Dad was called and they got Roddie out with a rope, but it was touch and go. He caught giardiasis from swallowing the water and was in hospital for a long time, with terrible diarrhoea and vomiting. He's never been the same since, he ended up losing his job, another victim of the Melvick curse.

Thinking of that night made me shiver, even in the heat of the sun. Dad was stunned, Mum was confused as to why, and how, somebody could be that stupid. We all knew how dangerous the faerie pools were, with their strange deep whirlpool current and the overhanging banks.

Roddie was lucky to be alive, Dad spoke to the police about fencing off the area. The police said that drunk folk do stupid stuff, and you couldn't protect them from their own stupidity. It was the first time I had heard that people had died there before. Death just like that, right here at the end of the garden. Then the eagles came back, then birdwatchers and sightseers were walking through the woods uninvited. Dad, the police and the council decided to build a lay-by off the road, Dad was donating the land, and the council would provide signposts to divert people around the Tentor Wood to the bridge.

That's how there came to be the lay-by where Mum was last seen, waiting to be picked up by a car driven by some man that we didn't know about.

I decided to walk back up to the house, see what Dad was doing for breakfast and put off the evil moment of meeting Jago, maybe ask Deborah about the keys. Molly and Anastasia walked slowly after me, their tongues lolling out the side of their mouths, panting. It was already too hot for them.

Dad was nowhere to be seen so I showered, answered some more emails of condolence and spent a long time out on the balcony of my bedroom, part of the long terrace looking down the long drive out to the Benbrae, waiting for somebody to appear. There used to be a routine in this house, it used to bustle. Melissa was always the noisy one, screaming with some tantrum or another. I was the apologetic one, Melissa had a sense of entitlement and never apologized for anything. Until her dying breath.

This has never been a house for bringing people together, it's too easy to stay apart. As a kid, I would sit alone in my room, in my soundless room, reading a book. They tried to send me to school but I didn't like it so the school sent me back. They sent me away to another school, I didn't like that so they sent me back. It was all too noisy and too difficult. Then I ended up at the local school, my parents had been talked into it by some of the villagers. That didn't work and it ended up with me having a scar on my forehead and being schooled at home, in a classroom of one. But it did bring Carla to my rescue.

It did mean that I was lonely, but at least I was at peace. And it meant that I met Carla eventually. I was a kid who ran around this big house on my own, she was cramped into a corner somewhere in shared accommodation. We should have hated each other on sight but there was always a symbiosis there. The recognition of two outsiders who needed each other.

Eventually the sun drove me off the terrace so I went back into my bedroom and opened *Lonesome Dove*; I was slowly getting through it. I needed to do something on my own, I was still heavy-headed from the bad sleep. I wasn't used to living with people, not used to having to wear my hearing aids and concentrating on listening to think. I actually wasn't that interested in hearing, but I only knew that after I had been bothered listening to it. Funny how those that talk think I will be interested in hearing; it's never that fascinating, believe me.

'Megan?' There was a knock at the door. I heard some muffled noise, saw the door open slightly. 'Megan? Can I come in?'

Deep tones, I adjusted my hearing aid and put *Lonesome Dove* down on top of the duvet.

'Come in.'

It was Dad, looking at the ground, smiling grimly. 'Megan. Did you sleep well last night?'

'No, why?'

'Can you come downstairs for a minute?' He stood up. He had his headmaster's face on. 'It's important.'

'What now?' Christ, had Jago told him?

'Yes, Megan, right now, please.' He stood by the door and opened it wide, ushering me outside into the hall, then down to the front room.

I was surprised to see Deborah, not Jago, sitting there, legs crossed at the ankle, looking more prim than the queen, despite her normal dress of jeans and loose white T-shirt. She was holding her hand to the side of her face, she looked a little red-eyed.

I thought she was having some delayed reaction to the events of yesterday.

Dad pointed to the sofa opposite Debs and asked me to have a seat. He sat on Debs' side, close next to her. I wondered what Heather would say about that.

'Megan, I think you should listen to what Deborah has to say.'

I looked at her but she was looking at Dad, eyes wide, almost frightened, not wanting to say what she was about to say. She looked incredibly young. Her hand dropped revealing a nasty injury, still bleeding at the bottom; crimson pansies of blood patterned the white handkerchief; from a distance I had mistaken the injury for a rash.

'Deborah, can you tell us what happened to you last night?'

She looked from him to me then back to him. 'She doesn't know, does she?'

'I don't think she does.' My dad looked at me, a curious mixture of guilt and shame on his face.

'Know what?' I asked.

'Deborah was out last night, checking the house before she went back to the lodge. It was dark by the time she went down the path between the house and the orchard.'

'It was very dark, so dark I really couldn't see,' Deborah explained, more tears rolling down her face.

'Are you OK,' I asked, 'were you attacked?' I felt the curse of the house come down amongst us. 'Was there somebody out there?'

'It was very late, it wasn't dark until after midnight last night. You know that, Megan?'

'Of course I do but I was upstairs in my bed . . .' And then I looked at their faces, reading what they could not say.

'Somebody was out there, waiting for Deborah when she went out to the bins, and hit her. It was only by chance that she managed to get away, a glancing blow rather than what might have been intended.' He pointed at her face. 'And the dogs did not bark, none of them, so it stands to reason it was somebody that the dogs knew.' He looked at me directly; he had a way of staring that used to bore through me when I was young, it was a look of interrogation. Nobody would dare to lie under the intensity of that stare.

Now it was my time to look from one to the other.

'Deborah thinks it was you, Megan.'

'I didn't say that. I just said—'

'Deborah, I am dealing with this.'

And she was immediately silent, hands in her lap, the cut on her face surrounded by blue and black petals.

'You must have followed her out from the house . . .'

'I didn't even know she was there . . .' I argued, but it sounded weak, I knew exactly where this was going.

'You did look very strange, I think you were asleep, Megan, I don't think you meant it or anything. I'm not accusing you, I'm not doing that.' And the tears started again.

'Nobody is accusing anybody of anything. We know that Megan has had issues in the past and we are going to get it sorted. Megan? Do you recall anything last night, anything at all?'

'No.'

'And when you woke up this morning, Megan? Did you feel odd or cold or were you more dressed than you were when you went to bed?'

'She had her nightdress on,' said Deborah. 'And her housecoat was over it but not tied closed.' She looked at me. 'I'm sorry but you did have it on, I think I startled you, you were sleep-walking, you didn't look like yourself. Your eyes were open. I gave you a fright, I didn't know you were there and you just lashed out at me, hitting me here. You had something in your hand, it was dark, I only saw it coming and I closed my eyes. There's a scratch, must have come from your ring . . . there was a lot of blood. I went back into the lodge and watched from the door. You strolled back to the house, into the kitchen, like nothing had happened. You closed the door behind you and didn't come back out.'

'I don't remember it at all.'

'Can you go upstairs and get your nightdress and the housecoat you were wearing.'

'I had them on this morning, they were clean.' I knew they were, I would have noticed.

'Ivan, she was sleepwalking, there is no need for all this.'

'One look at what she was wearing will help us.'

'In my washing basket, in the laundry,' I said. 'It was very hot, last night.'

'I'll go and fetch the basket,' said Deborah, looking relived to be out of the firing range, caught between Dad and I.

'Thank you, Deborah.'

And he waited until she was gone before he said, 'Megan, do you feel that you have been under stress, too much stress, with Melissa and everything? Maybe we have been neglecting you, there has been so much and—'

I droned him out, floating into my silence. It was happening again. 'I need to apologize to Deborah.'

'She says there is no need, but yes, I think you must.' He rubbed his face. 'I was talking to Donald Scobie. He knows your history of blackouts. I called him yesterday about Melissa, of course, but I am going to call him again and tell him of this recent event. I do not want you going backwards, Megan, you have been so well, holding down a job and living independently. I'm sure this was a single incident, an accident because you came across Deborah in your sleep and you both got a fright. The stress of losing your sister . . .'

The door opened, Deborah entered holding a folded-up white cloth under her arm, my nightdress that she had put out on the bed for me the night I arrived. She handed it to my dad slowly, her hand shaking. Dad unrolled it and saw the little spatters of blood down the right side close to the bottom. He looked at the back, at the front, and then rolled it back up again.

'I'm so sorry, Deborah.'

'I know it was an accident, Megan,' Deborah said, then turned to Dad. 'Can we leave it like that? And Heather has arrived, I met her at the kitchen door. You might not want . . .'

'Does she just let herself in?' I asked.

'The door was open. It's very hot out there,' she chided gently, back to her usual self.

'OK.' Dad voice was grave; he was getting this conversation back on track. 'And I was telling Megan that we are getting Donald Scobie to call and see . . . if we need some more help.'

'It's been an awful time for you all. No need for you to apologize, Megan. I gave you a fright, that's all.' And she put her arm out to hug me, rubbing my back. Up close, the skin of her cheek

had split, still open and weeping, not bleeding now. It was starting
to crust round the outside, the edges of her skin were puffed and
raw. The bruising was already starting to deform her cheekbone.

I said sorry again and walked towards the door, aware of a
scarring noise on the far side, the smell of Pomegranate Noir
hanging in the air. I hadn't smelled it when I was hugging Debs.
So I knew that the lovely Heather had been listening at the door.

NINE

Carla

So Megan can't trust her own memory. And she lamped Mum, good for her, maybe if she put a lot more effort in she could have stood them together and lamped Heather as well. If she fancies getting busy I can give her a whole list of folk that could benefit from a good slapping.

Megan, without me, is a bit unstable. I'm serious when I say that there is madness in that family. My family are all a bit bonks but we only suffer from the normal drunken madness of getting pissed, falling into fountains, stabbing our nearest and dearest and cockaleekie soup.

The memory of Frosty Pants dragging her down to the faerie pools, blindfolded, is coming back, slowly. There was a lot of screaming there, Megan's complex neurones had convinced her that she was deaf by then so couldn't hear herself scream for help. Ivan said it sounded like a wounded dog, inhuman, incredibly loud and piercing. When he first heard it, he had no idea it was his daughter making the noise. When he got to her, she was sitting in her own pish and shit, so mad with fear that she didn't recognize him. He had looked round for the animal that had attacked her, the one that had made the noise, there was all kinds of stuff going through his mind.

Totally missing the fact that this was a rerun of the incident where she had been struck deaf by the noise, in the same way some folk are struck dumb. But they never talked about it, nobody listened. I think Frosty Pants knew that and was evil enough to repeat it.

As I've said, the Melvicks hide their delusions very well, they play rugger and are gentlemen, inbred to the extent that they possess a real Heathcliff and Cathy kind of madness, Ophelia *going slowly nuts and then drowning herself. Megan met a boy that she really did like, and they starting seeing each other, he was really nice to her, he got on well with her family and had suitable breeding, was the right height, the right school etc. And what did she do? She woke up in the middle of the night and set fire to the bed while he was still in it.*

I guess that kind of put an end to that relationship.

His family and her family got together, of course. Ivan got Megan help, the best of help. Dr Scobie, the shrink, started treating Megan with a compound of drugs for some mental disorder. They get her well enough to leave the house, the minute she's back the madness starts to kick off. She needs to get away, but she's being pulled back in, her work say there's no need to come back, so the arms of the family are round her, trapping her. She'll think it through one day, that she's better off the drugs than on, better off away from the house than here. She's too trusting, I'd have seen through that quack in a minute, He is a right little shit of a man, he looked like a piglet poking his head out a hole. And I think, and Megan suspects, that her father and dear Dr Scobie are too close as friends, and it's really another way for Ivan to control his daughter. It's very much Donald and Ivan, not Dr Scobie and Mr Melvick and who can blame Ivan for giving his deaf daughter a get out of jail free card in case she does turn out to be bonkers?

Megan believes in those very people she should be suspicious of. I can hear her dad's voice warning her that she should have been suspicious of me.

Me?

What about her? When the news of that fire spread round the village, suddenly little innocent Megan walked onto centre stage of the tragedy of the wedding night. The poor little deaf bridesmaid, standing beside the more beautiful sister, then setting a fire and killing the other bridesmaid, burning her to a crisp, spoiling the day and the memory of the day for everybody. Did she do it?

If she did, was she aware she did it?

People will talk. And let's face it, when you are deaf people can talk about you all they like, you'll never hear it. But as far as Megan knows, her sanity is slowly unravelling.

I knew she'd fall apart without me.

The preparations for the funeral seem to be underway, people are coming and going, the gates of the Italian House are opening and closing like the legs of a French whore in wartime, as my gran used to say. The family do have a sense of occasion; no doubt this is all part of doing the right thing by Melissa. We have caterers, the distant family, the close family, friends, business people, fellow theatre types and, of course, Jago when he wakes up. That will be fun. Not. He's never forgiven me for pointing out what a small willie he had. It wasn't what I said, it was the fact I knew. And Melissa knew I knew.

So all that is coming back to bite us on the bum, except instead of it being Melissa's wedding it's her funeral, a bit like a replay. But the colours are darker.

A wedding and a funeral, five years apart. Almost to the day.

There was a rehearsal for the wedding, two days before it. All shite and hullaballoo about who was to stand where, sit where, speak to this one, speak to that one or in my case speak only when you are spoken to. Then I got lectures on how to speak. Try to say a 'T' at the end of the word if it is spelled that way, and try not to swear. My mum really stressed the not swearing part.

She was hanging around on the sidelines, looking across the stage waiting for her big break. I think I even saw her practising, putting on her new nude lipstick, rather than her usual tarty bright red. She'd always have that lipstick, even in the days when we had no food, nothing to eat in the house at all, she would always have bright red lipstick. Her own lips were thin and mean looking, as were the words that came from them. At that rehearsal I heard her practising, in her mad head she was rehearsing her own wedding, like that would ever happen now, as she put it 'with all the baggage I have'.

I think that was a small reference to me.

It was something she said a lot when she met a nice guy, his reason for not wanting to go near her with a bargepole was me. 'Why would a man want anything to do with me when there's a kid like you buggering around, all the nice men will go with women who do not have wee shits like you'.

On the wedding day, we were in the same church as the funeral would be. Both a summer's day in a plain church, a single figure of Christ on the cross, his face bearing down on me like a dog that wanted to be put to sleep. I always think that Jesus looks like he wants to be put out his misery hanging there on the cross, in pain. I'd prefer that he was happy, not suffering, not on my behalf.

I like this church. It belongs to the Melvicks. It was plain not fancy. It was a church of the people, while it was a Church of Scotland, but it was the Melvick family who kept it going. I bet any minister that didn't get on with Ivan Melvick never lasted more than a month. I wonder if Megan had any sense of the power her father had, he could have sacked my dad at any time and we would have lost the house, my mum would be in worse straits. He had the power of work and idleness. Did he have the power of life and death? Did Megan ever stop to think about the hanging tree and the madness in the family that all started somewhere? Did Megan ever stop to think how close that madness might be stalking her?

I doubt it.

It was a quiet church, a space to reflect and think, bit like the Benbrae but closer to the village and even here the Melvicks were the family, standing at the front, the congregation was subservient to them, separate. Again, there was a 'them' and an 'us', I don't think my mum changing the colour of her lipstick was going to alter any of that.

There had been seven rehearsals for that wedding, Melissa getting more and more stressed at each one, Ivan trying to look interested but looking like a clown at a christening. And Beth looking at her watch to see when she could get back to the ponies, pouring words of comfort while my mum poured something a little stronger if nobody was looking. Melissa wanted it all this way then all that way. Megan fretted about being in church, her hearing aids could pick up sounds the normal healthy human ear could not hear. And that was why she hated big echoey places like the church.

She preferred her world quiet.

The main players exchanged glances behind the bride's back, uncomfortable shoulder shrugging, awkward silences, and those little coughs that mean nothing and everything.

It was tedious beyond belief.

Megan and I were bored so we were studying Melissa's university pals and Jago's friends. We started marking them out of ten, then betting on who might have some weed on them and might be up for a wee puff in the toilets.

I suggested who might be up for a shag, but Megan took a quick look round and shook her head. 'I wouldn't bother.' As if she knew it would be crap.

Megan

Shit. It'd happened again.

I felt that creep of madness coming on. I had no recollection of hitting anybody but the evidence on my nightdress told its own story. Was this how it felt for Melissa? How it started, an inability to trust yourself and memory? There is something malevolent in this house now, it's poisoning me. I was well when I wasn't here but now it's happening again.

I felt banished to the long veranda outside my bedroom, the early-morning air was clear and still and the heat continued to build. I was sitting on my rocking chair, wrapped in another light housecoat and another cotton nightdress trying to catch up on some less troubled sleep. I had four of these nightdresses, pure Irish linen, crisp and cool for hot summer nights like those we had suffered in the last six weeks. They never left this house, they carried the scent.

The conversation with Deborah, the concerned looks from Dad, had convinced me that I was guilty. I must have been up in the night, walking around the house. Who was I looking for? Melissa? My psyche unable to accept she was gone. Mum? Because I wanted her to come back. Carla? I missed my friend.

I had gone into the shower the minute I woke up so there was no point in looking at the souls of my feet, the ground outside was burned to a crisp. My shoes if I had them on, or my slippers, wouldn't show anything. There was just the blood on the linen, the injury to Deborah's face and the fact that I felt overwhelmed with tiredness.

And now I had to talk it through with Dr Scobie. He would

talk about my blackouts, my unreliable memory and the anger of my deafness, his diagnosis of Dissociative Identity Disorder. He was shit hot on that one; the distress and the memory loss, the anxiety and the sense of being detached from myself. There would be a fight about resuming the medication, what I did and did not need, what I would and would not take. It hadn't escaped my notice that it was all starting to slip, just as I returned home. Like I was being poisoned by the very air that I breathe . . .

I needed to get dressed again, although I felt more tired than I had felt when I got up the first time. Dad never liked us walking around in unsuitable clothes, people like us didn't do that, we didn't get tattoos, women didn't cut their hair short and the men didn't grow theirs long. We didn't swear in public, we didn't get drunk either.

Such were the rules of the club.

I looked out on the water of the Benbrae and the Tentor Wood beyond; the word *tentor* derived from the Latin for 'to hang'. The trees sit there as a reminder of the best escape route when you cannot trust your sanity. As a family dyeing our hair was frowned upon but hanging yourself out in the woods was perfectly acceptable.

I had another shower, running the water cold for the last few minutes, in an attempt to wake me up. Then I put my hearing aids in and immediately heard the rumble of the water pipes around the house. They brought back old memories of lying in my bed, the duvet pulled tight up over my head as Melissa told me that the noise was the padded feet of the bogeymen, coming to get me. When they caught me, they'd drag me out to the faerie pools and drown me. The age gap between Melissa and I left me wide open to be scared about stuff like that by my lovely sister. I believed she would drag me out and drown me. She had done the blindfold thing more than once. As I got older, Melissa would get her friends in to help her be horrible to me. I was always on my own, I liked being on my own as a kid but Mum thought I should be with Melissa and her friends as it was 'good for me'.

All that led to was me being dragged along and making all parties miserable. The last time it happened, Melissa and her mates had taken me out on the *Curlew*. We could all swim perfectly well so there was no danger with us slipping off the boat and into the cool water. It was a rare burning hot day. I was swimming back to the boat and Melissa thought it would be funny to place the palm of her hand on my head.

It was very quiet under the water.

I liked it, so I stayed there in the silent, cool water.

And she got into a lot of trouble for that.

I was dressed for the second time, in a neat navy-blue dress, my hair tied back in a slim ponytail as people were going to be visiting today and as a family we were in mourning so a certain sense of propriety would be expected between now and the funeral on Friday. There was a sense of waiting, hanging around, in a vacuum. All the clocks were ticking, their noises echoing round this empty house, yet time was standing still until Melissa was put in the ground.

Dad was out on the terrace below my window, he had been on his mobile phone for about twenty minutes, making call after call. Tying up the final arrangements for Melissa's funeral, calling friends who he hadn't been able to contact yet, talking to the printer about the order of service. He was pacing back and forth, but with my hearing aids I could hear most of it, he was too far away to lip-read but I liked to practise and see how well my eyes heard. He was looking pale, anxious. This was a time for him to be strong and stand tall, the way the Melvicks always did.

I took my chance, feeling brave and caught him in between phone calls.

He smiled at me, like the earlier conversation had never happened. 'Ah, Megan. You look very well turned out. I've got hold of Donald, he's happy to come out to see you.'

'Donald?' I knew damn well who he was, but I was making a point.

'Donald Scobie. I'm sure he'll get you on the right road again.' His hand came up, cupped the top of my arm and I have to resist the temptation to step back, to pull away. I have never felt like that before. This was my own father. He would do anything to protect me.

Maybe he had.

'I'm afraid I lied to you, Dad.'

His eyes narrowed, the creases in his forehead deepened to a black plough line. 'I am sure you had good reason, thought I'd like to hear it.'

He didn't quite add 'young lady' but it was there, unsaid at the end of his sentence.

'I didn't mean to, it was just something that Melissa said when she died. I thought it was for me, between her and me, so when you asked I didn't want to break her confidence. As she said it, on her death bed, with her dying breath.'

Did I see a flicker of fear in those blue eyes? The hand cupped my arm tighter, comforting now.

'That wasn't a lie, Megan, of course you kept that confidence. That's between you and her. You kept it to yourself. If she wanted to say it to me, she would have.'

'She said "sorry",' I blurted out, and then I was sure. There was that little flicker of fear in his eyes, a slight narrowing before he covered it with a slow eye blink. 'Do you know why she would say that to me?'

He smiled and shrugged, relieved. 'You should know better than me, she once nearly drowned you in the Tentor Wood. She was a rascal.' He tapped my arm. 'You take it easy today, I've some phone calls still to make.' He sighed like a man who had been told good news at the doctors. 'Oh, and on a more delicate subject . . .' He clasped both of my arms in his hands.

'Yes?'

'Have you got the necklace?'

'No.' Again I knew exactly what he was talking about.

'It was in the safe, Megan, you haven't been in there?'

'No, of course not. The last time I saw it, it was—'

He put his hand out not wanting that particular memory to come back. 'I must have mislaid it.'

My mind flits to what else I was doing while sleepwalking, 'Dad? You can't . . .'

'I will have put it somewhere secure, don't worry. Too much coming and going. But I do want you to wear the necklace at the funeral. I'm sure that will be difficult, but it will be an honour for you.'

I hoped he couldn't read the ungrateful comments that were

going through my mind. It was more like a yolk than a piece of jewellery but he just nodded, it was a done deal, he added something about a phone call and turned his back on me.

I looked past him down the Long Drive to the Benbrae, the ever threatening Tentor Wood. I am going to inherit all this, I had just been promoted to the lady of the house, that necklace with its twisted lion and unicorn of the family crest, that gave me a job and a status.

His back was towards me now. I had been dismissed. I knew that my dad told lies, too.

I went back indoors, feeling like I was waiting for a hurricane, searching out hot strong coffee to shrug off the rest of the fatigue. Debs was in the kitchen, sorting out laundry into piles, her face now neatly made up, the cut in the skin covered by a clear plaster.

She smiled at me nervously, another person uneasy in my company now. She concentrated on her task, doing it slowly, making it last as long as possible, trying to keep busy as the kettle boiled. She was looking at a white linen bed sheet that she had taken off the line. Was it Melissa's bed sheet, the one she had died in? That thought struck me brutally, she was gone. Never to come back, throw a tantrum, scream at the top of her voice or fling plates at the wall.

Debs apologized, 'Oh my God, I am so sorry, I didn't mean you to see that. To see this.' She looked down at the wicker basket as if kicking it out of sight under the table would make it OK.

'You don't think about that, do you? The pillow where somebody laid their head before they passed away. Seems too mundane and yet so final. Is your face still sore?'

'Not really, it looks worse than it is. Carla used to sleepwalk when she was wee, you know.' She smiled at the memory. 'And because we moved about so much she never had a chance to get to know the layout of the house so we'd find her in all kinds of places. She'd sleepwalk when she was unsettled and that was always when we had just moved to a new place. We'd find her in the garden, under the table in the pantry, in the bath. We never woke her up though, I know that can be dangerous. Did you sleepwalk when you were wee?'

She was blabbering. 'I don't think so,' I replied.

She pulled her short blonde hair, as wiry as a Brillo pad, back into its rubber band and put her hands on her hips. 'I don't really know what to do next. I don't get paid to do nothing and I'm trying to keep out of Jago's way, your dad's way. I really don't know what to say to him when I bump into him. He asked me this morning when Jago was arriving. I had to say that he arrived yesterday but how easy it was to get the days muddled. He's been awake half the night. He really is the strong silent type but he can't hold all this in, it's not good for him.'

'You should know us Melvicks by now. Dad's been on the phone for ages doing the stiff upper lip routine,' I said, switching the kettle on.

'Here, dear, I'll get that for you.' She put down a pillow case she had picked up, clean ready to fold, pulling out a chair for me to sit down. Her fingers and hair and elbows and bruises all shook. Had it affected her more than me? She has more memories of Melissa being ill to forget than I have.

'No, I will get it myself.' It wasn't a clear order but Debs felt it, the hired help but she wasn't hired by me, and she and I, well, our relationship went back much further than making cups of coffee and folding the laundry. 'What were you doing with the keys for the gun cupboard?' The question rattled out as an accusation.

Debs bit her lip. 'I moved them. They are up there, in that jar marked salt.'

'Why?'

'I didn't want your dad to have access to the gun cupboard. He was talking about taking the guns out in the evening. I wanted to stop him.'

'Why?'

'You know he lost the necklace?'

I nod.

'I'm just a bit worried about him. The box for the necklace was up in his room, but it was empty. I'm looking for it, he'll have put it somewhere. I didn't want him putting a bloody gun down somewhere and forgetting it.'

I smiled at her. 'You are very good to us, Debs.'

'Yeah, well, I am making myself useful. And while you are

here, I need to know who to expect for dinner tonight. He told me last night, then again this morning. Then earlier he apologized for not knowing. I don't think he remembered telling me. Can you find out? I need to know who to cater for.'

'Yes, of course.' I did a mental count. 'Six for dinner.' I counted, 'Me, Dad, Jago, Heather plus his parents, his brother and his wife. Eight. Get the caterers in, I'll say we talked about it and decided. Salmon for starters? Chicken? Strawberries, cream. Something like that.'

'We could tell him anything and he'd believe it, he's so stressed out at the moment. And while we are being honest' – she pulled out a pan, burned at the bottom in a black flower – 'your dad left this on last night, he'd been warming milk. You wouldn't have heard the alarm. Luckily, I was still here, I was just putting the rubbish out when you . . . when we ran into each other. Do you think your dad is coping with all this?'

'He's very distracted,' I said, not wanting to think of the alternative.

Deborah, like her daughter, was more direct. 'I hope that's all it is, Megan.' She turned her head away from the door, I looked round, hearing the noise. Debs looked at me and rolled her eyes slightly as she swiftly turned away. Heather appeared at the door, saw me, then her eyes flicked to Debs, a quick scatter over the plaster and the bruises but they were smiling by the time they were looking back at me.

'Oh, there you are, Megan darling.' She slipped her arms round me.

Debs was busy spooning the coffee into my Snoopy mug.

'We were making a brew, do you want some?'

'I think I will wait until your father is off the phone. How are you bearing up? Did you sleep well?'

Was that a loaded question? What had my dad said? I didn't answer. 'I was up during the night punching Deborah in the face so I do need something to keep me awake.'

She gave a wittery little laugh, not sure if I was being serious.

'I was sleepwalking,' I explained.

'And I got in the way,' said Deborah.

'Oh, you should never try to stop them, that can be very dangerous.'

'I didn't try to stop her, we both got a fright.'

'Are you feeling OK, Megan?'

'It was Deborah who got punched.'

'Yes, but you are the one under the strain. And you do need to start eating properly.'

I wanted to tell her that anorexia is not catching.

'Deborah, maybe you could make sure that Megan has enough to eat. Ivan is very stressed, so Megan, please eat and make sure he sees you eating.' She turned. 'And Deborah, I think the minister is coming today and they plan to have tea in the study, so you could see to that, if you'd be so kind. And obviously the study needs a good clean, it's a terrible mess, and keep the door closed so the bloody dogs don't keep getting in. And you left this in the morning room.' She paused, putting a bottle of Gray Goose on the table, her brown eyes creased, making the chin of her heart-shaped face even more pointed. Her eyes darted over the mess on the side of Deborah's head. 'And could you cover that a little more, it looks bad. We don't want to scare the horses.'

Deborah and I waited until we heard the efficient click of her heels fade into the drawing room before we burst out laughing.

Upstairs, through the bedroom and onto the veranda I saw Dad was still down on the terrace, on the mobile, running his free hand through his hair, standing facing the sun. He looked older. Worse than that. He looked old. Worn out. Fading and failing. He was still a tall, strong man, long-legged, handsome-faced but older. I had been away, time had passed. He seemed to have aged about twenty years since Christmas when I had met him in Glasgow and we had shopped in Princes Square and gone out for lunch, soaking wet and laden down with parcels for . . . Melissa.

Bloody Melissa, she'd kill us all in the end.

How much of this forgetfulness was stress, how much was the start of something?

I watched him for another quarter of an hour, until Heather joined him, reaching up to place her tiny hands on his broad shoulders, high heels sinking into the grass. She looked like a dwarf trying to be seen in very long grass.

I felt a sharp tap on my arm, Debs letting me know she was there.

'It's OK, I have my aids in.'

'Sorry, I'm never sure. Well, I've put your clean clothes on your bed, I can put them away if you—'

'No, thanks, leave them . . .' I hadn't taken my eyes off the action on the terrace, Deborah followed the direction of my stare. Dad ended his call.

'Just leave him be, kiddo, he has no idea what's happening in his life at the moment.' Deborah put her arms round me and gave me a hug, I could smell the nicotine from her. 'And don't bother about my face, I've been hit by better people that you. It was nothing.'

I hugged her back, nice to feel the warmth of another human being. Suddenly I was close to tears. The scent of Deborah was very like that of her daughter. Memories came back, of the boat and the splintering of wood and the flames. I shivered, pulling away before my eyes welled up.

Heather now had her little hands clasped round my dad's arm.

'She drinks too much vodka that one. Her and your dad had a bit of a session last night. Doesn't do him any good.'

'You don't like her, do you?'

'Heather? No, I don't. She wants the dogs out the study, out the house, off the estate, blah blah . . . The study! She thinks when she's in this house she's in a bloody Agatha Christie novel.'

'Maybe she grew up playing Cluedo.'

We both stood up and leaned on the stone balustrade, watching the couple below. 'What happened to her husbands anyway?' asked Debs.

'One left. One died.'

'Of boredom?'

'Probably. I think she has been through a few husbands, not all of them her own.'

'If she marries your dad, I'll be out on my ear pronto.'

'Dad's still married to Mum.'

'Do you think that will stop her?'

'Mum will be back.'

'I hope you are right, kiddo, for both our sakes. But in the great scheme of things, it's not looking likely, you need to face that.'

'No, I'm not going to face it, she's coming back.' I nodded. 'She'll be back.'

'Megan,' her voice was soft. 'Have you ever thought that she might not be able to come back? Why would she leave all this? I mean it's paradise here.'

'It's a gilded cage. She escaped.' Then I processed what she had said. 'What do you mean, she might not be able to come back?'

She shrugs, not able to voice what was going through her head. 'Something might have happened to her, the police . . .'

'The police were here at the time.' I point out the window. 'They didn't look for her because she took her passport, left her wedding ring, took a photograph of me and Melissa but not one of Dad. She left the necklace, she left . . .' And then I started to cry.

'Here, have a ciggie?' Debs had a very straightforward way of coping.

'I'm sorry.'

She dug about in the back pocket of her jeans, lit up two cigarettes with her faithful DuPont lighter, and handed me one. We puffed, wafting the smoke above our heads so Dad didn't a get scent of it. He didn't approve of women smoking in public.

'Forget what I said, you are right. Your mum planned her . . .'

'Escape.'

'I can't imagine how she felt. Carla died here and I go down to the mosaic sometimes, have a think and a wee greet. At times I was awful to her. But we live and learn. But you watch her.' Deb pointed the cigarette at Heather. 'I bet a few women have set their cap at your dad over the years.' A worried little scowl drifted across her face. 'I know what he is going through, he's a dad who has lost his daughter. There's the same age gap between you and Melissa, Paul and Carla. It's a constant reminder.'

'I'm sorry.'

'Don't be sorry, kiddo, it keeps them alive for me, in my head. Do you remember the explosion?'

'In bits, I know I was on the ground, covering my ears. I remember the noise. It was like bring punched in the stomach.'

'The police grilled me and Tom, yet Melissa and Jago just drove away. They didn't seem to want to interview any of you posh lot, only us. But I did remember Heather there, she was smoking down at the boathouse that day. Funny how these things come back. One person's loss brings back the memories of another.' She closed her eyes, remembering something, the crow's feet at the side of her eyelids deepened, as she drew hard on her cigarette, as if her life depended on it. 'I look round and I think who got the better of it all, Tom went to jail, you lost a friend and a sister, Ivan lost a wife and a daughter. I lost a daughter. Heather seems to stroll through it all. Your mum told me that. Heather is the only one that comes out of this smelling of sugar, and usually that means the stink of shite is not far behind.'

TEN

Carla

*L*ooking back, I have witnessed bits of the madness in Megan.
We were down at the Benbrae, I was larking about. I slipped
into the water and thought about swimming to the deep, far
side of the pond. Megan had said there was a current down there,
like there can be a current in a pond like this. She had talked
about the wind and the trees. A load of crap. I was swimming,
expecting her to follow. It was to be an adventure. We usually
came off the Curlew at the island and made our way to the side
furthest from the house, and skinny dip from there. I crawled
over, to the deep bit, bobbing about in the water, it was cold and
coloured, my hands under the surface were peat brown, like I
had a really good tan. I turned and called to Megan who was
sitting on the top of the wall, her long brown legs dangling, eyes
wide open staring into the darkness at the far end of the pond.
I splashed to get her attention, shouting and shouting. She was
deaf, but she wasn't blind. I guessed there was something wrong
and I started a slow steady crawl back, thinking that Megan was
frightened. She had frozen. Megan had an angry, terrified look
on her face, the same face you see in a frightened dog before it
either cowers away or rips your face off. She was distant, yet
intent, her eyes narrowed, seeing movement across the water,
listening to a sound she could only hear in her own head and
whatever she thought she heard had traumatized her.

But when I got there and tugged her leg, she jerked out of
whatever trance she had been in and slid into the water to
join me.

Looking back, I know now that she'd been gazing over at the
Tentor Wood, it was the first place I had hidden when I had
broken in over the fence of the Italian House. Thank God I didn't

know then what I know now, or I would have been scared shitless. I had even seen the rope.

She's going to go down to the Benbrae today, I know her so well. She's confused about the injury to Deborah, her dad's sanity and the meal with Jago tonight.

Megan thought Jago was an arse; if he was not the cause of Melissa's illness, then he certainly didn't do much to help her. With him it was more a case of when the going got tough the tough buggered off to pastures new without so much as a backward glance.

The same way her mum did, hung around to get Melissa married, saw Megan through school, then was off. Or, maybe, she saw the way the wind was blowing with Megan's mental health and saw a future of babysitting daughter number two.

Maybe I shouldn't have shagged Jago the day before he married Melissa, him being her fiancé and me being technically underage, but some things have to be done and Megan and I had a twenty-pound bet on it. Then she trumped me by shagging him actually on his wedding day.

There was a lot going on the day before the wedding. Now, on the day before the funeral, there is nothing to do. And that made the day long and heavy. Megan is preparing herself to be told things that are hard to hear, in both senses of the phrase.

Before the wedding, like now, there had been solid weeks of sun, the grass was dry and brittle under foot and the roses were growing strong. There had been a bit of a breeze in the earlier hours of the morning. Megan had escaped down to the Benbrae after her tea, or dinner as they called it. I had met her there with some Buckfast and a packet of Embassy. We had a drink and a laugh, paddling in the Benbrae, looking at the dark brown petticoat of the surface, the rose petals floating on the top. We both slipped into the water, putting our heads under, linking arms and laughing. The water was biting cold, we started splashing, and then fell into each other's arms. We lifted each other up. Megan leaned forward, her dark hair framing her lovely face, the huge brown eyes, her white cotton blouse was sodden and draped off her shoulder. She looked like a winsome gypsy. Then she smirked and leaned forward, whispering in to my ear.

Stifling a laugh, I kissed her, long and hard, my hands clasped to the side of her face. When we broke off, we both turned to wave at Jago, standing at the fence watching us.

Megan turned her back and looked at him seductively over her shoulder, pulling down the top of her blouse even further.

I waved him over.

And he came.

Simple as that.

So I guess this dinner is going to be interesting, they can't dodge each other for ever. Christmases, they keep apart, and birthdays, they keep apart. Megan shagged the groom on his wedding day, and now they are meeting at the funeral of the bride who might have found out. Has it crossed Megan's mind that Melissa might have been asking a question? Now there's a thing. Sorry? As in, are you sorry now? Are you sorry for what you did to me?

To which I would answer, well you married a man with a taste for underage girls, but nobody ever asked me.

Melissa developed her anorexia rather late in life, or did it just not show itself until later? After she was married, after her career hit the big time, after the explosion at the wedding, after her sister slept with her husband, after she discovered what a tosser he really was. I guess Melissa had a lot to be angry about.

Or feel guilty about.

I guess that depends if Jago confessed to Melissa or not? Sorry dear, I shagged both the bridesmaids, one before the ceremony and one after. She certainly didn't go nuts so I, we, had always presumed not, until the inquest and the rumour mill started turning. My dad did time for the 'fatal incident' with some trumped-up charge like he was guilty because he didn't have a fucking crystal ball to see into the future, like he should have known a firework would come flying through the sky and land on a container of petrol that somebody else had removed from the boathouse and left open. I don't think anybody believed that pish.

It was deliberate, there was a chain of 'inflammable vapour' from the boathouse to the Curlew, the alcohol, they said, was already swilling in the bottom of the boat. I thought some drunken bugger had spilled it, I didn't see the danger. None of us did, apart from the brilliant mind who set it up.

Somebody lit the touch paper, somebody set Megan and I up that night, hoping for us both to be burned to a crisp. Melissa was unusually quiet, no big tantrums that evening. Was she planning something in her own wee mind? I'm not saying she tried to kill us but she was removed from the scene immediately afterwards. The might of the bank accounts of the Melvicks went round her to protect her from the full force of the law.

Was that what had eaten away at her?

Is that why we are burying her now?

Well, you know what, Melissa?

If I was you, I'd call it quits.

Megan

There are people at the house, but not the one I am looking for, every knock, every phone call I think it will be Mum.

Dad came racing out the study, pointing to the phone and ranting about something. He was throwing his arms about, his face right up against mine. I had never seen Dad like that and something in the back of my head started to laugh at the state of him.

Then it seemed to dawn on him, he took a step back, Debs was standing there. I could lip-read what she said, telling Dad I didn't have my hearing aids in, that I couldn't hear the phone. That was why I walked past it rather than answer it.

My dad went pale, and apologized. Debs and I exchanged a glance. She mouthed that she'd keep an eye on him. I said I'd put my hearing aids in and get the phone next time.

And went upstairs, to sit at the window and watch the gates. Jago, his parents, other family that Melissa had left behind. It was weird that I had no intention of leaving. It hadn't even crossed my mind. There was a beguiling sense of sanctuary here, away from the bustle of the city, the demands of work, as demanding as working in a private library for a friend of your dad's can be. I earned my pay. I was good at my job. I have a precise mind. I was a good archiver, a good researcher, and I could concentrate when the place was noisy. A distinct advantage of being deaf.

But now I can't trust myself to sleep. The bloody doctor will be coming soon, the period of experimentation with no medication has failed, the bruises on Debs' face are evidence of that. I know I will be put back on the drugs, the mirtazapine valium cocktail which sends me back to the tiredness and the fuzzy heads. My performance at work will stutter and Dad's friend will 'let me go' until I am well.

Then I will be truly trapped.

In the evening, they were having pre-dinner gin and tonic. In need of fresh air, I was out with Molly, loose sandals on my feet, strolling around thinking about what happened to Debs. It was what it was. So I thought about the walk. The inner perimeter of the estate from the end of the Long Drive to the east, up round the back of the house to the open woods where the eagles and ospreys could be seen high in the sky, as the rooks fought it out for the lower branches. Then across the fields at the back, then down to the house and on the small path beyond the field, saying hello to Lorimer and Marple, then walking on down to the boathouse. Beyond that to the far end of the Benbrae. The path here was bumpier underfoot than I remembered it being.

I didn't have my hearing aids in, they were in the pocket of my dress, and Molly was running around, ears pricked and happy. Then she stopped dead.

Ears forward. A low growl in her throat, then I saw her tail wag. I now had my aids in my hand and nearly in my ears when I saw a man coming along the path. I vaguely recognized him in the distance but couldn't quite place him. I leaned over and caught Molly by the collar.

And then I recognized him, he had the soul of creeping Jesus. He moved up to my shoulder.

'So you are here again sniffing around, doing whatever you are doing?'

'You got me, I'm not going to deny it.'

'And why are the misfortunes of our family of any interest to you, mysterious Mr Murray?'

'Because it is mysterious Detective Sergeant Murray. May I walk with you? And ask you a few questions about the night of the wedding, when Carla McEwan, Carla Sullivan died?'

'There was an inquiry and criminal charges, it was all covered at the time. Tom McEwan did time for it. You know all this.'

'Tom wants to see you. He feels there was a bond between you and his daughter. Or he knows that you and your family killed her.' He walked on, forcing me to follow if I wanted to hear. 'I need to get a feeling for what it was like. Carla sounds like a monster, drinking vodka, sleeping with older men, stealing, causing bodily harm, winding everybody up. What could a girl like you want with a girl like that?'

'Tom was the one who brought about Carla's death. Not my dad. It was an accident.'

That was the version I had to believe. Any other theory was for me alone. Surely Melissa didn't hate me that much. But when I was awake in the ebony hours of the night, waiting for the rooks to batter on the windows, leaving their blood trails on the glass, I know how alike Carla and I looked. Of all people, Melissa knew our habit of going out on the *Curlew*. We had seduced her husband.

She had said sorry.

Drew was walking on, holding back the overgrowth away from the path, inviting me to follow him round the Benbrae path back to the road.

'Tom swears he secured that petrol. Your dad had told him that there was going to be fireworks. Tom McEwan was not an idiot. He loved his daughter. So somebody tampered with it, I know we only have his word for it but he seems genuine to me. It was a wedding, all those people around. He was the only one who admitted seeing Carla get in the boat.'

'I guess the fact he loved her was lost on the original inquiry.'

'He loved her as much as your dad loves you. And yes, points were scored because much was made of Carla's reputation, and Tom had a new baby with a new wife who walked the minute he was convicted.'

'I had heard that.'

'You are not stupid, you must have theories. Petrol doesn't burn like that, not on water.'

'But it did, we saw it.'

'Because somebody made it happen, Megan.' He shrugged. 'Somebody had access to rope and petrol. The rope that was attached to the *Curlew* had been soaked in petrol and used like a fuse, and the boat had alcohol in the bottom. Carla went up like a roman candle. That's the gist of it. Pre-planned.'

We stood in silence, considering its horror.

'Tom is right that your dad was very keen that he was found guilty of some recklessness while he was equally keen to ignore the fact that somebody committed murder.'

'That's ridiculous; you're saying that my dad helped to derail a murder enquiry.'

'I've read all the documentation. Yes and no. The team did investigate, of course, and found nothing. All the material is there. Nobody saw anything. There was no evidence to convict anybody. And it was Tom McEwan's job to keep an eye on the petrol and the boats. So yes, he failed in his duty of care, and was reckless to the endangerment of human life.'

'But it was his daughter who died.'

'A point your father made many times, hence why Tom got such a light sentence. I doubt he served more than a few months, and that was in a low security establishment. He lost more than anybody. But that does not help us.'

My recall of that night walked a very narrow path. I can't dwell on the noise of my best friend burning to death. I refuse to revisit that but I do recall the way Melissa and Jago were whisked away. I've always thought that smacked of my dad's efficiency.

'Tom was sentenced when it was obvious he had very little to do with the big problem. Nothing else we could do, the team involved had looked at it closely and judged that any other prosecution was not worth going to trial with. And the fiscal knew your dad well, of course, a fact that didn't escape my uncle in the original investigation.'

'So what are you doing here?'

'Talking through it. I know the boathouse could not be seen from the house that night. Your dad told me that. He told the police that, he showed them the alignment of the house, the carousel and the boathouse. Who was paying attention to where anybody else was? All eyes were on Melissa. And nobody spoke to you, Megan, you were missed as a witness.'

'Melissa was missing for a part of the day. Never said where she was. She wanted to get some peace.' I walked on for a little way, enjoying the sensation of the pine cones crunching under my feet. Then I turned, still not used to the fact that others can hear easily even when they cannot see.

'That was what you said at the inquiry, and at the court case. The evidence did not support that.' He closed his eyes, ashamed of how brutal it sounded. 'Has your dad ever mentioned to you that he thought you might have been the intended victim?'

'Never.'

He looked away and nodded. 'I think if you ask him that question, he won't be able to look you in the face.'

The whole wedding day was a mirage for me, memories and dreams, falsehoods and images floating through my mind. I no longer knew what was real and what was not. The fire didn't start in sparks of little fires dotted over the surface, as if the embers fell from the sky and landed on the water. It was a still night, there was no breeze to drift the sparks away, they would have rained down on the Benbrae. There was one, only one, one match dropped.

'Carla is gone but I also don't want anything to happen to you.'

'What are you saying?'

'Be careful, Megan. I think your dad was very quick to get you away after the event. He made a huge play about reckless endangerment of the petrol cans being left unattended. He made sure that Tom was well compensated with a great new job. It all smacks of something but I can't quite put my finger on what. And now, you and I are here together right here where it all happened.'

'Are you trying to frighten me?'

'No, I am warning you.'

ELEVEN

Carla

*O*h, the lovely DS Murray. I knew he was a bloody cop the minute I saw him. He was walking around the Benbrae poking and probing like he was searching for something. From the look of his boots, he might well have gone as far in as the faerie pools in the Tentor Wood, which made him either very brave or very stupid.

He wasn't good looking but he wasn't plug ugly either. He does look a bit like his uncle, his features were soft and friendlier than the average Melvick face. Melissa was chiselled like her dad, and stunningly beautiful, but not the kind of face you want to be giving you a bed bath. What made Ivan so handsome even at his decrepit age made Melissa a little hard looking and haughty. Megan's face had a softer contour.

I was glad to be down at the Benbrae with her, strolling around the outer edges with the rather lovely DS Murray.

Megan was a worrier when she was born. I would never have grown up; as things turned out I never got the chance. But I lived life to the full, as they say you have one life so live it well and live it the best you can; I think I had that sussed.

As the Americans would say, I got all my bad shit in at the start.

Megan was born with a frown, as it turns out she was only trying to concentrate on what you were saying, and that took a lot of effort for her. Then she told me that people raise their voices to deaf people and in the human face that is the same as shouting. The face we pull as we speak loud is that of an angry person, imagine everybody you meet being angry with you all the time. No wonder deaf people kick off.

It's better, she said, to speak clearly and slow down, enunciate *properly. She was like that with the big words. So shouting at deaf people helps them hear as much as shouting at a Spaniard helps them understand English.*

One day we were sitting at the Benbrae and she was asking why people were so nasty to me. I had no idea. I have clear memories of the people in those houses, the bruises and the broken bones, but the houses, the bedsits and the hostels all roll into one mass of bad smells, bad men and shared toilets. I don't think I deserved any of it, I guess I was unlucky.

Once on the Curlew, *on a summer day like this one. She asked me why nobody ever told the deaf jokes. Well, I took that as challenge and gave her one of my best.*

'A bit of string walks into a pub, are you that wee bit of string that everybody is talking about, no, says the wee bit of string, looking forlorn. I'm afraid not.'

Her brown eyes stared at me, the furrow came back into her forehead and she said very quietly, 'And you wonder why it's good to be deaf.'

But she was smirking, I punched her on the arm. 'Here's one,' I said, 'listen. This man goes into a pub.'

'The same pub?'

'Yes, people in jokes are always in the pub, usually with an Englishman, a Welshman and an Irishman, but anyway . . .' I had kind of lost the thread, a fish had jumped and caught my eye, distracting me with a streak of silver.

'The man goes into the pub?' Megan prompted showing me that she actually was interested.

'Yes, he goes into the pub and he buys a talking centipede in a wee box.'

'Sorry, I heard that as a talking centipede?' she asked.

'Yes, that's right, go with the flow, it's worth it.'

'I was checking that I had heard it right, a talking centipede.'

'Yeah, so the guy goes home with the centipede and they watch some TV.'

'How does he do that, the centipede?'

God, she really took her jokes seriously.

'He opens the box and puts it on a cushion so he can see the football.'

'*OK.*'

'*So, the guy and the centipede are watching the football then the guy says, "Let's go out for a pint, my treat." And the wee centipede doesn't answer.*'

'*Was it deaf?*'

'*No, it could hear perfectly fine. So, the guy says again, "Hey wee centipede, I asked you a question, do you want to come for a pint or not?" And the wee centipede looked up and said, "Give us a break, big man, I'm just putting my fucking shoes on".*'

For a moment she looked at me, staring deep into my eyes and then she burst out laughing, I didn't think I had seen her laugh like that before.

She shook her head. 'So, the centipede was just putting his shoes on. That's great.' She rested her chin against the rim of the boat, her finger playing with the oar lock, twirling it round. Clicking and rusty 'He was putting his shoes on . . .'

At times like that I really wanted to be inside Megan's head, those quiet moments when she looked out into the distance as if she knew all the truths of the world, devoid of the spoken bullshit. What really did go on between those ears?

Megan

Drew and I were sitting at the seat over the mosaic talking about nothing in particular. I preferred being there with him, rather than up at the house with Jago and his family. I found myself telling him about the mosaic, and then all my Carla stories; he had to see her humour, her courage, her zest for life. She was a better person than me, by a long way.

Then I told him why my father's actions might seem like protection to him. I told him about my diagnosis and the confusion in my head.

I answered his questions: who was where, what had I eaten, where was Heather, how well did I know her and on and on it went. I realized there was something else going on here, a slow but definite interrogation. But I didn't mind, at the end of the day, whatever he got out of it personally, he would find some justice for my friend.

The sun was starting to lose its heat; a slight wind ruffled the surface of the water. It was hard to believe it happened here. The new boathouse, built of brick and wood with a sharp angled roof, looked Alpine; there were brackets of swinging colourful flowers hanging from the roof. The boathouse with the blue loch behind, the hills in the background. 'Were you involved in the investigation?'

'At the time, I was very much on the periphery. My uncle knew your family better, you and Carla. I knew you and Melissa by sight, of course.'

'Your uncle?'

'Yes, he had a few run-ins with Carla over the years. He always had less paperwork when Carla was out of town. She was a wild one. He never thought she was a bad kid, not compared to some. He died a few months ago, but it was one of his constant nagging thoughts, it ate away at him. Who killed Carla Sullivan?'

'And he knew her? I'm glad.'

'And he knew Deborah, of course.'

I feel myself smiling, somebody else who thought about her as I did. An unforgettable, elfin face. 'I remember your uncle. He took Carla away the day I got the scar. So you must have known me?'

'I had seen you around. All the boys in the village were very aware of you and Melissa, the local tottie.'

And there was the truth. 'Yes, all the boys liked Melissa.'

'No, not all of them. There were a few that preferred you, the odd ones!'

I found myself laughing. It was a kind of compliment, the type that rang true for its understatement. 'What? Did you have a league table?'

'Oh yes, you, Kylie, Melissa, a few Kardashians, Sally McGuire because she gave the boys free doughnuts in Greggs.' He was teasing me now. Then his face went serious, a crease appeared across his forehead. 'But your dad knew that Melissa was unwell, and that part of her illness was hating you. Maybe she regretted that in the end.'

Sorry. Her final word.

Drew went very quiet, hesitating about what he was going to say next.

'If the police have it closed officially, then why are you here, now?'

He turned and looked at me, wiped the back of his hand across his chin. 'Your mother. Nobody knows what happened to her.'

'She'll be here on Friday, for Melissa.'

'And if she isn't.'

'Not you as well. Look, Deborah herself saw Mum. Mum was on the phone. They had a brief conversation. Mum asked her if everything was OK. Debs got the impression she wanted to be left alone. Heather saw her, and spoke to her. Alistair Connolly saw her as he drove home. She left.'

'And nobody has seen her since. Her live footprint left the estate through the front gate on Thursday the twenty-sixth of May 2016.'

'Live footprint?'

'The last time we had irrefutable evidence of her being alive. Megan, it's impossible now to walk through life without leaving evidence, credit cards, ID, mobile phone. There's nothing, Megan, nothing.'

'Because she doesn't want to be found. She ran off with another man. She texted, she left her stuff behind.'

'That's what you've been told.' His voice was low, quiet. His logic was chilling.

'Is it not true?'

'It's not untrue. But it's not actual evidence of life.'

'So what happened to her?'

'What do you think?'

'She left Dad.'

'I have combed through your mum's life, she wasn't having an affair; she had nobody to run to. Nobody. Sorry.'

I looked at his face, his floppy fringe bright, the sunglasses pinning the rest of his hair back to the top of his head. His sleeves were rolled up, he had strong forearms, his fingers were devoid of rings. He was patting Molly on the head, properly. Stroking her, not patting her like he was testing a bed.

Mum had no live footprint.

And now Melissa was gone, Carla was gone. And here I was, not remembering attacking people and having a chat with a detective. For some reason I wanted to laugh, Drew Murray suddenly looked very young and rather foolish.

'Some people believe that your mother walked away from the family and decided not to return.' Drew pursed his lips. 'But my opinion is different. There is the outside world, then there is the Italian House. If you are in there, you have been invited. And somebody had access to your mother. You should think about that.'

I stood up and put my hand out, he placed his in mine. I shook his hand, thanking him for his interest.

He screwed his face up a little, maybe realizing that he had gone too far too fast.

'I must go,' I said.

'Megan?'

'Yes?'

'You look after yourself. Be careful. Here's my number and I want you to call me if you are' – he paused – 'uneasy about anything.'

I walked away, back up the Long Drive, looking at his phone number, committing it to memory before ripping the paper into tiny pieces and setting them free to the wind.

TWELVE

Carla

The trouble with my family was that it wasn't a family. My parents couldn't stand the sight of each other. Then, they couldn't stand the sight of me. But I should be grateful that they took turns when it came to disliking me. And my tiny world was wide; I could wake up in one country and go to sleep in another, to be dragged out my bed and stuck in a coach to be carried five hundred miles. I saw an awful lot of wallpaper, none of which belonged to us. I liked to think that Dad was back in Sandbank, in some rented little room somewhere, or living with Gran in Dunoon where I imagined that I was welcome-ish to kip on the floor in a sleeping bag he kept rolled up under his own bed. Then Fishface came along and although things got more complicated, the same rules applied.

My rules weren't their rules.

Mum and Ivan are having a chat in the front room with a vodka and tonic, the way folk do when they live miles from anywhere. The curtains are open and all the lights are on – they are like a couple of monkeys in the zoo.

Or a couple of fish in a barrel.

I know exactly what my mum is doing. Ivan Melvick is ripe and vulnerable. Mum has clocked the misplaced necklace. It hasn't dawned on Megan that Heather doesn't drink Grey Goose, my mum does.

Mum has that thing that men like. A kind of sex appeal, a charm, something like that. She likes men, God knows she has had enough of them, most of the time they were either complete tossers or they were someone else's. She always believed that they would leave their wives and their kids for an uneducated *deadbeat like her and, from the width of her smile, she was about to go back down that lane again.*

I wonder what Ivan Melvick was making of all this.

Then I saw the look on his face, that same look he used whenever he saw me. Ivan Melvick was a man for whom doing the right thing was lodged deep in his genetic make-up even when he didn't like it.

Ivan hadn't seen me as anything other than an inconvenient playmate for his deaf daughter. He only did that because he employed my dad. Now my mother was wandering around the house dusting and removing the keys to his gun cupboard.

But this was not our world, we could walk through it, see it, hear it and taste it in little doses but we would never be allowed to stay there – it was not ours to inhabit.

Ivan had inadvertently invited me into his family, and he had very quickly regretted it.

We could not be both inside and outside, we can never be in two places at the one time. But I think I know exactly how two people can be in the same place at the same time. In fact two people can be, they can inhabit the same place in the same time exactly.

I know that now.

Megan

The evening meal had been a torment for us all. As agreed, Debs had brought in a caterer as she doesn't really do big posh food, it took me back to the way things used to be here when we had dinner parties and the Melvicks all dressed for dinner in old Agatha's time. I guess that was the way of things in those days but it seems so odd in this world to spend all night eating, talking and drinking in your own house when you could be doing something useful like reading a book.

Heather was there, of course, either balancing the numbers or practising getting her feet under the table. She could be relied upon to be the hostess and do the right thing. Dad was his usual self, Jago was there with his older brother and his wife; she was a stressed ball of neurosis, maybe all the Harrington men were attracted to neurotic women. Jago looked a little sad and obviously

more than a little uncomfortable when I appeared, awkward in
conversation, silences that went on too long, missing the social
cue of pleasant conversations. I was used to it, it happened to deaf
people all the time. But I felt Jago looking at me across the table,
leaving his eye on me as he caressed the stem of his wine glass
over the chicken and haggis medallions, the conversation moved
on, the odd laugh, the small chat about absent friends, mutual
acquaintances. Melissa was largely absent from the conversation,
but his eyes stayed with me as the talk rolled on to another topic.
His parents were there also, his dad was cut from the same stuff
as my dad, and I think they even had friends in common.

Jago did broach the elephant in the room by asking if anyone
had heard from Beth yet.

There was a jagged silence, the chink of silver tapping china.

'Not yet,' I said, as cheerfully as I could.

'She'll be back if she can. I mean, she might not want to until
it can be a private family affair. She will want to say her own
goodbye.' Jago's mum, Dorothy, patted the back of my hand with
hers. I think she even cast a quick glare at her husband. I liked
Dorothy, she was a rather dumpy little cheerful woman who always
made a point of talking to me, and she seemed genuinely interested
in what I was doing. She talked about my deafness and the visual
system I used at work. She nodded and said what great leaps
technology had made. Then she said, as she often did, that as she
had no daughter of her own, could she borrow me for a while.
She had said that at Melissa's wedding, to which I heard my sister
say, There's no point in talking to her, she can't hear you.

'Oh, the deaf are very intuitive,' said Jago's mum, smiling and
fiddling with her pearls, I think she had taken me by the arm and
marched me off to look at the ponies. I guess she was more like
my mum, and she loved Dad's Munnings; joking about sticking it
under her arm and running off with it when nobody was looking.

Carla

*It was weird to see Jago again, I think he had lost weight, matured
since I had last seen him. He used to be like the fat boy in the
class that you had to speak to because he had money and his*

dad had a nice car. Jago was never one of the cool kids, rubbish at sport so not really part of the gang yet somehow you always knew that he would grow up and get on, leaving us all behind in his wake. Stuck here in our little village while he visited the capital cities of the world, doing deals in his handmade shoes, such was the way of the Melvicks and the ridiculous double-barrelled Harrington bullshit.

And here he was returned to the big house, and technically he was fair game as his wife – ex-wife, estranged wife – was lying dead over in Dunoon.

And men don't change, they like the taste of young flesh.

It was easy to do, the Italian House was an absolute paradise for sneaking around, the outside veranda ran the full length of the building outside all the bedrooms with their French windows, and some of them didn't open now. The balcony at the far end had been declared unfit and crumbling, but he was in there, my prize.

It took me a long time to prepare, a long hot bath, I poured in some oils, brushed my dark hair, beautiful make-up, deep red lips like he liked on Melissa. It was easy to go into Melissa's room, her clothes were still there, her nightwear piled up, washed and ready for someone to decide what was going to be done with it. A quick ruffle through, a silky navy number, setting against my pale skin.

I climbed onto the veranda, Melissa's housecoat pulled over me, dark air piled on top of my head. The door to the bedroom was locked, as they always were, but the window was open, as always in the hot weather, but I stood there looking right at him.

He was sleeping, eyes closed, bare chested, his head slightly back so that the arteries and veins of his neck were visible. His ribcage was easy to see through the thin sheet which covered his body. Jago. The object of our foolish teenage desires, that crush we had on him because he was unattainable, unobtainable and yet here he was naked and as vulnerable as a baby.

He turned over, maybe aware of my presence, my observation of him, he stirred slightly, and his hand outstretched towards the window, towards me . . .

'Melissa?'

THIRTEEN
Thursday

Megan

I was still half asleep, drowsy, dreamy. It was warm, the house had not woken up yet. I sensed rattling in the hall outside my door, then the handle was jammed down and the door burst open. Jago stormed in, furious, but then closed the door behind him gently. He turned to me, his face red and incensed. He was dressed in jeans, unzipped, a white T-shirt flung on. He was unshaven, red-eyed as he strode over to the bedside, and pointed at my hearing aids and then at his ears so I heard him when he said, 'So you get this, you sad little bitch.'

'I'm sorry?' I said, pulling the duvet round me.

He sat on the side of the bed, leaning over me, spitting saliva into my face as he spoke.

'What the fuck do you think you are doing, how dare you?'

'Jago, I have no idea what . . .'

'And don't give us that shite, you take a long hard look at yourself, right! You are one diseased, evil, little whore.'

'I have no idea what you are talking about. Get out!'

His voice went very quiet, his finger was right in my face. 'You were at my window.'

'In your dreams. Get out of my room right now.'

He grabbed my arm and pulled me out of bed, over to the dressing table and the mirror. He yanked out the stool and sat me down on it, spinning me around so I caught sight of the woman who looked back at me. Red lipstick drawn across her face, smudged down onto her chin, panda eyed.

'Do you see? Do you see that?'

'Oh my God. Oh my dear God . . . Jago, I have no idea.'

He grabbed hold of the sides of my head, forcing my face into the mirror. 'You are not Melissa, do you understand? You are

nothing compared to her, standing there, pretending that you
were . . .'

'Jago, no, no.' I was horrified. 'Jago, no!' And then the tears
started to come. 'I didn't, Jago, I have no idea. I went to sleep . . .'
I looked back into that face, the face that wasn't mine. I never wore
lipstick like that. I never wore my hair like that . . . the way Melissa
did. 'Oh my God. God! Jago? I never.'

'Look.' He stood behind me, grabbing the side of my head and
forcing me to look straight in the mirror, confronting this version
of myself. 'Look, who is that? Who are you? If you think you
can be Melissa, fill her shoes, then you have another thought
coming, young lady. You are nothing. You should be ashamed of
yourself.'

I tried to open my mouth but his fingers gripped tighter,
around my jaw, his thumbs pressing deep into my cheeks,
preventing me from speaking. It hurt, it really hurt. I squealed
but he didn't ease off the pressure. I could see my skin blanching
under the force of his fingertips. He squeezed tighter and tighter
muttering obscenities into my ear. Suddenly I was Melissa and
this was the violence she had suffered during her marriage.
Was this what she had to endure every day? No wonder she
left him, threw him out. No wonder she killed herself. How
dare he.

'Trying to look like her.'

Well, that was as far as he got. I pulled back my elbow and
rammed him. I was aiming for his testicles but caught him in
the lower abdomen. He was still shocked enough to let go.

I stood up and whirled round. My finger stabbing him in the
face. 'How dare you touch me.'

'You are one fucking psycho. I didn't believe your little deaf
girl act for one minute, you are one fucking screw ball.'

'Why the hell would I want to come near you, you disgusting
little pervert? I know what you did to us, when you used to stay
here, so don't you play the innocent with me.'

That pulled him up short. He sat down on the corner of the
bed, his T-shirt rumpled, dark rings round his eyes, hair sticking
up showing his bald patch. He looked ridiculous. I started to sob
uncontrollably. 'I have no idea why I am like this, dressed like
this. I have no idea.'

'Megan.' Suddenly the fight went out of him. 'Megan? I am serious, you were standing at my window last night.'

'I have no memory. Yesterday I hit Deborah. I don't remember it, but I spent a long time yesterday talking about Melissa, going through it with the police.' I don't know why but I enjoyed saying it like that.

It had the desired effect. His head whipped round in shock.

And I enjoyed repeating it. 'Didn't you know the cops are reinvestigating it? They are re-interviewing everybody. Without Dad's protection this time.'

I thought he was going to walk out. Instead, he rubbed his face, scraped his hair back, covering his bald spot, trying to clear the confusion in his head.

'Well, maybe that is a good thing,' was all he could say. 'Megan, I have a lot of respect for your father but you are unwell. Very. You need help.'

'I don't know if I do,' I cried. 'People always say that when I point out something unpleasant. I sleepwalk and last night I walked along to the room where my sister died four days ago. I don't think that's so odd.'

'Oh, is that the story? Just look at yourself. I'm glad the police are onto you, Megan, you and your deaf girl act, you don't fool me for one minute. You and your pseudo dose of Melvick madness. I have always suspected that you killed Carla. It was all a bit convenient that she died, wasn't it? And then you gave Melissa no peace, driving her to her death.' He nodded, looking out the window. 'Yeah, you are responsible for the shite and crap that Ivan has had to suffer over the last few years. God, not even your own mother could stand the sight of you.'

I stared him down. 'That's not true.' A little voice in my head said, Or was it?

'Look at the bloody evidence, Megan. Melissa got married and Beth couldn't stand being here with you. Your dad and the others who looked after Melissa need to grieve in peace without you' – he struggled for the words – 'doing what you do.' He stood up and closed his eyes, as if he was counting to ten. 'I'm going to talk to Ivan now, he needs to know. You made Melissa's life miserable, Beth's life intolerable and I am not going to let that lie. You can stay here until after the funeral, then after that you can get out.'

He walked out the door, leaving it open, then putting his head back round.

'I pity you as much as I hate you. Stay away over breakfast, I want to talk to your father.'

Carla

Oh shit, well it really is all going a bit tits up, isn't it? Poor Megan, I didn't really think that he would do that but I doubt that he is going to go and run and complain to Ivan in case Ivan says, 'Why did you not come and tell me this during the night, why did you not wake Megan up at the time? My precious daughter.'

To which Megan might just ask why Jago shagged the two bridesmaids – underage bridesmaids.

So good luck with that one, Jago.

But I know he's not thick. Why is he banning Megan from a house that she will inherit? He has no power here, not now.

I think Ivan will be on to him pretty quickly. Megan is his daughter, his only daughter now and he will always protect her. Jago is angry at himself more than anybody else, and Ivan had probably told him that Megan had gone a little peculiar since the death of her sister and that she had started sleepwalking again.

And chatting with anyone who has madness in the family is usually quite amusing, it has a raw reality. They can say, 'Oh, he went mad and hung himself in 1952' as easily some folk would say, 'He popped out to the shops and came back with skimmed milk instead of semi-skimmed . . .'

Conversations with Megan used to go like that, 'Oh yes Agatha, she topped herself in the Tentor Wood, as did my great grandfather and Uncle Sebastian'. She'd say that as we sat on the Benbrae looking at the dark and not so distant trees of the Wood. I could imagine somebody walking out of that silent house, down the Long Drive in the bright sunshine and round the path into the wood. They don't need to bring the rope with them, it's already there, hanging off the low-slung branch of the tree, swinging out over the water, the noose pulled back and then left on the bank side of the tree for the next suicide to come along. Is that my memory or is that Megan's memory? We get blurred now and again. I mean why does anybody need a ready-made suicide spot at the bottom of the garden?

Funny that all my memories of Megan and me are always down at the Benbrae and always in the sun. I'm sure we must have met up in the winter time. But I can't recall any, not really, never at Christmas, never at New Year, never in the snow. Did I ever exist in the winter at all or would that have been a different story?

Megan

Was he right?

I was looking in the mirror.

Am I a monster?

I knew there was something wrong with me.

I am not a monster. My disease is a monster. It was terrifying.

They were downstairs talking about me, whispering behind my back where I couldn't see them. I put my hearing aids in. I was getting paranoid. I remembered Dad saying to somebody that they should not talk in front of mirrors as I can read lips. Suddenly I saw a meaning in that that I didn't know before. Be wary of Megan.

Was any of that true?

Was I jealous of Carla?

Jago believed that I, in some way, was responsible for her death.

I was not sure.

I know what I thought happened, but there were bits where I had no memory, nothing at all.

And why did my mother leave? Did she leave Dad? Did she leave us? Or me?

I lay on my bed, *Lonesome Dove* open on the pillow. The sun was shining across the floor, making cube patterns on the light green carpet, and everything seemed the same.

Dad would already have called Dr Scobie, telling him that Megan is having her issues again. And I knew that I had to see him and that I would become my father's puppet.

He would be in command again, just as I was spiralling out of control.

Carla

M and M had no chance as Beth wasn't totally right in the head either – although I think she might actually have been the sanest of them all. Given she had the wits to get out. I see history repeating itself with Megan. If a member of the family deviates from the normal behaviour then a private doctor comes in and says they are bonkers and they are medicated until they come back into line. There is an all-powerful evil overlord that gives that family, the name, and they operate a secret code of silence, an omerta. The family member doesn't count as an individual, they have to keep in line. Or else.

It was all rumour but even my dad said it and he doesn't gossip but he does pick stuff up from the pub so he's pretty reliable. Beth Melvick was supposed to be having some kind of affair, no problem there, as long as the children had the right DNA then it didn't really matter who went on to shag who. Talk was Ivan Melvick kept a lady in a flat in Glasgow. Beth's problem, so the rumours went, was she was seeing one of the local vets and that was a bit too close to home. That kind of thing went over Megan's head. She thought Beth and the hunky vet were together a lot because of the Benbrae Highland ponies, fat chunky wee beasties that were better looked after and had more attention doted on them than her own children ever had.

As Drew said, Beth was not having an affair. She got up one morning and went through her usual routine, feeding ponies, looking at ponies, patting ponies on the head. Then she put a few things together and disappeared. Seemingly when somebody pointed out she wasn't back at teatime and nobody knew where she was, Ivan's first response was to put on a jacket and walk down to the hanging tree to check, so I guess there must have been something going on behind the scenes.

Mum was there at the time, helping out, doing a bit of laundry and a bit of cleaning – nobody with the surname of Melvick did that sort of thing.

Beth had taken a few things with her, but her wedding ring and the Melvick necklace were left behind. She took some clothes though. The most difficult thing to believe was that one of the reliable witnesses who last saw her was my mum. At ten past eleven that morning. Mum loved being part of the drama. She tried to hide it but you could tell she was struggling to keep the smile from her face. Apparently she passed Beth on the road. And Mum said Beth was on her phone. Just as well Heather Kincaid and a friend of Ivan's saw Beth Melvick after Mum did, as Beth then disappeared off the face of the planet.

FOURTEEN

Megan

I felt banished to the upstairs of the house. I had nipped down to make some toast, pour some coffee to take back to my room. I could tell from the dishes and the pans left out that the dining room had been set for breakfast. I caught the scent of fried bacon out in the hall but I didn't go in and look. Jago might have my dad deep in conversation already so I slipped up the stairs, sneaking under Agatha who cast a beady eye on me wondering what I was up to. Once in my bedroom I could walk out the French windows and looked along the veranda where I must have walked. It looked the same as it always did.

But from here I could walk the full length of the upper floor of the house, listening to any conversation that happens to drift my way from unsuspecting guests, as long as I had my hearing aids in and there was no other background noise. Jago's parents were probably around somewhere, chattering in the garden beneath me. As kids we learned early that it's not easy to see from the ground floor up to the balcony. As long as we stayed low under the level of the balustrade, we were invisible.

So it was second nature for me to walk along there, keeping to the side of the wall to see the big picture and then I could duck down and tune in. It hadn't happened often now that we were all adults and grown up but over the years there had been many a time when I'd sit there and spy on the guests at Mum and Dad's drinks parties, then I'd spy on Melissa and her parties when she was a teenager when her mates would sneak off down the Benbrae for a swim or a sail or a snog.

But I knew this house well, I knew all its little spying secrets. Now, grown up, nobody's life was so interesting that I needed to hear it, but when I did, this was still a very good place for eavesdropping. Even without my hearing aids. I could keep an eye on who was coming and going.

More than one person had commented how this house could have been built for spies. The kind of person who asked exactly what my dad did for a living, the words 'civil servant' and 'foreign office' not quite cutting it. People who were curious about the men in black cars and good suits that came and went when I was a child. These were people who were suspicious, those who had seen too many James Bond films. Or maybe, when Papa was alive, Dad really did drive an Aston Martin.

Then I spotted a car coming up the Long Drive. I thought I recognized it. By the time it pulled onto the gravel, I was running the shower, adjusting my hearing aids and closing the French doors behind me so anybody would think I was still in my en suite. Outside, crouching, I heard the front door open and Dr Scobie's voice drifting up over the balustrade. Then he was standing outside, with Dad walking around slowly, no doubt thinking that a moving target was more difficult to eavesdrop on. There were low level mutterings for a few minutes, loud enough for me to catch the odd word but obscure enough to not make any sense.

Then the volume increased slightly, I heard my dad tut and could imagine him shaking his head; in my mind's eye I could see him dislodging his long grey fringe then swiping it from his eyes.

'What do I think might have changed her behaviour so violently? Losing Melissa?'

'I think she was bound to crumple one day, maybe it's better to have happened here, where the damage she can do is minimal.' Scobie's voice, quiet and insistent, loud enough for me to hear, said, 'What you need to understand is that if the world was silent, then Megan would be sane. But it is a noisy world and she misses out on so much, things like social conditioning. She is frustrated and angry, many deaf people are angry and that might—'

'Excuse me, but that seems a very long reach, I know my daughter. I know what she is like.'

'She likes being deaf, have you never thought that a little strange, Ivan?'

My dad did not answer. For a moment or two, the silence was

interrupted only by the rushing water of my shower and the chirping of the garden birds.

'Have you ever thought that she might have found out about Melissa and Beth?'

At that moment, I felt my heart skip a beat. I exhaled slowly.

My dad's voice was quiet but determined. 'She doesn't know, we have been very careful. Jago is the only other person who knows, and you. I hope. But now neither Melissa nor Beth are here. Megan tells me Melissa said sorry when she died. I think that's why she apologized. Beth and Melissa always felt bad about it.'

'Ivan, all I am saying is that Megan was a complex child. As an adult she was a complex patient, maybe not totally cured or even curable and she discontinued treatment before she was better. She has Dissociative Identity Disorder. We have been through this, it's not a walk in the park, Ivan, it's a serious condition and you allowed her to disengage from her therapy. You made it possible. It was not advisable. So this time, she sees it through.'

'You said it was rare and there was an experimental programme. She's my daughter, for God's sake, not an experiment, Donald. I know Megan, she's struggling at the moment, that's all.'

'Do you know her, Ivan?' Dr Scobie's voice was firm but empathetic. 'No dad really knows what their daughters are like, it's a self-protection mechanism. Do you think your brain would allow you to imagine the pain that Melissa was in, something so bad that she starved herself to death? Of course . . .'

They were now walking in the direction of the woods, but walking under the long balcony, easy for me to track them from above, knowing they couldn't see me but I could hear every word.

'. . . you can't. You have spent the last ten years trying to find a cause for the deadly worm of psychology that ate her up. And there is no cause, it's not your fault, nor Beth's, nobody's. She was what she was. And then look at Carla, how did her dad cope with that little monster?'

'He loved her, despite everything.'

'He loved her and lied to himself, that's what parents do. He coped by lying to himself about her. I was reading that Keke Geladze convinced herself that her son was angelic. He was Stalin.'

I heard my dad's response, quieter now, thinking. 'It's a bit of a jump from Stalin to Carla but I take your point. How Tom must have deluded himself about Carla, lied to himself time after time.'

I sat down again, behind the balustrade, placing my head against the marble upright, eyes closed, painting the words in my head.

They had all lied about Carla.

And I had no idea just how they were lying about Carla.

Just as they were lying about me.

Carla

I've always been a nosey bitch, always been on the big outside, always looking for a way in, then when I got in I discovered that most folk are awful once you get to know them. Being a nosey bitch, I had only been staying with my dad a week up in Kilmun when I discovered that with Mrs Adamson's binos I could look out right over the top of the loch to the trees that surrounded the Benbrae and, if I fiddled about with the focus and lifted it up slightly, I could see the Italian House, but not close enough though. Then I thought if I could cycle round the loch and maybe to the folly, I could see it closer.

If I knew there was a party coming, I'd pull on my big jumper and climb out gran's bedroom window and down the drainpipe, holding the leather strap of the binos between my teeth, a wee bottle of something in my pocket. Then on my bike round the top of the loch and onto the roof of the folly. It was always awkward getting onto the top but it was nothing a monkey couldn't manage and then I was up, crawling on to the roof, feeling the cool tiles on my bare feet and under my fingers. The old folly sat slightly up the hill, it was a good viewpoint to see everything that went on. I climbed along for the best view and then I'd sit and drink, and watch. Watch the perfect family live their beautiful lives.

I really enjoyed it when they had one of their house parties; I watched the rich and glamorous float around like ethereal creatures, iridescent faerie people at the bottom of the garden, and get pissed as farts.

Megan was never invited. Melissa was there if she was back in Scotland for a holiday, spending her long summer holidays with her lovely young friends. It was a difficult angle but sometimes I would catch sight of Megan standing on the veranda, above the heads of those out on the terrace as they sipped drinks and danced to the music that blared out of the French doors. Melissa liked jazz, that syncopated stuff where men snapped their fingers and nodded their heads with their eyes closed. No hokey-cokey for them. I kind of liked it. I'd sit there for ages, watching, pretending that I could hear something so far away. I couldn't, of course. I was experiencing it as Megan would.

As the summer rolled on, and Megan and I got to know each other, she knew where to look and would wave. Although she could not know I was there, she couldn't see me, not from that distance standing on the veranda, hiding.

Megan could know stuff she couldn't know.

She said there were not five senses, more like twenty. People said that the blind have acute hearing. Megan said they probably didn't as nobody expected the deaf to have better eyesight. But Megan could sense stuff, what was in the air, a drop in temperature, the variation of the airflow across her skin. Megan said that we could all do that, but we didn't have the words, the vocabulary, to explain it. But I knew that feeling of being watched, of knowing that somebody was there when there was nobody to be seen.

I knew.

So I didn't doubt her.

I bet she could 'hear' over the air, like a shark does with its special senses.

And sharks are dangerous things.

Megan

We were sitting in the main living room, the room with the modern sofas from Ikea, the big television screen in the corner. There are new pictures on the wall, prints, nice things, flowers and men walking over a desert in dull light, their camels stick thin against the sand.

Dr Donald Scobie was sitting in the chair opposite me, holding a cup of tea, one leg over the other, showing three inches of creamy woollen socks, in this heat. He had no neck, just rolls of fatty, pasty flesh between his shirt collar and his chin.

I didn't know if he knew about last night and Jago.

We had gone through the pleasantries, well Melvick pleasantries about the latest round of tragedy, the loss of Melissa and the feeling of being back in the lion's den. The feeling of being trapped was a constant theme of mine.

'Megan, you know that your condition gives you selective amnesia, anxiety and you do experience a sense of being out of your body, hearing things that you cannot possibly hear. You do not have a split personality, you have DID that can lead to you having two distinct personality states but you don't, not as yet. We must keep you safe, you are a bigger danger to yourself than anybody else and you need support and treatment, the drugs are there to get you through until the counselling and behavioural therapy can work. I was reading a paper that suggests ninety per cent of cases stem from childhood abuse maybe war, or health problems in childhood, maybe a disability in childhood. You can see the boxes I am ticking.'

'My sister trying to drown me, and the fact I am not sad that she has now died?'

'Maybe more the fact that you are deaf and are back here as the lady of the house, abandoned by both your mother and your sister. In this house which you admit feels like a prison to you.' He smiled slightly, as he continued, 'With a pond at the end of the garden where your sister used to try to drown you, I'll give you that. But now that you are back, I'd like to touch on Melissa's wedding. And Carla, do you remember the first time that you met Carla?'

'Yes, I was lying on the ground bleeding.' I lifted my fringe to show the scar that was still there. I needed to chat, otherwise Dr Scobie would stare at me and intimidate me. 'She rescued me. Then I rescued her in Frasers. I had never met anybody quite like her.'

'Were you friends?'

'Yes.'

'Did you admire her?'

'Yes.'

'Seems to me you had more to give.'

'I had more to gain. Carla was always there, down at the boathouse. I first remember seeing her when she pulled that boy off me. He was kicking me in the face, he was stepping back for a big kick. I closed my eyes, waiting. But it never happened. I thought I was going to die and then there was a noise. Something small and fast hit him in the chest. It was Carla, rugby tackling him right in the guts.'

'Do you know why she did that?'

'She was protecting me.'

'Maybe, I'll read you this.' He unfolded a piece of typed A4 paper. 'By this time in her life, her father, Tom had remarried and not told her. She was living with Mrs McEwan, who was in her early seventies, and she was struggling to fit in at school.'

He cleared his throat.

'"I was all ready for the school dance that Christmas." This is Carla talking about the Christmas before the incident when she came across you. "The rest of the class had shared limos, the girls had fancy frocks and piled-up hair that fell in ringlets over fake-tanned shoulders. I was chalk white, skinny and not one of them. I was dancing around on my own, already on the floor when a slow Adele song came on and Wullie Campbell came up to me and asked me to dance. Me. In my charity dress with my hair washed and everything, he chose me. He led me onto the gym hall floor, right to the middle, as the lights went down, everybody was watching, amazed at my good luck.

"He put his arms up as if he was going to give me a hug. Then he shouted that I was a stinking wee mong and he ran away, holding his nose. So everybody was laughing and the teacher put the lights on. The rest of the class were all laughing and chanting 'stinking wee mong'. They had all been in on the big joke, they were all laughing at me".'

'Poor Carla, that's horrible.'

Donald Scobie looked over. 'It goes on: "the teacher was rushing to catch me before I got to Wullie Campbell. But I was quicker, he was singing about me, my mum and how she'd seen more pricks than a cactus when I knocked his teeth out".'

Scobie folded the paper.

'That was the brother of the boy who attacked you, it was nothing to do with you, Megan, it was about her. Her and him.'

And I looked at him with this paunch and his face like a pig, thinking where the hell did you get your degree? Could he not see, it was about the hunted and the hunter? It was about redressing the balance. Poor Carla, the humiliation if it, I could feel the burn of anger for her. I would have put that boy in a faerie pool for doing that to her.

'Did you feel responsible for her after she saved you?'

'I think she was always saving me. She never stopped.'

'Would you have liked her to be your sister?'

'No, then she would have been Melissa, and one Melissa was enough for any of us.'

'Did you prefer Carla to Melissa?'

Like I was stupid enough to answer that.

'We have to talk this through, Megan, you know that. You need good, effective psychotherapy.'

Well you had better find a good effective psychotherapist then. Sometimes I can hear Carla's voice in my head very clearly. But I don't repeat her words, I am too well brought up for that.

Scobie crossed his legs and continued, enjoying the shit he'd just thought up. 'But she was not a part of this family. There must have been some sense of her looking up to you or being envious of you? Maybe that got to her after a while, the more she saw yet the more she was locked out.'

I looked at him. 'Envious of me?' I pointed to my own chest. 'Me? You don't know Carla. She's not envious of anybody. She was a hedonist. She hated the structure I have to have in my life.'

'I saw Carla at Melissa's wedding. I wonder if I spoke to her?'

'You would have remembered if you had.'

'People have commented that Carla at thirteen was a scrawny wee spotty girl with pale skin and blue hair. The Carla I saw at the wedding was groomed and tanned and dark-haired and healthy looking. She could have been a Melvick.'

He thought I was stupid. 'She was my friend. I know how scared I was walking home, it was a long walk, and Mum had got caught up in traffic after taking a pony to the vet. The local kids were walking behind me, I knew they were there, a gang of them. They were shouting. I couldn't hear the names they were calling me. You have no idea how that feels.'

He looked confused.

'It was only when I turned around to see them, I saw their faces and I realized how much I was hated. I wasn't used to that. I was used to puppies and strawberries, not being spat at. Carla knew how that felt.'

And I was there for an hour talking shite about Carla, stuff we had talked through a hundred times before. I knew it off by heart. I knew the lies to tell.

Dr Donald Scobie was so full of crap.

Carla

Dr Scobie is going over old ground, there's a load of stuff he cannot fix, but gets paid a fortune for talking it over. Megan's dad is flinging money to try to get her better, when I think I know the one thing that will get her better is not being here at this bloody house and all the gawping ancestors that she can never live up to.

It's this place and its malevolent memories, it's toxic to her soul.

Like Dad and Gran said, they tried everything to get Melissa better but it was like tossing money down a hole.

Does that make it sound like we were gloating? We weren't really. It was more like the feeling of inevitability, that 'if it can happen to them, and then it can happen to anybody'. And that if you don't have your health, you don't have anything. OK, a few folk made comments like, 'so if she actually had to work for a living, or pay a mortgage, she might smarten her ideas up a bit', but those comments stopped eventually. They saw her in the village, the smallest of clothes hanging off her, cheekbones and shoulder blades sharp ridges under fabric, paler and weaker until she stopped being seen out in the village, then she stopped being seen outside the house, then she stopped altogether.

When Ivan Melvick married Elizabeth Rose Nicolette Palmer that should have been them set for a life full of love, laughter and privilege. They would never, ever have to worry about money.

They had the Italian House and a small collection of paintings that were worth a fortune, so it was rumoured. Some were on the wall, although the talk around the village had it they were only copies, the originals were in the bank.

Oh yes, Beth had landed well on her little feet that time. She was from a good family up north, she spoke dead birds and shotguns fluently, she was perfectly capable of breaking the necks of dying animals, and shooting her own horses through the head. I'm not saying that she was heartless, she loved her two daughters very much. I don't think that she realized how fragile Melissa and Megan were. The family had the Italian House, the land, the Benbrae and the Tentor Wood, the fields and the stables that would be home to the ponies, it should all have been perfect.

Then, to make the lovely family complete, the daughters were both adorable. Beautiful little girls, olive-skinned, dark-haired, brown-eyed.

It was those two that messed the whole story up. Somehow, after everything the parents had, it was only fair that the generation after them would be cursed.

Megan

I saw the door open out the corner of my eye and looked round, it was Drew holding his finger up to his mouth, telling me to be quiet. He tapped his ears, enquiring if I had my hearing aids in.

'Should you even be here?' I said, trying to wipe my tears away. I had gone back to my bedroom for some peace and quiet and here I was sticking my hearing aids in to hear the interruption more loudly.

'I said to your dad that I needed to have a word with you, he said you were upset.'

'Really?'

'And then he told me why.'

'Oh right, so you know.' Everybody seemed to know bloody everything.

'Well, I don't know if what he said was true.'

'Are you accusing him of lying?'

'No, I am accusing him of protecting his daughter's reputation. Have you been speaking to the doctor?'

'The psychotherapist, yes. Again. He's an arse.'

Drew didn't argue. Just nodded as if that was his opinion of all psychotherapists. 'He said that you have had a couple of episodes recently.' He closed the door behind him, carefully using both hands, one on the handle and the other, higher up, making sure it closed without making any extra noise. 'So, what happened?'

'Why do you want to know?'

'I'd like to hear it from you, not what your father chooses to tell me.'

'Did he ask you to come here and look into my mum's disappearance?'

He doesn't flinch, he's either about to tell the truth or he's a good actor. 'He mentioned to one of my superiors, but the case has never come off the books. He has often mentioned it. Cases like that have to be prodded by some new information, because it seems to us that someone like your mum might have wanted to walk away. There has been no sign that she was a victim of foul play. It's been three years. I thought it warranted another look. But I do not answer to your father, a fact that I don't think he is aware of.' He smiled at me, giving me some belief that he was on my side.

I explained it to him, all of it, all that happened when I stood at Jago's window, and then back to when I had attacked Deborah. I told more than I intended, but his face stayed totally impassive. He got up and starting walking round the room, looking at the veranda and the view.

'And what of that do you remember?'

'Why do you care?'

'I am interested. And I have a degree in psychology so I know some big words.'

He made me smile at least. 'I remember nothing, none of it at all.'

'And that's not the first time that you have had a blackout that has resulted in somebody else getting injured.' He was looking at my picture of Carla and me, flying round on the carousel, arms out, laughing.

'It's not the first time, but I have no memory.'

'What is your dad going to do now?'

'I'll be put under some kind of house arrest. I'll have to leave my job. Then Scobie will mess about with all kinds of medication. It takes ages.'

'I didn't think meds worked well for DID.'

'They don't, but he does it anyway. They make me sleep, keep me calm until I do get better. Or get my mind back under their control.'

'Have you thought of getting a second opinion from somebody who is not a friend of your dad?' He picked up some of my dirty dishes that Deborah had not cleared away.

'Like that would be allowed.'

He raised his eyebrows. 'There's a few forensic psychologists at work that might be able to recommend somebody. But maybe for now you should stay here. For your own good, until after the funeral and they have all gone home.' He looked at my plate, into my Snoppy mug. 'You posh folk are disgusting, I'll take these downstairs.'

'Fill your boots. Maybe I should go on more medication and walk around like a zombie, I can't go around attacking people, can I? Maybe I should be locked up.'

'Are you sure you did it?'

'I don't think somebody crept up and put lipstick on me. So yes, I must have done.'

His eyes narrowed. 'Why? Why not some other . . . personality?'

'Oh don't you start. I don't know. Do you think I wanted to see life as Melissa saw it? Should I want to look like her? No, that's pathetic because I don't. But I did put all that stuff on my face, didn't I?'

'Keep quiet about that. We've never had that conversation. Could you develop a personality that cleaned up after itself?'

I nodded slowly. A wave of relief that Drew, at least, was treating me like a sane human being. 'Who would do that?' I asked carefully, looking at the dressing table. 'Who would do something to her?'

'Who are you looking at, Carla? Or your mother?'

FIFTEEN

Carla

T hings were odd up at the Italian House. Once Melissa and Jago were an item it was as if the power of her personality, her rather unpleasant personality, had been multiplied by his presence and that hatred liked to focus itself on me, because it was easy.

Mum had driven me up to the Italian House for what was becoming a regular event, another bloody meeting about the wedding and Melissa telling Megan and me how to behave. Mum would pop in to say hello and get a shufti at the house, enquiring if there was anything she could do as mother of the bridesmaid, and was told to try and keep me out of trouble.

Mum said she'd been trying that for the last thirteen years as she was ushered out the door.

She was happy to leave, knowing I'd get a run home.

One such night, Melissa had been getting ready for a ball or a concert or something. She had a long black dress by some poncy designer and the dog, Marcie, had got into her bedroom and lain down on the bed, on top of the dress. Melissa went nuts, totally tonto in her now hairy dress, called Jago and demanded to be picked up right here and right now.

He didn't, he talked her down and there were all kinds of accusations about who did this and who did that, who left the door of the bedroom open (her), who let the dogs upstairs (the dogs always went upstairs) and why was her life so difficult, (answers on a postcard) and why was she born into this god awful family (awful but loaded) where nobody understood her (she was mental).

She strutted and screamed around the house. Beth nodded. Ivan went off to his study. I am sure Megan slipped out her *hearing aids and crawled off to curl up in the corner of a settee somewhere, reading, and I followed, burrowing myself under huge cushions, watching their very small telly.*

Once Melissa had banged a few more doors, silence fell over the house. Marcie, the old golden retriever that had caused all the trouble, was alive and well when everybody went to bed, but after that nobody saw the dog for a while.

Marcie was found on the front terrace of the house, right in line with the front door. The dog had her throat cut. Unlike me, Beth never believed that it was Melissa. I guess that was the way it was meant to look. Melissa had been in the company of Jago, or upstairs screaming at the top of her voice.

So it couldn't really have been Melissa and the attention then turned on Megan. Quiet, silent, little Megan who stood in the corner and took everything in through those wide brown eyes.

Oh yes, I think Beth was scared of what Megan would do if Megan ever found out why she was deaf.

Megan

Everybody seemed to lie to me.

The water was cool against my toes, the Benbrae looked as though it was losing water through the intense dry weather. I was not worried, it had been there for years and it would outlive us all.

The house was full of lies and liars.

I hoped I was better than that.

Things were strange in the house, tense. The funeral was hanging over us all, Debs backtracking everywhere Dad had been looking for the necklace. The drawing room had a constant buzz of people drinking tea, eating scones, Heather hosting, asking Debs to refill the tea or coffee pot. Dad walked through, passing the time of day, but kept going back and forth to the study.

There, there was a lot to be said but nobody was saying it. From the corner of my eye I could see the tree beckoning to me. It was a low tree, an old oak that had grown there for many, many years, where Melissa terrified me as a young child. I can remember the water going over my head, the different kind of deafness under the surface and me letting the air out of my lungs, watching the bubbles float past my eyes, thinking that I was going to die.

And I wasn't scared.

Then Dad's arms scooping me out, holding me close. He was so scared, he was crying, I could still taste his tears on his face as he held me close to him, pushing my face against the crispness of his shirt so tight I couldn't turn my head to see. I have never been down that end of the Benbrae and the faerie pools, not since. I was scared of it as a child and I am scared of it now.

She had a cruel streak, Melissa.

Generations of our family have hanged themselves in the wood once they felt the creeping madness get too much for them, even Papa, who used to sneak Oodie Jaffa cakes, killed himself in there, swinging from the hanging tree, so somebody not in the family told me. Our family doesn't talk about such things. I wonder when I will get that mad.

Or do we kill ourselves before we go insane on the basis that if we were that mad we wouldn't notice?

Not intentionally but I had followed Jago about most of the day. Both he and I were out in the estate, walking, remembering and forgetting but not forgiving. We were treading water before the funeral. He avoided me with little sidesteps and pulling out his mobile phone, pretending he was busy. But then in the late afternoon he walked down to the Benbrae, strolling along with hands in his pockets, shirt open. He walked very slowly on the grass beside the long drive heading towards the mosaic. I could see that he was reflecting on Melissa and how and where it all went wrong, from the glorious day of their wedding to the mess we were then in.

We had all lessened as people.

In my bare feet he didn't hear me, he hadn't developed those senses of listening to the movement of air, feeling the fluctuations of pressure, knowing without hearing.

I waited until he was at the mosaic and I stood at the side as he looked down at the cracked tiles that mean nothing as individuals but everything when viewed together, they are such a pretty picture.

He saw me out the corner of his eye, smiled as if he had known I'd been there all along. 'Hello, Megan. Please go away.'

'You talk like it is my fault, all of this.'

'Some of it is.'

'I want to know what you know. That little secret about me that you and Melissa and my mum know about. I heard Dad talking about me on the veranda earlier today.'

'If you heard it there's fuck all wrong with your hearing.' He responded, then saw my face and added, 'We have been chatting about a lot of things.' He kicked something invisible away with his foot like he was wanting to kick me then said something but his face was turned away.

I grabbed him by the arm, forcing him to face me.

'What?' he asked.

'I want to know what you know. You, Dr Scobie, Dad, Mum, Melissa. "Do you think Megan has found out about Beth and Melissa?" was what Dad said. What was he talking about?'

'Ask him, ask your father.'

'Is it the reason Melissa told me she was sorry?'

He looked up at the house, then down to the Benbrae, searching for eavesdropping ears and eyes. Or maybe a way out.

'We only have your word she said that. My wife was not a great apologizer. And you're deaf so who knows what she said, or what you heard?' He smiled a rather cruel smile. 'You like your secrets in this house, don't you? They killed your sister, the secrets. Have you ever thought of that?'

'I doubt that. I know she had a shit of a husband that fucked off at the first hint of trouble.'

'Maybe you don't know all that—'

'All that what?' I asked but he turned away from me again and this time I hit him on the upper arm to get him to face me.

He raised his arm. 'I have never hit a woman, but don't tempt me because I might make an exception for you, Megan.'

'Tell me.'

'Go to hell, Megan.'

He walked away. I looked back up the hill to the Italian House where Dad was standing out on the terrace. Heather came up behind him, wrapping her arms round him, no doubt to comfort him, the anger of our exchange must have been obvious even from that distance. Dad knew, and he never told me.

Not a word.

I wondered if Heather knew as well. Maybe they all did, everyone except for me. I saw Deborah standing at the door, cloth in hand, holding it open for Jago's mum. They must have been going somewhere. They've all moved on and now there was only me standing in the middle of the mosaic feeling very alone. I closed my eyes with the sun on my face, and I missed Carla so much.

Carla

For a load of folk as intelligent as they were, why did nobody spot that Melissa was barking mad? I understand them missing it in Megan as she's a bit slow, a creeping quiet madness. Whereas Melissa would have a nibble at a corner of a slice of toast and then go running for six miles to work it off. She used to moan about how slim she had to be as an actress and that the theatre lights could put the pounds on the figure, the dresses she wore were so figure hugging. Not one buggar pointed out that it might look at bit better if there was actually a figure to hug.

But it's not about that, is it? It's about having the power to decide your own fate and when that is taken away from you, then you attempt to control things that you really can control, like the nourishment of your own body. They feel they are not good enough. Well, I confess that I don't understand that in this case, as Melissa Melvick was one of the most arrogant people I have ever been ignored by.

Megan thought there was a huge freedom in the fact I could be anything that I wanted to be, I could say what I wanted to say. I had to tell her that she was bloody naïve, yes I was able to say what I wanted, but what was the point when nobody ever listened to anything I said? Whereas Bloody Melissa, who everybody listened to, never had anything of any interest to say. She was only ever really interesting when she was speaking words that somebody else had written, usually that Shakespeare bloke, who if I understood Megan correctly, was from Birmingham.

Melissa used to go running so often she actually wore out the grass in a track round the inner boundary of the Italian House estate. Her parents forbade her to do it, they tried all sorts of things like locking her in, but Melissa was too manipulative and conniving.

No surprise then that as soon as Melissa got ill, they prevented Megan from going anywhere near that path. I guess they had their reasons.

Megan

There is always sanity in doing normal things. Like making the bed. Then that falls apart when there is a small box on the pillow, left there with a note signed by Debs, saying she'd found the box in the bin in the study and the necklace in Dad's bedside drawer.

It took me a long time to open it.

The Melvick necklace, worn by the eldest female in the family. Mum had left it when she walked out, that was a gesture we all understood. Agatha has it round her neck, I think she removed it before she hanged herself. I had witnessed Dad taking it from Melissa.

Was there a pattern here, each rejecting the house, the family and escaping in their own way? I opened the box and looked at it; it was so familiar to me, gold, unicorn and lion, entwined together, elegant and timeless. The chain has been changed many times of course. I held the lion to my lips, just as my mother had done, and as Melissa had done.

I thought they were entwined, the unicorn and the lion but studying them now, close up, it looked as if they were fighting, hooves against claws. At least if they were fighting there would be a winner. If they were entwined, they were stuck with each other.

Poor sods.

I was now the lady of the house, and nobody but me knew how bad that felt.

My work was with a friend of Dad's of course. They will have a conversation that I am not needed back, as I would be employed here and end up running the estate.

Trapped in this hellish paradise.

No wonder Agatha killed herself.

I found myself thinking that if Mum did appear at the funeral, I would get my freedom back. I was too young for all this. I should have had my life in front of me.

It was a weird thing to look through my old wardrobe, past the everyday clothes to those occasional items that lie half hidden in the corner. I was looking for a black suit I knew I had somewhere. The Megan Melvick funeral suit, a jacket, a skirt and a small hat that went with it. It had been made for me when I stopped growing, one of the daft traditions of the family. If I looked at any picture of any family funeral over the years, all the members of the family are wearing the same clothes.

It should have been in this wardrobe, protected in its plastic envelope. On a velvet coated hanger and may even have the dry-cleaning tag from the last time it was worn. That would have been Carla's funeral, they tried to keep me away but I made a point of going, enjoying reiterating to my father all his talk about respect and duty. OK, she was not a member of the family, but I had lost somebody very special.

I toyed with the idea of not bothering and wearing something else for Melissa's funeral and saying to Dad that times move on and so should we.

Yeah, as if I was going to say that to him now. I could never find the words to explain to him how this house was starting to feel toxic, squeezing the life out of anybody who lived within the walls. Oh and ask him at the same time, what's the big secret?

I reached my hand in, and felt the wall. The suit was not there. I moved through to one of the spare bedrooms which had two huge wardrobes, massive things in carved walnut that looked seaworthy, dating from 1845 or something, vast. If I hid in there for hide and seek I could be lost for a couple of generations.

I opened the wardrobe doors both wide, looking at everything. The full expanse of clothes were laid open before my eyes, like a curtain coming up on a play. There they all were, the Melvick funeral fashion hanging up. Appropriate shoes underneath. We didn't wear normal shoes at a funeral but highly polished court shoes with small polite heels, nothing zany, nothing outrageous, or fashion forward in case the empire collapsed at the sight of a stiletto.

And then I saw it, wrapped in its polythene shroud. The green bridesmaid dress I had worn for Melissa's wedding. The one with the headdress of twigs and flowers on our hair, I could hear Carla at my side, laughing. I pulled it from the rack, pushing the other clothes to the side as if they had no right to be intruding on its space, and I held it to my face, breathing in deep, thinking that I could see Carla in the dead space. I missed her so much.

SIXTEEN
Friday

Megan

Funerals are tense enough, more so I suppose when there has been a split in the family. I could sense the expectation in the air that my mum might put in an appearance. We were not here to celebrate the life of Melissa Melvick plus her middle names, we were here to see if my mother came back. The whole village was here to see that.

Something ironic in the fact that Melissa was upstaged at her own funeral by somebody who wasn't even there.

It was very traditional, the organ was playing 'Abide With Me'.

I had already seen the order of service, now neatly placed on the seats, on the front was a beautiful hand-drawn pencil portrait of Melissa. It caught her wistful beauty perfectly, and the translucence of the image suggested that she was already slipping away.

It was incredibly touching.

I saw villagers looking at a few actors who had turned up, subtle selfies being taken to engineer a famous person in the background, I heard my dad swear under his breath and Jago told him to stay calm, it was the way of young people today. Jago glared at me. I glared back. He mouthed that he was sorry, Melissa was my sister long before she was his wife. I gave him a wistful smile, whatever, there was bigger stuff going on now.

Today was for us.

The hearse drew up pulled by Lorimer and Quest, people stood around, their ebony clothes at odds with the brightness of the sunshine. I swear that as soon as the back of the hearse opened, and the coffin was gracefully slid out, one single cloud drifted over the sun. Even in death she was in control.

Ten light yellow roses, nothing vulgar and nothing like 'Melissa' or 'daughter' spelled out in dense petals.

I felt Deborah's hand on my back, comforting me. Then I noticed Dad standing to attention, doing the right thing.

I noticed a car parked on the same side of the grass verge as our funeral car, Dad's Rolls-Royce Phantom, the one that had taken Jago and Melissa as a married couple from this very church. It had been in the family from way before my sister or I were born, before Mum was born in fact. It was Dad's favourite car and if it gave him some comfort on the day he said goodbye to his eldest child, then I had no quarrel with that.

Jago went forward to help take the coffin on his shoulder, the crowd all moved, like a murmeration, to either side.

Then there was a slight change to the sombre atmosphere, a tickle of excitement, a vehicle was drawing up pulling into the kerb, the mourners looked at it, then looked back at my dad.

I watched him carefully, as he watched the strange car. The door opened, a foot appeared, a female foot in a low-heeled black patent shoe. It was exactly like the ones I had on my feet at that moment. The Melvick family shoe. Then the door opened further and a leg emerged, a black skirt. At that point, I felt my heart give a little stutter. Was it Mum coming back?

I even opened my mouth, even took a step forward. I felt Deborah's hand increase her pressure, warning me.

Tears of sadness, replaced with tears of happiness. Mum was coming back.

Then Heather's auburn bob appeared as she rose from the passenger seat and looked at the crowd in the front of the church with a shy smile, a hand raised to apologize for being late. She dropped to say something to the driver and the car pulled away.

The murmerers retracted, deflated.

My father's face retreated to its mask of calm passivity.

I think my heart might have snapped at that moment.

Carla

And then of course, we were all waiting with bated breath to see if Beth would turn up at her daughter's funeral. The whole village was pretending that they were there to pay their respects, but in reality, it was a day off work, a great bun fight and a swally, all wrapped up in the big will-she, won't-she.

She didn't.

There was a rumour that Big Barbara was running a book on it in the Oarsman. Malkie from the garage said that Babs had a vested interest, and insider information was she was shagging Ivan and the last thing he wanted was the first bloody wife showing up.

There were rumours at the time that Ivan had done her in and buried her in the compost heap, or given her a necklace of breeze block and dumped her in a faerie pool. But he had paid to have that searched by divers, probably because he was unable to believe that any woman could have had the balls to walk out on him. We liked the angry husband theory, Ivan was so ruggedly handsome and charming, quietly in control, so I liked the idea of him going totally bonks and stabbing her with his gold-plated fountain pen. It was just my fucking luck that the one person who could say that was not so, was my own bloody mother. She was his alibi. Mum had seen Beth that morning and Ivan had been in the study with somebody called Alistair at the time. Or so he said. And so they said, 'But money can buy an alibi as easy as it buys friends'. Mum saw her walk away, 'As if', she said, 'she was going to meet somebody'.

Heather saw her there as well, had exchanged a few words through the car window on the way in, had waved and driven past on the way out. I fancied the idea of Heather getting out with a mallet and battering Beth to death before stuffing her in the boot.

Our minds were running riot behind Megan's back, and sometimes to her front, as she could never hear us anyway, about her mum and sex parties and the druids in the pony club.

But in the end, with the passage of time, I guess some fancy man came along who decided he would take her away from this terrible weather.

They kept things in the family, they liked their genes to be passed on and Beth had always felt she wasn't quite up to the Melvick standard because she had not produced a son, or a daughter who wasn't nuts.

I wondered if my dad felt the same. I was his daughter, his family was complete, then he told me that Fishface was pregnant.

I think he felt kind of bad about that.

'So you are going to be a big sister,' he said.

'I have been that before,' I replied.

He nodded, sorry for his mistake and patted me on the head. He wasn't a bad man and sometimes stuff just doesn't pan out.

So there was Beth Melvick, very smiley and pleasant, she wore sensible skirts and green quilted jackets. She smelled of vegetables and pony clubs, community halls and flower arranging. And there was Ivan Melvick, he was all waxed jackets and yachting, he was a tall and handsome man, getting more so as he got older. Looking back, he has been grey in all my memories. He was a bit of all right, a silver fox, with his slightly long straggling hair that he swept over his head with a very aristocratic wave of the hand, pinkie out of course. I would have shagged him myself if I had been older and if he didn't have a bad hip. While he was kind of rugged and handsome, there was solidity about him, a sense that he could be depended on to do the right thing. I wished he'd been my dad.

They were both good people, but like I said, sometimes stuff just doesn't pan out.

The real truth of it all, a truth that cannot be admitted, is that Beth was taken by the kelpies, those great mythical beasts with horses' heads, and dragged into the Benbrae, drowned and scoffed. The Italian House had everything money could buy so why not a few monsters in the Tentor Wood as well? That was the chat in the Oarsman after hours when the home brew came out. Malkie from the garage and Minty Minto had even retraced Beth's steps that night, away from the road and down by the side of the Benbrae. They had both ended up wet and half drowned but for different reasons.

The kelpie theory had even appeared on a few websites.

Even before all that, Beth's disappearance had become a bit of a legend around here.

What exactly did happen to her?

Not that anybody talked to Megan or Ivan about it. Must have been tough that, knowing that your mum didn't love you enough to hang around and wait until you grew up. At least it was my mum who tended to drag me with her when she legged it, away from whatever man was beating her up and stealing the money out her purse while she was out earning it. And there had been a lot of men. A lot of houses, spare rooms, step-dads, step-sisters, but there was nobody like Megan. I guess she was the one constant in my life by the end, trapped because there was nowhere else for her to go. She said that, more than once. She had grown up in the Italian House and had come to, well, hate it I suppose. Now Melissa had gone, she would be expected to stay here. Not grow up and get married, not leave and live another life outside the village.

Yes, Megan now knew that her life was here, just as Beth, the incomer, had got stuck here. Beth had seen life outside that house, then arrived here as a young bride, full of hormones and delusions. Then the girls arrived and neither of them were exactly what she had hoped for.

The only thing Beth must have worried about was which daughter was the bigger disaster. My money would be on Melissa.

One thing was for sure though, I know because I saw it with my own eyes. As the Highland ponies pulled their sad carriage behind them into Kilaird Kirkyard, Ivan took one slow, last look up the street, his blue eyes closed slightly against the glare of the sun. He looked like an African hunter surveying the veld for a shy leopard, but we knew he was having a last look down the road, to see if his wife was going to turn up to bury their eldest daughter.

Ivan had expected her to be there.

Megan

'The flowers are beautiful, Megan, just beautiful.'

I knew it was Debs. Her little habit of giving me a soft tap on the upper arm, to let me know she was there and that she was going to say something. It gave me advance notice to turn around, so I didn't miss the start of the conversation. She was thoughtful that way, Debs.

'Was Melissa fond of yellow?' she asked, her finger tentatively pointing at the pale yellow roses wound into a wreath, like the headbands we had on at her wedding, the same green threads weaving and wafting their way through the softly coloured petals. 'It's the same colour as her bedroom, so pretty.'

I looked at the roses, then at Deb's fingers, red and cold looking even in the heat. Then at her wrist, at the silver bracelet. I recognized the silver band, the complex clasp, the engraved thistles.

'Your dad asked me to wear it,' she said, seeing the look on my face. 'I'm not sure what he meant but I didn't want to refuse.'

'It's fine,' I said, hoping the shock didn't show.

'Can I give it back to you at the house, and you can put it back in the safe? I really don't want it lying around.'

'Yes, of course. What is my dad doing?'

'I've no idea, but he gave Heather a choice of pieces to wear. I thought he had told you.'

'He never said.'

'Sorry.'

We had been whispering, Debs and I but our caution had drawn some attention.

'She was fond of colour full stop. But she did like the smell of these roses,' I said, loudly.

'Oh, are they the ones from the garden? I never noticed they were gone,' answered Debs.

'They are now. Cut, dying. Killed for their beauty. They will wither and fade now, just like Melissa. She faded with the colour of the flowers.'

'Sometimes you worry me, Megan, why can't you think like a normal person.'

I could hear the amusement in her voice. Deep down, Debs thought I was the sane one of the family.

'Shame I never knew Melissa, not well. Not when she was well, I mean,' said Deborah, walking away from the flowers and the sad little tags. The throng of people who had gathered, I wondered what we looked like Debs and I, the sister and the hired help. 'You should be over there with your father.'

But I had already spotted Heather with her arm on Dad's shoulder, as if he was an old man in need of care. She was guiding him, consoling him, looking as though she was making decisions for him, leading him this way and that, thinking she was protecting him. My dad was the strongest man on the face of this planet. He did not need the help of Heather and her empathetic smile.

Or was I deluding myself.

Suddenly I felt a huge rage against her, I wanted her gone.

'Calm down.' Debs must have noticed my reaction. 'She's very good at it, isn't she, playing the lady of the manor.'

'So she thinks,' I answered.

'I was a bit worried about him this morning, he seemed very stressed, even a little confused when I set the breakfast table. He asked me if we were having guests.'

'Really?' That chilled me, he knew we had a house full.

'I don't think he's been sleeping.' Debs watched as Heather took my dad's elbow to guide him to speak to another mourner, navigating him through the crowd. 'How does she think that looks behaving like that? He should be with you; she was your mum's best friend.'

'Maybe that's why she thinks she can. Dad has no close relatives, neither had Mum, I guess she's the closest we have to an aunt.'

Carla

Melissa's send-off was beautifully orchestrated. The church was busy, there were even folk standing outside in the sunshine once it all got underway.

When Baby Paul was buried, there was Mum, me and a social worker. That was it. Mum was upset afterwards but we went out for a fish tea and that cheered us up. At least we would get some sleep.

Of course, there was a big hoo ha when the baby died. In the dirty bedsit with the knobbly wallpaper, and there was little Paul in his cot in the corner, his face turning as blue as the paint on the skirting board. Looking back, now that I am older and have had the time and the experience of life and death to reflect, I know that they suspected Mum or me.

After talking to Mum they just suspected me.

There was a lot of sitting in rooms, my mum's snot-filled face always red-eyed from crying. She appeared to be very upset. A nice woman, Joanne somebody, with glossy hair and big warm jumpers would sit beside me on the settee in the police station, asking me how much I liked Paul and did I kiss and cuddle him. Did I cuddle him hard, did I take him to bed with me and when I woke up was he cold? I answered that I didn't like him that much as he was bloody noisy and woke me up when he cried. And that Mum cried a lot after he was born, and she cried herself to sleep at night. Some instinct of self-preservation must have clicked because I didn't tell them that since Paul had died Mum was sleeping very soundly, she was almost content, even happy. Then they got Mum to talk to me, then Dad got involved and said, as he always did, that I wasn't like that. Then a psychologist appeared from nowhere saying how did my dad know what I was like as he didn't live with me? And how did we know Mum was telling the truth about me as she did live with me and would be biased?

It went round and round, like a bluebottle at a window, busy buzzing but settling nowhere.

And nobody was there when Paul died, nobody but me. But babies do fall asleep and some of them do not wake up.

Round and round, going nowhere.

Like the horses on the carousel.

SEVENTEEN

Megan

After the funeral, there were a lot of people back at the house. It felt like an invasion. I knew I was now watching my father through different eyes. I headed out the back courtyard, round the corner to the wall where we used to grow the sunflowers, to what we called the orchard where there was an old swing standing amongst the cherry blossom, and the graves of our faithful dogs, still tended to, still cared for in death as they had been in life.

And there was Deborah.

'Hi, how are you? Do they have enough tea through there?'

'The ladies from the church guild have taken over the kitchen. Heather is in charge.'

'That will stop them gossiping. Or give them more to talk about once her back is turned. I am having a bit of a breather, a quick fag.'

'Can I steal one?'

'It's a disgusting habit.'

'Yes, I know, it's your habit, not mine, so it doesn't count.'

I sat beside her, pulling up the other swing, keeping the back and forth momentum. Her feet were up on the seat beside her, her red shoes kicked off to let her feet cool down. They were tanned and she had her toenails painted. She had a small tattoo on the side of her ankle, a little dolphin, and the word Carla underneath and a date. The date of Melissa's wedding. Which of course, was the day Carla died.

'When did you get that done?'

'Last year. You could afford a mosaic. I got a tattoo. I like it, God knows what it will look like when I am old and wrinkly, it's going to stop looking like a dolphin and start looking like a bloodhound.'

'Heather thinks women with tattoos are little more than harlots.'

'Well, she should get out more.' At that moment two of Mum's friends from the flower club walked through the courtyard, looking at the flowers, talking about how some people can have everything, but not happiness. Debs nudged me. 'Let's walk.' She pulled long and hard on her cigarette, as she slid off the seat. 'Don't fuel their gossip, they have tea to make.' She stopped after two paces, standing at Oodie's grave. 'You Melvicks really do love your dogs, don't you? This was your collie.'

'My childhood dog, my friend. Her mother was called Fern. She was the dog lost in the faerie pool.'

Deb pointed at the small cairn. 'No grave, just a memorial, like the mosaic and the tattoo.'

The next one was a grave covered by a well-trimmed bamboo plant, a stone statue of a Labrador peeking out from between the leaves. 'Martha,' I explained. 'She was murdered.'

'Really?' Debs looked alarmed, 'Come on,' she said, and we walked in silence for a while, habitually taking the path out to the stable then turning towards the water.

'Why is Heather here so often, she's swanning around in there like she owns the place? How long has that been going on for?' I asked, well out of earshot.

'About eighteen months or so. She's a dead man's slippers kind of woman, as soon as somebody dies she's right in there.' She placed her hand on my arm. 'Sorry, kid, but you know Heather wants to be the next Mrs Melvick, Christ knows why.'

I smile at her mockney accent. Debs was always cheery. Always had a glass half full way of looking at life. 'I know it's hard and she's a right royal pain in the arse but you have your own life to lead now, you have your flat and a job. Maybe Heather and your dad will do just fine.'

'I'm not sure I will be going back to work, with Dad the way he is. Maybe it should be me looking after him.'

She didn't look at me. 'That might be for the best. But you shouldn't if they do get together. Like I say, you will be away one day and he'll be left here with me, a couple of ponies and an incontinent dog. I know how fucking useless he is. Your dad can start a combine harvester but can't programme the microwave. So no, Megan, don't you mind what your dad does, he needs his happiness and you need yours. I always thought Melissa was tied to this place too much by being Melissa Melvick from the big house after she left, or tried to leave. She was whiplashed right back. I hope things are different for you.'

She was right. Mum had not come back. It was all very different now. I was thinking about what Drew had said, and I knew deep inside that she would have come back to see Melissa if she could. 'Debs? Why do you think Mum left?'

'There were lots of rumours at the time but honestly, I think she had her reasons, kiddo, and she will come back when she wants to. And if she knew about Melissa, I'm sure she'd be back right now.'

'Of course she must know.'

Deb's head flicked round. 'Why? The only person who has heard from her is Heather. Would you tell Beth what was going on if you were her? Heather's sitting here, all doe-eyed helping your dad to get through the trauma, using Melissa's passing to get him to change his will. I wouldn't put it past her to offer to be your responsible adult, you know, with your history. Of trouble. That Scobie guy saying you were incompetent . . . mentally . . .' she added lamely.

'Really?'

'Yes, one of those suits at the house yesterday was a lawyer, a new will to protect you if he gets married again. You still inherit everything, at the end, any new wife will have an entitlement but nothing that will affect the house or the estate.'

'Or the Munnings, get your priorities right. Bloody hell, so he must be serious about her.'

She laughed, 'Or lonely, maybe just lonely. But still technically married. Drew was being all sensible, stressing that he thought your dad wasn't thinking clearly, you know, this is not a good time for him to be making decisions.'

We walked on in the baking sun, hard to grieve on such a beautiful day. 'And what about you, staying at the lodge?'

'I'm here all the time, I had a flat in Dunoon, but when Melissa's illness took hold your dad offered me the lodge. What with Carla and my alcoholic boyfriends, shit and vomit don't bother me and I could be on hand to look after Melissa. I don't have a lease for the lodge or anything, so don't you go rushing back to Glasgow, or I could be out on my ear. And your dad needs you.'

'You think?'

'He needs somebody. When you are not here that somebody becomes bloody Heather. I always get suspicious when that lawyer, Lawton, appears at the house and they disappear into the study with strong coffee and instructions not to be disturbed.'

'So how do you know about the will?'

'He asked me to witness it.'

'And he told you what it was?'

'I asked him. I wasn't going to sign anything that didn't look after you properly. Since Beth left, I've always thought it was my duty to look out for you.'

'And I've always thought it was the duty of our family to look after you. After Carla . . .'

'So we are quits then.' She continued, 'And they were looking at Melissa's will.'

'Really?'

'Yeah, your dad said I wasn't to say anything but Melissa did leave me a few quid.'

'You are kidding?'

'I hardly knew her. I thought it was weird. I was around her, you know, when she came back here, she was so weak by then.'

We strolled in silence.

'How weird do you think that is? You did look after her for a while, but not enough to warrant an inheritance.'

'I know what you mean, it crossed my mind too. Melissa hated Carla, and she leaves me some dosh. Blood money? Almost as if she was sorry.'

'Melissa was always strange,' I said, not wanting to think about that. Princess Frosty Pants.

For a while, we walked on the other side of the fence almost at the bank of the Benbrae, the aroma of cigarette smoke mingling in the air with the warm sun, a bee buzzed nearby. There was a strong resonance of what had gone on before. She was looking at something, her eyes slightly narrowed, she shivered in her black blouse, and stuck another fag in her mouth so she could rub her upper arms to get some warmth back. Or to comfort herself. Funerals tend to invite thoughts of those absent. 'Carla?' I asked.

'No, not Carla. Carla was Carla and that was that. I was thinking of those trees over there, they always give me the creeps.'

'The Tentor Wood? They give everybody the creeps.'

'Yeah, but you more so surely.'

'Why? Why me more?'

She looked at me with surprise, her blonde fringe falling into her eyes. She looked at her feet. 'Oh shite, you don't know?'

'Know what? There are a lot of things I don't know. I'm getting a bit pissed off with it. I think I grew up blind as well as deaf, I sleepwalked through my entire existence seemingly.'

'The Tentor Wood has a dark past, in your family.'

'But not recently?' I raised an eyebrow.

'You had better ask your dad that one. It's none of my business.'

I looked across, aware of Deborah getting onto her feet and drying them on the grass before she slipped them back in her bright red ballerina pumps. 'No, Debs, you tell me. Please. Just because I'm deaf doesn't mean I should be kept in the dark. Ignorance is not the default position of the deaf.'

She smiled. 'Have you been practising that?'

'I heard it somewhere.'

'I like it. But still, ask your dad.' With that she got up and left. Not like her not to finish a conversation that she had started, she was the straightest person I knew.

I looked over at the Tentor Wood, vague memories dancing around me. Dad lifting me up out the water, but I was dressed up. I felt the lace at the bottom of the skirt wet against my legs. I never had that on, not down at the wood. That was my birthday frock. That memory rises and then the dark water, slick like ebony oil, covers it and it sinks from my consciousness.

That hadn't struck me before. I would go anywhere in this house that I wasn't allowed to go. I crept into Dad's study, went into his wine cellar and climbed up onto trees but those other trees, those that crouched in the dense darkness, I never went there.

Carla

There is always a turning point, that moment in time when enough becomes enough. The moment when the shit hits the fan. And that was how I ended back up in Dunoon. Mum got a taste of how bad the big wide world can be. She was in court and I was in high dependency.

Dad was good, of course. In his own faltering cack-handed way, he came to the rescue. He stood up for Mum in court, as the ex-partner, saying that he thought she was a good woman who had lost her way. The social workers had created this wonderful fiction of my new life in Dunoon, in a place where the big city couldn't reach me and I would learn to be responsible and turn into a useful human being. Dad was going to look after me. Well, he was going to get Gran to look after me as Fishface Norma couldn't stand the sight of me.

Mum was deemed to be irresponsible after taking up with a new partner who was involved in a paedophile ring. He was in jail of course. Now. A real hateful bastard called Keith. He was one I couldn't fight off but anything can become normal if you are exposed to it often enough. Not so different from M and M, all their demons came from the inside, mine were right out my bedroom door.

I never like to play the victim, these things happen, I wasn't the first kid and I wouldn't be the last. I survived all that, I had Megan somewhere, to hold on to, to run to.

Things didn't change though, I was passed on. Somebody else's problem.

It was a fuckin joke, back in Dunoon. Next thing Mum is back also, saying that she had changed and it was all different now, telling the social worker that she was a better mother after the rude awakening of her dangerous lifestyle. She asked Dad if she could have me back, as she was staying above a pub in Dunoon (like that was a good idea). Dad wasn't keen. He said he'd ask his boss if I could go to work with him for a few weeks so that I could get into a routine and I might even be some help with the dogs and the horses. It had been proven that kids with a tough past do well with animals.

Ivan Melvick said no.

So he must have been well chuffed when I rolled up anyway,
the heroine who saved his daughter. Not.

Megan

I spent a fair while down at the Benbrae, on my own, sitting on
the bench at the mosaic and watching the cars leave the house.
The mourners were all going home. I strolled back up, released
Molly from the stables and let her run around the home field. I
sat on the fence as more people came out the front door of the
house, shaking hands with Dad, leaving him alone on the step
as they drove off. I was surprised to see Jago's parents go off in
a local taxi back to the airport and then Jago himself, leaving,
shaking hands with his father-in-law, climbing into his Jag and
away.

My dad looked very small and alone, standing in the big double
doors of the house. Then Heather appeared behind him.

I waited for a while, until I was sure they were all gone, no
cars left on the gravelled forecourt. Then I saw Dad leave, walking
down the Long Drive and felt it was time for me to see what
was left of the buffet.

I ran straight into Heather, standing at the bottom of the
stairs in the great hall, looking up at Agatha, straightening her
black skirt, and patting her hair. She was tilting her head, trying
to pose like Agatha. I think she might have been looking for
hints for being a Melvick, pulling faces and practising the
insincerity.

'I think she would have approved of it today. Quiet, tasteful.
All very tasteful. The women's guild did us very proud.'

Us?

'Is there any food left?'

'Deborah is seeing to that in the kitchen. Megan?' she said,
linking arms with me. 'Your dad and I were just saying that it's
all going to come down to you. I noticed at the service how
beautiful that necklace looks sitting around your neck, like it
belongs.'

'Does it?'

'It does. You're the only child, you will be the one to inherit.'

'I'd rather they were all here to share it with me. And Mum is not dead. She's still married to Dad. It will take seven years, legally.'

'Three years have already passed. Drew mentioned that.'

'Did he really?' That needled me. Why had this man become some kind of magi?

'But you won't leave here, will you? Your dad wants you to stay.' Heather tilted her head to the side the way Molly does when she wants the crusts of the toast, as she was a greedy little madam, and I was thinking that she wasn't the only one around. Heather was standing there, her lovely legs crossed at the ankle, looking every bit like the lady of the manor. In a minute she'd be asking if my dad was in good health and if he was well-insured.

I knew the answer to the last question would be yes. I wasn't so sure about the former. I wasn't even sure if he'd changed his power of attorney after Mum disappeared.

'He's so broke up about your mother not coming back for the funeral. I wonder if it's now time to break free from that.'

'Do you want him to start divorce proceedings now?' I shook my head. 'The week his daughter died?'

'Sorry.' She took my hand in both of hers, despite the heat of the day her skin was dry and cool, like snakeskin. 'I didn't mean that. What I meant was, do you think he'll be able to break free of Beth now?'

'Mum got out of bed that morning, took off her engagement ring and her wedding ring, and this.' I held up the necklace. 'This is what the current Mrs Melvick is supposed to wear and off she trotted. That's a pretty clear sign to the family. She rejected us. I think she had somewhere to go. And she has gone there. And stayed.'

'Do you really think she would do that? To you, to Ivan?'

'It's not what I think. It's what she did. Melissa was married and away, I was turning seventeen, she felt she'd done her bit. She was miserable here.'

'Why do you . . .?' Then she stopped, and there it was again that little lie. The evasion that everybody thought I wouldn't notice. 'Are you going to stay around this afternoon? I don't think he should be on his own. He has some people to see later, he didn't say who.'

'Yes, of course, I'll be here.' Was she hinting that these 'people' might upset him? Had she already noticed something not right about him, or did she put it down to the strain of the day.

'Well, I will go then.' She went up on her tiptoes and kissed me on the cheek.

'Bye,' I muttered, 'don't hurry back.'

They arrived about six o'clock. Two men. Walking around, men on the outside of the estate, I saw them take Dad to one side, have a few quiet words, a nod then they would part, Dad walking back to the house and the men back down to the gate and to continue their circuit.

I asked him what was going on but he said it was nothing to worry about but there was such a crease of concern over his forehead it was obvious that there was plenty to worry about.

They did underestimate me, I had already gone into the study and looked in Dad's desk diary. It was written there in fountain pen with his precise italic hand. He really did believe that people lived to his standards, not reading other folks' diaries was one of them.

He was having the estate valued.

Valued.

I know, he was distracted after the funeral. He had been in mourning before, but now he was worried. Something had happened and he wasn't telling me.

I watched as he turned away from the men. He stood for a long, long moment, looking up at the house then down to the Benbrae, staring at the sky as if the rooks were offering the answers to all the questions he had never asked.

Or totting it up in his head.

Then he seemed to come to some conclusion and began the walk back up the Long Drive, his shoulders down, walking reluctantly, as if he was walking back to a situation he would rather avoid.

I was going to hide back up in the bedroom but then, too restless, I strolled round the house, looking at the familiar, resenting the changes. Everybody had gone home. Deb to her lodge house, the dogs to their beds, even Heather had buggered off.

Dad had disappeared too. Off hiding in the study with a bottle
of malt and a glass. He said goodnight to me, clasping my upper
arms, kissing me on the forehead and said, 'Do you know where
my car keys are? I know I left them in my study.'

'They will turn up, it's been an awful day. Use the spare set.'

'They were the spare set. I have already mislaid the other
ones.'

'What did you want them for? You've had a drink?'

'Just in case.'

'I'm sure they will turn up.'

He rubbed his chin. 'I was sure I had them in my hand this
morning.'

'I'll keep my eye out for them. It's been a very long day.'

He hugged me and told me that he hoped I loved the house as
with Melissa gone, it was all coming to me. 'Please don't hurry
back to work, I have spoken to Edward and he's happy for you
to stay here, maybe work from here. I really want you to be here.'

He didn't add it is your duty, but I could see it in his
eyes. He's not asking me, he's telling me.

'I think I'd rather go back to work and finish up for myself,
there are a few clients I'd like to see through, people I was doing
some research for.'

'I'd rather you were here.'

Cold.

'I'd rather go back. I have good clients. I'm not leaving them
to one of the others.'

'I got you the job, Megan, and I will have it taken away from
you, you have a job, a job and a duty and that is here.' He nodded,
a dip of his chin as if he was dismissing one of the lower orders.

'I think that should be my decision.'

He smiled again, blue eyes creasing. 'Of course it will be, and
you will make the correct choice, I am sure of that.' Then he
closed the door back over, and the hall went dark.

I walked around making sure the doors were locked and the
windows were closed, Molly was with me, still hyper after a day
of being locked up in the stables and resentful of missing all the
comings and goings. She wouldn't sleep, she was restless, walking
up and down panting. I went back downstairs and Molly ran up
to the door of Dad's study.

I was feeling very uneasy, not really sure why. My dad had been under a lot of strain and it was very odd that this house should be so empty, like it had been cleared. Intentionally. I went back upstairs and looked round Melissa's room. Her bed had been remade, the yellow duvet cover millpond smooth. All the equipment had gone, the porcelain jug and wash stand were back in place, all was back the way it was, as it had been for every minute of my childhood. It was as if Melissa had never existed.

Her photograph, which usually stood on the dresser, was missing. And even in the heat trapped in that room, I felt a chill.

I ran my hands along the top of each picture, tapping them in turn, one of Melissa was missing. Nope. It was still here but moved to the front. The one of Melissa and Beth together was gone.

The house was empty. Just Dad and I.

How many times had it been said to me today? Stay here.

The carousel was moving round. I fingered the necklace, looking out the window. The estate had been measured up today. And valued?

A sense of a house being put in order.

I pulled out the mobile and called Drew.

EIGHTEEN

Megan

Ten minutes later, dressed in jeans and a warm jumper, I was down at the Benbrae with Molly. It was dark, Drew came out from the woods, looking like he had climbed over the fence. I was going to ask him why he didn't drive in. Where had he been to get here so quickly?

'Megan, somebody has walked round the house, they might be making their way down to the Benbrae. I think it's your dad.'

I thought about getting up but Drew held on to me, telling me to wait to see what way they went. He didn't seem surprised by any of this. 'What do you know? What is he doing?'

Drew told me to be quiet, pursing his lips and shaking his head. 'Let's see what he does, where he goes.'

So he was here, but not for me. Yet some other secret of the family. 'Do you think it's something to do with Mum?'

'Let's wait and find out.'

'He's been very worried. Where is he going?'

'Quiet.'

I watched as Dad walked past us, hidden as we were, crouching down in the lie of the land. He didn't keep to the road, he veered off.

Into the Tentor Wood.

All I heard was Drew swear under his breath and he took off, into the darkness. I had to hold tight to Molly's collar to stop her trying to follow him.

I tried to stand up but my legs were stuck, my feet not moving as I commanded them to, I tried to make my way slowly, pushing branches aside, my face getting scratched. Drew had seen something, under this very dark sky, twinkling stars making it seem even darker.

Molly was beside me, shivering. Sensing my tension.

I heard voices, shouting in the distance.

Then they stopped.

Drew came running past me, fast, stopping for nothing, he shouted at me to get out the way.

So I ran in deep into the Tentor Wood, running behind Molly who had caught a scent. I almost stumbled into the clearing, just in time to see my dad lift the noose and slowly put it around his neck.

I stopped dead.

Someday it was all going to be mine, and that day is today. Carla died the day of Melissa's wedding, my dad will die on the day of her funeral.

I said nothing. I couldn't move.

I felt the screaming in my throat but it would not come out my mouth and I didn't know if I was seeing what was actually going on. Or was this in the past? Was I a kid again in my lacy party dress, my fourth birthday, standing, weeping as the black noise rolled towards me and behind it was Papa dancing on his rope, his twitchy, jerky dance?

And the hand that pushed him . . .

The noise echoed around the woods, the trees on either side were shouting or laughing at me, the rooks taking off, their wings swamped by the tsunami of sound.

But there is no noise at all.

Carla

Why does Megan believe what people say to her so readily? No wonder her personality fractures into tiny pieces if that is what it takes for her voice of reason to get a fair hearing.

She's thinking about her dad, she's thinking about the madness and thinking about the family history of suicide, and I know that she's scared for him. She believes he is ready to kill himself.

I know that the minute she pulls on a pair of jeans, her big jumper, and walks down to the kitchen to pull on her outdoor boots. The great thing about only existing in someone else's head is that where she goes, I have to go. The downside is that I can't actually stop her from doing anything that she wants to do. I have a stinker of a feeling what this might be. It's not often in my life that I am scared, but I am now. I am witnessing that terrible long moment before two cars crash and you are powerless to prevent it. You may see the driver put their hands up to protect themselves, an arm outstretched, an instinctual act to stop the passenger from going forward. And me, the helpless onlooker just watching the carnage unfold in front of me.

She slips out the door, she immediately slides along the side of the house, keeping in the shadows. There is a full moon tonight, the Long Drive is open, flat on the left and right sides, but Megan is moving quickly, her dog at her heels, cutting across the front door and heading out to the right by the wall. She's going to follow it all the way round, down to the gate where she can cross again onto the Benbrae. She's keeping out of sight, tucked in, being secretive, waiting for Drew.

Then Drew arrives and with his clearer head, he gets a grip on the situation quicker, and runs for the boathook.

Megan is on the narrow path, the path Melissa made while running off her calories. She's moving slower as if she's less certain of herself now, and then her hand goes up to her mouth and she backs away. I can see exactly what she is seeing. And I feel that sense of fear again. I can see Ivan dangling from the tree over the dark ebony depths of the Benbrae, swinging gently in a breeze, in the dark air, a single teardrop of a hangman's noose.

For fuck's sake, here we go again.

Megan

I turn round thinking that Drew must be close by but he's nowhere to be seen, nowhere behind me or beside me. I am alone with my dog in the Tentor Woods and am unable to take a step forward, watching my father twitching on the end of a rope, out over the water.

I can't save him.

He stops twitching.

Still now.

His body swaying back and forth with the slight breeze or

some inner momentum, he hangs like a doll somebody had lost and pegged out on the washing line by its neck.

My legs have turned to stone, all I can do is watch in horror. Then I am thrown to the ground myself, a punch on the back. I lie there and close my eyes, the skin on my face forced into the grass. There is no point, Dad gone, Mum gone, Melissa gone and now it seems to be my turn. The dog has taken off, Drew has gone. I close my eyes.

Why had it all come to this?

Because it was inevitable.

Carla

Drew is sharp. He twigged what was going on long before Megan did, he ran back, round the north bank of the Benbrae to the boathouse where, clamped onto the wall, were the long hooks. With one of them under his arm he ran back, the path, that very narrow path, was underused and overgrown so he was really pushing his way through. It didn't help that Megan was standing right in the middle, not hearing Drew shout to get out the way. So he shoved her.

And she fell.

Simple as that.

But she couldn't hear him. Nothing weird about that except I know she had her hearing aids in.

Megan

I watched, hardly breathing as Drew pulled Dad to the side using the boathook. He hauled him on to the bank, crouching low to get a grip, like a macabre tug of war. The sight of them rolling on the grass was what brought me round. The fact Dad had lost his shoes. He had attempted suicide, I was concerned his feet would be cold.

Dad was wet, dripping with sweat, shaking and panicking. Drew had to pin him on the ground until he calmed. Then we helped him to his feet, and we stood side by side supporting Dad as we started the long slow walk out the wood, then up to the house. My ears were full of silence, I felt I was under water again.

The Long Drive stretched for an eternity in front of us, the three of us walking slowly, we didn't speak. We were half carrying, half dragging my dad, he was struggling to breathe. I saw Drew's mouth open and close, but his head was moving too much for me to lip-read. We were trapped in the silent dark night with this old man, this shrunken effigy of my father, the pale wrinkled skin of his neck striping purple and pink, flecked with blood.

Up at the front door, Dad seemed to come round, maybe the familiarity reducing his confusion. He rubbed his head as Drew took him into the study and closed the door behind him, giving me a look that said do not come in here.

So I followed them in, angry at Drew. More angry at Dad.

'How dare you. How dare you,' I said.

'Calm down, Megan. Just calm down.'

I think that's what Drew said as he pushed me back into the big chair.

And I watched them talk, snug in my silence.

Carla

She is one drama queen, the little mare, now that Melissa has gone we seem to have found another actress in the Melvick family. I didn't see it all, of course, but I could work out what was going on. Drew, as well as being quite good looking, has come from a family of police officers that had worked in this part of the world and knew it well. All of Dunoon and the banks of the Holy Loch are, by definition, close to water. He, and all the emergency services round here, knew the dangers of the water sinkholes and faerie pools, the bottomless, dangerous, soft, overhanging banks, once in there's no escape.

And he knew the people, the families, the Melvicks. The faerie pools and the hanging tree.

What was not expected was that Ivan had lost the plot so quickly. It's always the same with these stiff-upper-lip types, they never show any emotion until they fall apart and top themselves.

What I was fully confident of was that Drew Murray was a good guy. I had known his uncle, a fair man. He had walked me into the school office the day I kicked Wullie Campbell in the teeth. Being older, he was the type of cop that would have taken me up a back alley and given me a stern talking to instead of reporting me to the child protection agency. But Drew Murray is younger, more dynamic.

And much more shaggable.

NINETEEN
Saturday

Megan

Breakfast had been a trial of things unsaid. The house is empty and echoey. Dad and I didn't exchange a word until I told him I was going out for a drive. I haven't slept. Well, not much. I think the three of us spent the night in the study, drinking coffee and dozing. We brought Anastasia in with us, her wee heart pumping like a piston, Molly curled in the corner. I noticed, and was grateful, that Drew locked the door although I wasn't sure if he was keeping Dad in, or keeping somebody else out. Either way, I was grateful.

My hearing came back during the night in fits and starts.

Dad was quiet, I don't think he said more than a few words to me. We put a blanket round him, a good malt in his hand and tucked him in. Drew lit the log fire and pulled up the wing-backed chair.

Despite the circumstances, it was the most homely, the warmest, I have ever felt in the Italian House.

Drew left early, after making plans to meet. Dad said he was going to bed for a couple of hours. I went round the house, locking the doors. With keys on my mind, I starting searching for Dad's car keys, through the drawers in the sideboard in the drawing room, the living room, down the cushions on the sofas and eventually found them in the middle drawer of the Welsh dresser. It was all coming together, I thought, as I put them back on the rack, where they should have been all along.

We were through the worst.

It was Drew's idea to meet at the Benmore Gardens. It says something about my life that I put some make-up on, just in case it was a date. My car hadn't been driven since I came home so it was full of dry, hot air and by the time I drove into the car

park, my lipstick smudged down my face. Reapplying it, I caught
the colour. Nude. Carla. What a laugh we had.

I was walking among the redwoods when I heard Drew behind
me, I could tune into his footfall now.

'So you heard me,' he said, lifting his sunglasses then hastily
replacing them in the glare of the sun.

'I did. I'm like a radio tuning in and out, but mostly in. How
are you?'

'Tired.'

'What the hell happened last night? Did he mean it?'

Drew shrugged. 'I think a lot of stuff is coming home to roost.'
He dismissed my question as if he knew the answer. 'How is he,
this morning?'

'Eating breakfast when I left him. He's tired, he looks so old.
He's wearing a scarf round his neck. Debs is looking after him, I
don't think she knows. He hasn't said anything to her, he said I've
not to tell Heather, he's too embarrassed.'

'Not what he says though, is it? He says it's a brave thing to
do. He says it's liberating to take your own life. You might have
missed that speech last night. Unmitigated shite. He thinks there
is some comfort in the act, that topping yourself is noble.'

'I suppose it might be compared to dribbling incontinence in
a care home. We have a choice.'

'You sound just like him.'

'The failure is embarrassing, you stopped him.'

'He needs to get help. Try that Dr Scobie. Your family needs
to get out the mindset that hanging is a good way to deal with
things.'

'He'll seek help when hell freezes over.'

'Aye, but he's happy to subject you to all that psychological
crap. What a bloody family. Come on, let's get a coffee before
I fall asleep.'

The gardens were handy for coming over on the ferry, making
it a destination for Glasgow day trippers for a toastie, a look at
the plants and to let the kids run around.

Drew was swithering over the brief menu, the noise in the
small cafe loud and reverberating, my left ear started zinging a
little. There is always peace in my retreat to the silent world but
this time the noise stayed, screeching in my ears, like a nail down

a blackboard. My hearing had gone from zero to hypersensitive
in a matter of hours.

'Get me a coffee, I'll wait outside.'

He nodded. It was a rare thing for me to be out with a member
of the opposite gender; even in a garden cafe rapidly filling up
with fat-legged ladies in a coach party from the woman's guild.

'I decided on a sugar rush instead,' he said, handing me a
vanilla and chocolate Cornetto.

'OK,' I said, standing up, my brain juddering at the noise of
the chair scraping back on the floor.

It was a million miles away from all the crap. People being
normal, a small boy feeding his cone to somebody else's corgi.
One lick to the dog, one lick to him.

We strolled in silence with our ice cream, I walked a few paces
in front of Drew. Looking at the plastic statues and the fake
storks, the hundreds of potted plants lined up, then up the path
to the tranquil beauty of the Japanese garden and the gentle noise
of the water from the spray hose, a restful sound. I sat down on
the wall at the koi pond, watching the nozzle move left then
right, the jet of water giving an elegant flick, leaving a hanging
moment of silence when there was no noise at all. The water
and I occupying exactly the same space.

Suddenly, I felt very tired.

I got a nudge in the ribs. 'Ice cream's good.'

'It's been a long time.'

'It has indeed.'

'So you are a detective? What rank are you again?'

'Sergeant. My uncle was a constable.'

'Hairy Monkey, that's what Carla called him.'

'They called him that round the station as well,' Drew laughed,
looking over my shoulder. 'Your dad and my uncle got to know
each other quite well over the years.'

'Over Carla? Is that where this story starts?' I am watching him
intently, staring right in his face. Two old ladies walk past thinking
that I am arguing with him. I pull away a little, finger to my ear
making an adjustment.

'There was one thing in the case that always stuck with my
uncle, I didn't know if I should tell you. Your mother said to him
once that if anything ever happened to her, we were to investigate

it. It was a long time ago, years before she disappeared. I mean years.'

'Are you serious? Nobody ever told me that.'

'Why would we, could we, say anything when she went? The investigation had its hands tied. There's still no evidence of foul play that I can take into a meeting and argue to get a budget to investigate. I've been looking, there's nothing. It does look like she walked away, that was what the family said. She's never filled out a tax return. That's the kind of thing we notice.'

'I thought that she got away to a better place, she waited until I was settled and then went. But now I am back, I doubt it.'

'None of that is good enough for me. I need to know what happened to her.'

'For your promotion?'

He doesn't flinch. 'It would help, be a feather in my cap so to speak. Cold case. Sensitive. Your dad being who he is.'

I got up and walked over to the shadows of the redwood trees but that was not where the chill was coming from. 'Do you suspect him?'

'Of course we suspect him, we always suspect the husband. I am well aware that all that care and concern could be a smoke-screen. He was in the study when your mother was last seen. His friend, Alistair Connolly left at ten past eleven. Heather popped in to see him, he and Alistair passed in the hall, Beth had spoken to Heather as Heather drove in, your mum was still waiting when she drove away later. Heather claims she went for a drive but didn't see your mum in a car on the road.'

'I am astounded that nobody is asking why a woman married to a Melvick was waiting for anything.'

'She never said,' I replied. 'And she didn't answer when Heather asked. And she did ask.'

'You don't know that, Megan, we only have Heather's word for that.'

'It's odd that. What was she doing, where was she going that she didn't want you to know?' Drew pursed his lips, leaving a pause for me to consider the options. It had seemed there was only one; she was waiting to be picked up by somebody that we didn't know. 'Your dad said he was around the house and it was only when somebody phoned looking for Beth about six thirty that they realized she wasn't anywhere to be found. He was concerned and went out to the Tentor Wood and checked the faerie pools. On his own. He found her stuff later up in the bedroom when he was going to bed, so he could have returned to the house with it himself.'

I took a minute to digest that.

'But Heather said, at the time, your mum took clothes that she would wear. And your dad wouldn't have a clue about that. So it seemed to her, and us, that your mum packed her own bag.'

'As if she was going somewhere. Have you seen the Munnings?'

He looked puzzled at the change of subject. 'Indeed. He's very passionate about it. It's a pretty picture, one of Munnings' finest from my rather uneducated point of view.'

'I always thought that Dad had bought it for Mum, but it was actually Papa who bought it for my grandma shortly before she died, and then he died.' The picture of Papa, on the rope, comes through like a gust of wind, crystal clear but fleeting. 'Mum bred these beautiful ponies and it stopped as a breeding line when she walked. It took about a year for Dad to come to terms with selling off the youngest three colts and that pretty filly Mum had high hopes for. We kept the two oldest brood mares as we couldn't bear to part with them. Like having teddy bears in the home field. Dad loved what Mum loved. He wouldn't have hurt her.'

'And you are a very faithful daughter. Did your dad get on with Carla?'

'Oh, my God, no.' I laughed at the memory, a welcome break from the serious chat. 'Just before the wedding, we were so pissed off with Melissa having tantrums left, right and centre Carla broke into his wine cellar to get some booze. We got a bit carried away and emerged very drunk. Dad was tight-lipped and a few hundred pounds poorer. He caught us, took us into his study. We were so, so pissed, holding onto each other giggling. He gave us a very stern talking to, lots of finger wagging, from behind the big oak desk. I'll never forget it, saying that it wasn't about the wine, it was about respect, "respect for other people's property".' I mimicked his voice. '"And you should both know all about that. I thought I had brought you up better than that, Megan Melvick". And then Carla said, clear as day, "But you didn't bring her up, the nanny did. If you had brought her up you might have realized she was deaf".'

'She actually said that?'

'Right in front of him, she didn't swear, she didn't shout. It was so unlike her. The worst of it all? Everything she said was true.'

'Out of the mouths of babes. And what did your dad do?' Drew wiped some ice cream from his lips with the back of his hand. 'Run her through with a sabre?'

'He said, "You can go now", rather coldly. He stopped me as I went to go out the door just to give me one of his looks. I've not seen that look on his face since.'

'And when was the wedding, in relation to that?'

'Four days later.'

'So four days after Carla accused him of being a bad father, she was dead. Yeah, that fits in with my thoughts.'

We didn't talk much after that.

TWENTY

Megan

I parked the Merc up at the house and walked back to the lay-by. Drew and I had decided to have a look around, there were a few demons that I needed to lay to rest. Drew was leaning on the top of his Red Fiesta, looking at his tablet then looking over his shoulder, making sure that the car was parked in the exact spot where my mother was last seen, in the spot I first saw him.

'So this lay-by was new three years ago?' he asked.

'Yes. The eagles had come back three years before, the bird-watchers needed somewhere to park and Dad had this strip of land. It was spring then, overgrown. Just this road, the lay-by, then the high wall. Not really that many options. Somebody must have picked Mum up.'

Drew walked up to the gates of the Benbrae Estate, looking at the road to the right, to the left, on the inside was a slight lessening of the undergrowth between the wall and the thick tree trunks of the Tentor Wood.

I pointed to the gates. 'This was where Carla always got in. My dad put the spikes on those cross struts after she died to stop others getting in the same way and here is the start of Melissa's path.'

'Not much to see now. But both Melissa and Carla knew that path well, it was better established in those days, I guess.'

'It was, five years have passed.' ·

'We need to figure this out. Somebody filled a tub with petrol, soaked a rope then tied it onto the *Curlew*. *Curlew One* that would be.'

'So we are talking about Carla now, not my mother?'

'We never stop talking about Carla, her death was horrific.'

'Are you sure that's what happened?'

'Yeah, the lads at the station and I have tried it. Petrol floats, it will burn but it's not directional, the vapour on the surface burns but the water doesn't ignite. Somebody knew that and thought it through. That rope had to take care of that, connect shore to boat, and the boat went up in a blue light because something flammable was already in the boat, caused a mass of flame that nobody could have escaped from.'

'I know, I was there.'

'Where? Where were you, Megan?'

'I was with Deborah, I do have a very strong memory of that.' I saw him smirk. 'For what that is worth.' The memory though is strong and terrifying, it comes back, a silent film in my head. The carousel in full colour, the lights and colour flickering on and on in a dark universe. Ebony and sapphire sky, the lights down the Long Drive, sparkling their way, a faerie path, the candles on the table flickering and inconstant. The darkness of the Wood and the evil dark of the loch to the left. The Benbrae beyond, faerie coloured lights strung over it, red and yellow and blue and greens suspended in the darkness. Fireworks, flashes and sparks. I felt very alone, looking up in the dark sky and seeing something flare and fade. Deborah, a hand held out, she fell, I was running, there and back, with ice . . . A drink, it goes wrong. And I had no memory after that until I was at the top of the Long Drive, being comforted by some friend of Mum's.'

I knew I had a gap there.

Drew kept quiet, letting the memory return as I looked round at the familiar view, trying to see it as I had five years before.

'I was intending to go down there, meet Carla, have a float around in the water, escape from everybody else and have a good bitch. Carla had been humiliated at the wedding, asked to stand out of a few photographs, told to get out the way full stop.'

'She was not family, fair enough.'

'It was embarrassing. Carla was not the person to take that lying down. Deborah wanted a word with her, I think to tell her to stop drinking. Debs was complaining about sore feet and we both walked barefoot. The fireworks hadn't started at that point. We went behind the fence and had a ciggie, then we walked down to the water. She slipped and hurt her foot. I went back up for ice. I think I passed Heather on the way.' That memory did come back. 'I did, she said that Mum would prefer it if I put my shoes back on.' I looked at my feet. 'I did make it back to the water before the explosion happened. '

'Did you now . . .' said Drew thoughtfully.

'I know they said it might have been because a cigarette was flicked out in it. Tom smoked, so they thought it was him and he was in charge of the petrol for the boats. But he was a careful man.'

'That was what the investigation said, they had nothing else to go on. It's not good enough for me. It was a terrible crime.'

'I know, I was there, I saw the boat burn. I am deaf, not blind.'

'And sometimes you are not that deaf, like now.'

I look up. 'Yes I know, they are my bloody ears, you know,' I snapped.

He rolled his eyes. 'Why are you so difficult?'

'Because I can be.'

'I mean you can be selective in what you hear and what you don't.'

And that punched home. That was two people who had said that to me. Him and Carla.

'Do you think I fake it? How interesting.'

'Not that at all, I think it takes a lot of concentration when you need to hear; you have to work hard at listening. Why should you not tune out, God there's enough shite spoken at work in meetings that I wish I had the integrity not to listen to.' He turned towards me. 'My uncle was under the impression that you were protected during that investigation, your dad maybe didn't go so far as to pull strings but you were always "too upset to talk". Your friend had died, at your sister's wedding, you were fifteen and you were a Melvick so nobody was going to give you a hard time, were they? Not if they didn't want to be transferred to Glasgow and a four-hour commute.'

'I was very upset.'

'I don't doubt it. But the fact remains, your dad did protect you. Maybe he didn't want you talking as he thought you knew something, or that you did it.'

'What? Why would I kill Carla? I loved her.'

'The ten-year-old Megan loved ten-year-old Carla. Maybe as fifteen-year-olds you had started to drift apart. Would you be friends with her now? I doubt it.'

I stopped walking, realizing how much he had misunderstood. It was black and white to him and he had never known the evil that is exclusion. Carla had been rejected by about everybody she knew. No family she could trust, a mum who ditched her every time a new man came on the scene, pulled back and pushed away by her dad and her stepmother. Maybe there was a bigger picture there that my youth had never suspected, Carla was a vulnerable child. I had never known rejection but I had never really belonged in the first place. I was always hanging on the coat-tails of the Melvick family; I was the one standing at the bottom of the stairs, as they all went out the door. 'Oh don't bother about her. She's staying behind,' Melissa would say as I asked them to wait for me. Not unkindly, just matter of fact.

Well, I was staying behind now, Melissa had moved on, to somewhere she could not come back from.

And the exclusion of deafness can be isolation in a crowded room, nobody ever repeats gossip or chats in inconsequentialities to a deaf person. 'She was the only one who ever told me a joke, you know, the only one. So yes, I think we would have still been friends, maybe something closer than that.'

He raised an eyebrow.

'She believed in fluid sexuality. We were young. Close.'

That surprised him.

'She had a bit of a reputation, as I am sure you know, she was too young to be running around like that. Children who are abused sexually are often seen as promiscuous and over friendly,' Drew said.

'Abused?'

'Is that a surprise to you?' His eyes narrowed. 'Why do you think she kept moving, all those social services, all that child protection?'

'Good God, I hope she felt safe here.'

'I think she did feel safe here,' said Drew, non-committally, 'which is ironic as she died here.'

'She should have had the chance to grow up, got a chance to live rather than fight for survival. She had never known the good things in life until she got to know us.'

Drew smiled but I could sense no sarcasm in the curve of his lips. 'Did it cross your mind that your family might have thought that Carla was not the best influence on you? Like the wine and the haircut.'

'And they had her killed?'

'You were proving to be a very loyal friend to her, you wouldn't just dump her. Would Melissa have caused her harm?'

That was a bigger question.

'And I have seen the later pictures of you and Carla, almost identical. Would Melissa have wanted to cause you harm? She knew you would both be in the *Curlew*?'

'She said "sorry" just before she died.'

'Sorry for what?'

I shrugged. 'Who knows?'

Drew nodded slowly, savouring the word. 'Dramatic to the end. Was she apologizing for killing the right person or killing the wrong person?'

'She's gone too far for us to ask, hasn't she?'

Carla

Hard to hear but true. But I refused to be a victim, I had the smarts in those days. Or I liked to think that I did. Maybe I was mistaken, things that went on and shouldn't have. There was that evil shit called Davy and he was evil. So yes DS Drew Murray, you are right. But what happens if a kid has no support and no help, no stability and well . . . nothing.

Davy was tattooed with gold chains round his neck. He had a permanent suntan and spoke with an accent so weird I could hardly understand him. He was much older than Mum, he had money – or so he said – and lived in a flat, one of those conversions, an old villa split into four where the residents all knew each other. It was the beginning of the end for me, I was already eleven, maybe twelve. Back on the road with my mum after being settled for the summer in Kilaird. OK, the cooking was shit, Gran was annoying and Dad kept trying to pat me on the head but I did get to go up to the Italian House.

Mum was trying to get herself together and Davy was trying to help her, or so it seemed. They would ply me with cheap vodka

*until I fell asleep and when I woke up I knew something had
been going on.*

*I told Mum and she went apeshit. At me. She liked Davy,
said I was making it up.*

*Sober she was fine but on the drink? Looking back, I felt I
was in control because I knew. I was getting thinner, the social
worker noticed that all was not well but it was only when I went
into a coma that somebody really noticed and, at that point my
dad came to the rescue and picked me up lock, stock and barrel
back to bloody Kilaird and a sentence of death by boredom.*

I guess I was lucky, caught before I fell too far.

Megan

We spent an hour or so standing at the bank of the Benbrae
mapping out in our minds who was where when the explosion
happened. The whole exercise got us nowhere but left me with
a vague feeling that Mum was being side-lined for Carla, again.

Drew took a phone call and left, so I walked back up to
the house, wondering if the call was personal or not. At the
house Dad immediately said he would go to bed, he had a
headache. Deborah was in the kitchen trying to tidy up the bottles
and glasses after the funeral. It would seem the ladies from the
guild had a bit of a taste for vodka. Anastasia was rolled up on
a kitchen chair, Molly was outside the kitchen door so I presumed
Heather was around.

'Oh yes, she's been doing the Florence Nightingale bit.'

'Do you think Dad's OK?'

'Nope.' Debs fished for more information. 'Heather was
saying . . .'

'Yes.'

'That your mum was younger than your dad, by a fair way,
and that maybe, you know, after yesterday, he's realized that
she's not coming back. Maybe it has just hit him.' She sat down
across from me, ready for a chin wag. 'She was kind of saying
that your dad was left a laughing stock really, half the village
sniggering at him behind his back, because she'd run off with a
younger man. For a proud man that must have been hard to take.

I mean, he's been sitting looking at that Munnings, it reminds
him of your mother, doesn't it? The way the three shell seekers
reminds him, and me, of you and Melissa and Carla. He never
forgets Carla, you know.'
  'Nobody forgets Carla.'
  'I'm not saying those memories were fond but they are there.'
She smiled, recalling her daughter's pixie face and wicked
humour. 'Heather has been helpful. Been a shoulder to cry on,
but she always angles for a way to spend the night here. Do you
think she had designs on your dad before your mum left?'
  'Don't ask me, I'm learning that I have no idea what goes on
in this house.'
  'I've always been shite with men.' She took a slug of vodka
from a nearly empty bottle. 'But then they have always been
shite with me.'
  The doorbell went, Molly gave a half-hearted bark.
  'I'll get it,' I said.
  It was inevitable after the events of the previous night that
Dr Scobie would come back, same face, different patient. I took
him upstairs, not speaking, not listening to his chatter. I
took him into the room Dad was using as a bedroom, I thought
I could smell the lingering scent of Pomegranate Noir.
  Bloody Heather.
  'Ivan? How are you, I was a little stunned by the call. I got
the first ferry over.'
  'Feeling better today,' said my dad from the bed, swinging his
legs round, ready to stand up. 'You can leave us now, Megan.'
  'No.'
  They both turned to stare.
  'Would somebody please tell me what the big secret is? I'm
finding it more than a little disconcerting, you seem to know
why I am deaf and nobody has told me. I think I should
know, I have that right.'
  Donald Scobie looked at Dad, then said, 'She's going to find
out sooner or later,' he said with a shrug.
  My dad looked very uncomfortable.
  'OK.' He breathed out a long sigh. 'Does it have to be now?'
  'Yes,' I said, knowing I was taking advantage of his
weakness.

'It will clear the air,' said the doctor and walked out, patting my dad on the shoulder, as he went past, like he was the one about to get the bad news.

Dad slowly stood up and moved to the unlit fire. This was his 'listen because I am going to say something important pose', and we had to pay attention when he did this, when I say 'we' I mean me. There was only me.

'Your mother was never inoculated against rubella when she was small and when she was pregnant with you, Melissa wasn't well but she was desperate to go to a pony club event. Nanny Brooke was going to take her and the pony. Melissa was running a fever – there had been an outbreak of German measles at the school – so naturally your mum kept out of her way.

'But Melissa was young she wanted to take Morse and he was a bad-tempered little beast who really only liked your mum, so Melissa pestered and pestered. In the end, she had a full-blown tantrum and Beth ended up relenting, going to the pony club show with Melissa and Morse in the horse box. He behaved like an angel, she got first place.'

Dad closed his eyes slowly, a lowering of emotion, ready to come up with a well thought out argument. He placed both his hands over his face, pulling them down; the face that emerged was quite different; ashamed. 'You know, Megan, we didn't notice. We never noticed you were hard of hearing. Beth was well during the pregnancy. When you were born you were such a beautiful wee thing, you were so perfect. And you grew up to be obstinate and defiant and everything that a toddler should be, we shouted and you kept running in the opposite direction.

'You would fool people very easily, you'd turn when people walked in the door but the rest of the time you'd switch off. Eventually, we took you to specialist. Do you remember going to Harley Street in London?'

'I remember the doctor with the hairy hands, he had a light strapped onto his forehead. I thought he was a miner.'

'They scanned you. You had every test under the sun. But Megan, you are my daughter, I think you are wonderful. I really don't care what he thought or what you scored on this chart or that chart and that it was a different score to the previous Wednesday. We had you tested, there was nothing that we could do to help, and no operation was going to fix the problem. We bought you the most sophisticated hearing aids that money could buy and . . .'

'I stood on them.'

'Indeed, the next advice was to use the cheapest. You were young, of course you would break them, you would have tantrums and kick against it all but one day you would want to walk into a hearing world. I don't think that day has ever come. Has it?'

'Not really. I hate the hearing world.'

'You were so quiet. After the whirlwind of Melissa I thought you were a God-send quite frankly.' He bit his lip. 'That specialist had told us to watch out for other signs of any mental instability.' There was a long pause. 'Then you set Dan Miller's bed on fire. We all did our best. Donald Scobie did his best but I think we all realize now what a mistake that was.'

TWENTY-ONE
Sunday

Megan

A nother day, another quiet breakfast in the kitchen with Molly. Now I was back up in the bedroom, trying not to think. It had been a difficult night.

It was, in a sad way, very funny.

So my sister and my mother were the reason I was deaf. Mum had tried her best, but Melissa, well, she should have taken a telling. Or was it all Mum's fault, she had been the responsible one? Melissa had been five years old. Had I been a constant reminder to Mum of her shortcomings as a mother? A constant reminder to my sister what a selfish bitch she was?

Sorry.

It was dark today. It looked as though the weather was about to break, huge black clouds rolled on the horizon, advancing their way up the river; pushed on by an ever-rising wind. The air became very close, rain was not far away. It was as if this was the day that everything was going to change.

I felt nervous, scared of something but not sure where the danger was coming from.

And thinking about Carla, more familiar territory to fret over. The only person who had ever asked me what it was like to be deaf.

I doubt many people know what deafness is like, and I didn't count myself among them. I know I have some hearing, I am not that delusional.

It was what it was.

The rain was starting to hit against the glass, I could see the rooks flying quickly for the Tentor Wood like they had been caught out in the rain. I watched them, looking down at the Benbrae and thinking of the hot summer days that seemed to inhabit our youth, watching the fish jump, tickling the trout as the sun flickered through the overhanging branches of the willows. We had been out on the *Curlew*, both of us had been leaning over the same side of the squat little rowing boat. The boat tipped us silently but gently into the bitter cold water, another way to cool down on that long hot summer day.

I told Carla that the easiest way to become deaf was to stick your head underwater and listen. So she dropped like a stone. The water swirled over her head, her hair, short blonde this time, floated out underneath the surface, an anemone of straw. I saw her eyes, mascaraed and fragmented, crystals of light dancing around them on the surface. She drew her knees up to her chin and she opened her eyes wide, then sank down further, I saw a trickle of bubbles escape from her lips. She was twisting, treading water, spinning, enjoying her deafness.

It's a very arrogant thing to think the deaf want to hear.

I can walk into a coffee shop to read a book and the distractions are minimal. I am where the book takes me, I don't need to suffer chattering people, mobile phones bleeping, young kids being spoken to loudly by their parents so the entire place knew that Findlay or George was a true genius and the constant, irritating clattering of fingers over a keyboard because the cafe had quick and free Wi-Fi for two hours if you bought a coffee. The noise of feet on the floor, the toilet door slamming open and closed, the screech of chairs being dragged across the tiled floor. People coming back and forth, do you want milk on the side or in the cup, so you want it hot or cold, cheese melted or not and more screaming of children as their buggies were clattered closed or wrenched open. For all that time I was in the novel.

I had no need for noise and nonsense. People talk far too much, and very few ever say anything of consequence. I decided to live a quieter life, but one that is fuller.

Hearing loss is a very different thing, a very different thing to never having had it. Or choosing not to have it. People listen to you talking so they know when they can start talking, they do not actually listen to what you have to say.

As humans we are despicable, we hear better with words of hate than we do with words of love so we are better not to hear at all.

Oh yes, people should talk less and listen more, especially Carla who always had too much to say for herself.

But now, for one of the few times in my life, I needed somebody to talk to.

I texted Drew and asked him if he was free.

Had I sensed it in the air? Did I know I needed help?

Again he appeared very quickly, this time his car drove up to the front door. I was upstairs at the paladin window, waiting for him and watching the weather as the skies darkened to indigo, the rain was staring to pour out in a constant stream. I hoped he was on my side, I wanted somebody to be. I can't trust my own memory. I can't trust my own family. I can't trust my memory of the night Carla died. I knew that I hadn't hurt her, I could never have done that, but those who knew me were not that sure.

I saw Drew come up the drive then Deborah brought him up the stairs chattering about the parched earth and how good this downpour would be. She asked us if we wanted anything to drink. Then trotted off downstairs leaving us under the eye of Agatha Emmaline.

Drew sat on the opposite chair.

I told him what my dad had said. 'Yes, seemingly my sister's need to run up and down a field on a fat little pony dropping potatoes into buckets was more important than the health of her unborn child.'

Drew nodded, slowly. 'I have heard that rumour. From my uncle. Did Melissa have German Measles?'

'She had been off school all week. But she really wanted to go to the pony club on Saturday. Mum knew she was pregnant with me. But it didn't stop her.'

'I'm sure she regretted it, people make these decisions all the time thinking that they will get away with it. We do it every time we drive a car or get in a plane.'

I stared at him. 'No, she should not have gone near Melissa until it was safe. It's not as if we didn't have staff that could have taken Melissa to the club, but no, Mum wanted to go.'

'I still say she regretted it for every day of her life. I can see Melissa being that insistent. And' – he put his hand on my elbow gently – 'do you think that had something to do with the way she viewed her own life? She was very hard on herself. Maybe it wasn't easy for her.' He sighed. 'Was it ever spoken about?'

'Not to me it wasn't. But from what you've said, the whole bloody village knew. Everybody but me.'

'I was talking to an audiologist after a case I worked on, a woman was struck deaf by shock, and there is sometimes such a thing as psychological deafness, brought on when there is a huge stress to the system, mentally or physically, to somebody in their formative years. You can be struck deaf just as much as you can be struck dumb, but the former is not as obvious, so who knows?'

'Not in my case, nothing as exciting as that, there was just that wee infection, that nasty wee virus, and a sister and mother who really loved their ponies. I guess I was unlucky.'

'I was thinking, about Carla. Reading the file after yesterday. When she had turned into the girl you needed her to be, she was the one who spoke out when you were too polite to. She said no. Did your family think you killed her because she was some-body you wanted rid of, you had found your voice as all teenagers do? Or did your sister kill her because she was getting too close to you and "the family"? Or because she had slept with Jago on the day before the wedding?'

I stared at him.

'We do have a file on all this.'

'Sleeping with the hired help?' I muttered, wondering how much he knew.

'Weird you should say that. I mean, for a Melvick, what is worse than sleeping with the hired help? Sleeping with the groom on his wedding day?'

So he knew. 'Do you really think we are monsters?'

'No, I think you are human beings, but I worried about Jago's morality in that, you were only fifteen.'

'Dad's sleeping with Heather.'

'Is he? Is he really?' Drew sounded very surprised then changed the subject slightly. 'Your family's got where they are by killing people, never forget that, Megan. This land you have is from the backs of slaves and the tobacco trade. Have you ever read the real version of your family history, where the money really came from?'

'Why do you hate me so much?'

'I don't bloody hate you, I am pointing out the obvious. I don't think Carla died by accident.'

'According to you they should have formed a queue.'

'In the file are a few pictures of you two, when you were younger, you and Carla. You were starting to morph into the same person. I really thought how easily you two had drifted into the ying and the yang, night and day, the streetwise and the intellectual, the locked in and the locked out.'

I looked out the window, back to the *Curlew* now bobbing on waves in the Benbrae, the rain was stabbing at the window. The rooks low over the water. 'She saved me in the end, she saved me.'

'She saved you from trouble that you wouldn't have got into if it hadn't been for her in the first place. That's what your dad thinks.'

'Does he?'

'My uncle got quite close to your dad, over the years after the wedding. He thought your parents were good parents, attentive, wanted the best for you.'

'I suppose that's true but they wanted what they thought was best for us not what we wanted.'

My heart started to pound in my chest, I was being led down a road that I didn't want to go down.

Carla

I think Drew is onto something here. What is that phrase about the suitable lie, the convenient truth. I'm sure if the Melvicks wanted to believe the real truth, they would have asked themselves why Megan could speak so well, and read so well, if she had suffered from hearing difficulties from the moment she was born. It was a question the specialists asked often enough. And here's a new boy on the scene talking about a form of deafness that is brought on by a big fright.

And the Melvicks removed her from treatment.

So what were they scared of?

And that got me thinking, of the Megan I knew, the girl who never went beyond the island on the Benbrae. Why was that?

She was brave in many things. We did so much shit together but that was one thing she would never do.

What was down the other end of the Benbrae that scared her so much? Where the willows hung low and the branches of the oak fell down to kiss the surface of the dark water. No sun ever shone there. It stank of fermenting grass and death, the silence was stifling and the freshening breeze that fluttered over the open parts of the pond, never penetrated the Tentor Wood.

Silent. It was the quietest part of the whole estate, no path went there, there were no seats on the overgrown bank. It was a wild, lonely place.

Exactly the sort of place that Megan should have liked.

So why didn't she?

Megan

Drew wanted some fresh air, which I took to mean he wanted out the house and I hoped meant that he didn't want away from me. He suggested a walk, in the rain, he had his waterproofs in the car. And we should take the dogs. I think he liked dogs and didn't have one in his life at the moment.

We had started by taking Anastasia and Molly out for a walk, but the rain had the wee dog scurrying back inside the minute I had my wellies on. Molly was made of sterner stuff.

We pulled our hoods high over our heads, the noise of the rain made any conversation impossible. The ground was covered in puddles, deep puddles. The deluge of rain was lying on top of the ground, the earth too dry and parched to absorb it. It might as well have been raining on concrete. But as we neared the Long Drive, I noticed that the world had changed. I did stop, look, then look again.

Then I pointed.

The Benbrae had gone. The water had emptied out. I ran down, feeling the panic rise and the tears fall. There was a huge void, a basin of stones and sludge, the side bank of the Benbrae nearest the loch had opened into a sucking, squelching bubbling hole. An underground channel had drained out, the lie of the lay had drained the water down to the loch. The ledge overhung, creating a lip, and the earth has been eaten away over the years, the grass at the top, clumped and sunburned, a verdant base where the water gave nutrition and sustenance to the soil.

Gone.

The Benbrae was empty, dead fish and mud banks of green algae and weeds. And the powan.

It would break Dad's heart. The ground was wet after the onslaught and below, there was the breach in the bank wall, and I guessed, it went all the way to the Holy Loch, the high tide has pushed in, the ebb had drained us of everything. There were some fish, flipping and flapping, in small pools trying to stay alive. I couldn't stop crying, this could not be happening. The island, dull and pathetic, wilted in the middle of the mud making a wee brick wall protecting it from nothing. It looked old and arthritic.

And there, in the middle was the *Curlew*, reduced to a sculpture of skeletal charred ribs, a black fish dead, her side exposed, brown algae furring the solid parts of her underside. She looked fat and ugly, not the graceful little boat she was on the surface. *Curlew 2* had beached near the pontoon, on her side, like she was drunk or a turtle that couldn't right itself.

I realized Drew was moving, towards the boathouse and the hose which he unwound from its reel and turned the tap on, unravelling it as fast as the water was moving. He handed it to me and I stood on the narrow pier spraying out a weak jet of water, easing the situation, not very effectively, but better than nothing. It eased my pain. The sandbags at the top of the bank to protect the road were too heavy to move in their sodden state.

Sobbing, I played the hose into the little pools giving the fish some cover from the birds that were already gathering in the trees, waiting for the rain to cease. I felt I had to save the little fish, tears and snotters blinding me as I slid and fell trying not to let go of the hose as it writhed away in the opposite direction and twisted around, like a demented cobra. I tried to hold onto it with one hand, then secured it with the fold of my arm as I searched about for my mobile phone. We needed help. We needed Dad or Debs or even bloody Heather if she could be bothered dirtying her designer wellies.

Dirty.

Dad would be so upset if he saw this. Suicidally upset.

I fell again, sobbing my heart out this time. It had all gone so wrong, Carla had gone, then Mum, then Melissa and now the Benbrae. We were cursed, the hose jerked and I fell, lying on my front in the soft mud, looking at the angry sky.

'Megan?' I heard the shout. 'Megan, stand up you stupid bitch or you will drown.'

He was an unlikely guardian angel, but I was in no position to argue.

I couldn't get to my feet, every time I tried I fell down again my feet slipping in the stinking, sticking, treacherous mud. The mud swallowed my wellies, sucking them from me, then suddenly a sandbag was beside me and Drew was holding out his hand.

We were both covered in fish shite. 'Give me a hand with this and stop being so bloody pathetic.' Drew lifted me by the hood, steadying me as I got on my feet. 'Let's drag the sandbags over, leave the hose, let go of the hose. It's pissing down now, the rain will fill it.'

It took on a dance of its own twisting up and down the whole Benbrae, spraying it with clean water. Drew was pulling one of the sandbags across to the breach in the wall, a collapsed sodden mass.

I tried to roll the other towards him. We got them together and pulled the sandbag across the breach. Then we put one, then two, on top providing a small triangle that allowed the Benbrae to retain a few inches of water, enough to save some of the fish. Drew walked round and picked up some of the stranded, gasping fish and moved them into dips that had more water, or at least were starting to fill up.

Then he spotted the canvas trolley in the boathouse and we moved the sandbags in that. In the general scheme of things, it was nothing but it made us feel that we were doing something. He caught hold of the writhing hose and wrestled it so it was spraying a definite mist all over the bed of the Benbrae. He moved it back and downwards, a bit here and bit there, saving a little of this and a little of that.

Then I saw it. The bank where the mosaic was. Missing. Devoid of support the outer edge of the mosaic had crumpled, broken bits of blue sky hanging, jagged in the air. Hypnotized, I squelched towards it, moving slowly, being sucked in by the mud. The bank had collapsed at this point and I looked at the hole in the earth. A tunnel into the fabric and foundations of the mosaic.

I saw it clearly for what it was.

Some woollen cloth, black and grey. That used to be black and white.

But I would have known it anywhere. I couldn't help but see the ribbed cuff and what lay behind, a few bones held together in a little knot. Then holding my head to one side and wiping the tears from my eyes, I peered in. It didn't look like a human hand. Animals do die, they can be buried. But they don't cover their bones in a funeral shroud.

I looked, thinking what I was seeing. Something woollen.

'Drew?' I pointed at the broken blue tiles hanging off the bank at the waterside, now a small precipice of sienna and cerulean.

'What is that?' He put on the torch on his mobile phone and looked more closely, digging around in the sandy earth of the bank with the end of his pen. Then he jerked his hand away.

'What is that?'

'The bones of a foot. A human foot. Be careful,' Drew said, 'just be careful.'

I clambered closer, through the mud. I pointed to the blue tiles, two of them had come away, the rest, held together by some fabric webbing the mosaic had been glued onto. That formed a roof over a hole about a foot in diameter where the water had eaten away the side bank of the Benbrae. The tidal water had got in and worked its way in to the soft earth, earth that had been disturbed when the mosaic was built and then restructured when the boathouse and the pontoon where rebuilt a couple of years after the fire.

I felt Carla was being taken from me all over again. Our sunflowers had gone.

I closed my eyes, willing Carla back. But it stayed dark, nothing, Even the memory of her had gone.

Drew pulled on a pair of gloves and placed a finger onto the overhanging tiles at waist height. He pointed his phone in, noticing a muddy piece of fabric poking out.

'Did you look at that?'

I realize he had spoken to me.

'Pardon?'

'Can you see that?'

'Yes.'

But I didn't want to look.

'There's more in there, it's the cuff of a jacket, isn't it?'

The cuff of a nylon jacket, a quilted nylon jacket, muddy and sodden.

He shone the torch in a little more then he switched the torch off and swiped a number into his phone. 'David? You know where I am? We need a whole crew out here. Now.'

'Why?' I asked, knowing the answer.

'Maybe you should look.' He pointed. 'Have a look in there. I think the bottom of the mosaic was filled in by sand, the water broke in and swept it away.'

I looked round, not making out anything, just shapes here and there, indifferent shades or darkness. Then the beam of the torchlight glistened over something, red and golden, a familiar shape, a pretty pony, not like the Munnings on the wall. And the small clasp. A Past President's Badge of the Highland Pony Society. Not many of them going around.

'Well, Megan, if we haven't found your mother, at least we have found her clothes.' He spoke down the phone again. 'And can you keep this low key for now? I want to talk to Ivan Melvick. We'll get there quicker if we "do the right thing". You always get further with sugar than with vinegar.'

After that, things moved very quickly. Drew made a few phone calls but never let me leave the boathouse, or out of his sight. He didn't let me speak to anybody. He made me hold the hose to give me something to do, spraying it around, watching the deep parts of the Benbrae fill up. It was stinking.

Then Drew was waving over at the long grass, signalling to a man.

'Who is he?'

'He is a scene of crime guy, Megan. We can't keep this between the two of us, we need a witness.'

I recognized the man from somewhere. He was carrying a small case and something that resembled a rolled umbrella or a small tent.

'It's going rain all night, and this area has high evidential value, it has to be protected.'

'I recognize the jacket, her quilted green jacket.' I said, quietly. 'And the badge.'

'You need to show me again.'

It was difficult for me to walk and follow a conversation, so the three of us walked in silence along in single file, in the grass around the side of the Benbrae. Anybody looking out the upstairs windows of the house would have seen us easily, as would anybody out on the high veranda, but I doubted there would be anybody up there in this weather. They were safely tucked up on the sofa or watching the telly, in the kitchen having tea and kippers. I trudged round to the Benbrae, its well of emptiness open, dying fish flickering, birds starting to dive and feast. The smell was strong. I heard some chatter, stunned words of amazement passed between the two men following me. Then I stood to one side and pointed to the mosaic that looked as if it had been corrupted by an earthquake, looking again at the little bones of a human foot, wrapped in a rotting sock.

Carla

I can almost feel it all slipping. Dying is worst, this time I am calling for her but she does not hear me, this confident young woman. Me with my permanent scowl and bad hair.

But I loved her, the one real constant, one day we cut each other's arm and mixed our blood, children's stupid games from something we had seen on the telly but to me it really meant something. It made me almost a Melvick. She was the anchor I could have based my life around. And there was a sense that she needed me.

As much as I needed her.

Dying for the second time was going to be painful. This time I am going to be forgotten.

Megan

Dad was dressed and sitting in the study, a tray beside him of toast triangles sitting in their polished silver rack, a cafetière

of coffee and a cup on a saucer sat beside it, and a folded up
copy of the *Telegraph*, not read yet judging from its neat folds.
He was scrolling through his phone, something that caught his
interest, his hand was reaching out for the coffee when he noticed
us squelching in through the door. He looked at our feet, at
the mess, folded his newspaper, but had the good sense not to
comment.

He was back, the master of the house.

The study was a dark, quiet room, it's Dad's place of
seclusion. Never to be entered without knocking or without good
reason. It had reverted to its custom formality after the cosiness
of the previous night.

'Megan. How lovely. Have you come to join me for breakfast?'
His eyebrows arched over his rimless reading glasses in quiet
curiosity, then narrowed on seeing Drew behind me, but being
my father, his mouth did not miss a beat. 'And Drew, would you
like a coffee?'

'I'm afraid I am here as DS Murray.'

Dad flicked his eyes to me then back to Drew, there was a
glimmer of fear there, at our clothes, our muddy faces. I couldn't
help but wonder how hard had he tried to look for Mum. 'Of
course, do sit down.'

'Better not, too dirty. I'm afraid we have some bad news for
you, Mr Melvick. Megan was out walking this morning looking
at the damage of the storm and the high tide.'

'As I was also going to do after breakfast.' Dad nodded
impatiently, he flicked his fingers against an invisible speck of
dust on his trouser leg, wanting Drew to say his piece, but he
was here as a police officer and wasn't going to be hurried.

'If you took your normal early walk this morning, you must
have noticed the damage to the mosaic down at the Benbrae?'

Dad's eyes settled on me then moved back to Drew, seemingly
relieved that this was only about property damage.

'I noticed the sink tunnel had opened and had drained much of
the water, and I noticed some damage to the mosaic but I was more
interested in the damage to the roof and the stables. Why?'

'The Benbrae has gone completely now, and there's damage
to the mosaic and it has revealed something underneath. Bones
in fact.'

Dad twitched a little at that.

'Human bones' – Drew took a deep breath – 'and sir, we believe, have reason to believe, it may be the deposition site of the body of your wife.'

Dad's eyes narrowed, a slight rotation of the head, in disbelief. 'But Beth wasn't murdered, she left.' Even as he spoke I could see a different version of events dawning on him.

'Nobody actually knows anything,' I said, and Dad looked at me, as if he had never realized I could speak. 'The president's badge, the one she wore, is on the lapel of the jacket still in the hole, Dad. I think it might be her. I think it's her.' And I started to cry.

Dad looked at Drew for help, in return Drew studied him intently as if he was looking for a sign of guilt.

There is no help coming. 'And there are signs of human remains.'

'Dear, dear God. Bloody hell.' He sank back in his armchair, the great wings seemed to devour him. The skin of his face went very pale, he closed his eyes. He looked old and defeated. I went towards him, he stretched his hand out and covered my small hand with his, and closed his eyes. For a long moment there was only the ticking of the grandfather clock in the study, then he opened his eyes and patted my hand. 'So, DS Murray, I guess we are on professional terms now.'

'Indeed we are.'

And the power shifted, just like that,

'I presume you now have a protocol to follow, and you must follow it. I want no favours or entitlement, you do what you have to. Please.'

'Of course. I have already set the wheels in motion. We will need to do some tests to confirm to whom the remains belong, we do need to tick that box, sir.'

The 'sir' did not fall naturally from his tongue and my dad gave a brief nod of consent.

'And I know that you are great friends with the deputy chief constable, he shoots on your land, I believe.'

My dad shook his head. 'That means nothing. You do what you need to do.'

'Of course we will, but I was thinking, that with your consent there might be a better way. I was wondering . . .' Drew was leaning forward in the chair, his auburn fringe flopping over his forehead, Dad leaned forward to meet him halfway. 'I don't want anybody to know what we have found, just you, me, Megan and our scenes of crime for now. I feel it's very important that this stays with us, and at the highest level only.'

Dad's brows furrowed.

'The banks of the Benbrae have been breached in four locations, I noticed that.'

Dad nodded.

'So I am thinking it would be helpful if we put some tents up on the other three areas, making it look as if we were doing some engineering work. The mosaic was a breach. Let's leave it at that. And the fourth tent can be the scene of crime tent.'

'Can you do that?'

'Physically yes, it would help us if there was no gossip or rumours – that stuff seems to follow this family around. We, and only we, and whoever put that person in there will know. Just a small controlled group of people. You must tell nobody else. We will do plain clothes. We will say a sewer has been breached, that will explain face masks and keeping people away. But I cannot do that legally, I will need some help from above, your friends in high places might be able to swing it for me. Or to be more precise, for you.'

'And why would he?'

'Because it gives us an advantage. And you could ask him. He'd do it for you.'

'Would you mind showing me where . . . The mosaic?'

'Of course, sir, and to be clear, say nothing to anybody else, not Deborah, not Heather. Nobody.'

I handed him his scarf and his hat, his jacket would be on the stand at the kitchen door.

We walked quietly along the hall.

Heather popped out the drawing room door. 'Ivan, what's happening?'

'A problem down at the Benbrae that's all. I'll be back soon.'

He couldn't quite bring himself to lie, so I did it for him.

'There's a broken sewer, it stinks,' I said, watching as Heather withdrew like she could actually smell it. Or was it alarm, had she been found out?

Dad took my hand and we walked out the front door together, side by side.

Carla

And here she goes, Megan on her daddy's arm. Where she belongs. With the events of today her fate is sealed, there's no way she's going to walk out on her dad and the Italian House now.

The house itself has a buzz around it. Heather is walking back and forth, Mum has been in and out that gate, then out once in the Land Rover. The women are like the birds, they are circling for their advantage, ready to pick off the vulnerable.

But it's all slipping from Megan and now the house is being affected as well, the Benbrae has gone, it's like the end for Megan and me, all those summer days lying on the boat. Ah yes, even the Curlew, *the boat that burned underneath me had reappeared like some deadly phoenix.*

There will be something symbolic in all this, something that the minister will drone on about at Beth's funeral, now that they can have one. But I feel diminished.

I will be the last to go and I know that as the breaches in the wall of the Benbrae are filled, repaired and strengthened, as Beth is buried, as the door closes shut on the Italian House, the gates will swing closed on me, too. The cross struts where I placed my feet to climb these gates have now got spikes on them. I have been removed from the wedding photographs. I wonder how long it will take Drew to remove me from Megan's affections, replacing me with every memory, every touch, every kiss. I am being erased, slipping from everybody's memory, I am slowly, but permanently, being rubbed from history.

And there's nothing I can do.

Absolutely nothing.

But wait, watch and wait.

TWENTY-TWO
Monday

Megan

We had been stuck in the house all day.

I stayed up in my room reading, ignoring the comings and goings below, easy for a deaf person to do. At one o'clock Dad knocked on the door and said that Deborah had made sandwiches for everybody and that we would be eating in the drawing room.

'The drawing room?'

His eyes flicked nervously, he was in a situation out of his control, and he didn't like it. When I came downstairs I was surprised to see who was there. Dr Scobie, the ever-present Heather, and Tom McEwan, Carla's father. He stood up, ready to shake my hand but I hugged him. We had a bond, I would have liked to sit down, him and me together, just the two of us, and talked about his daughter.

Debs was moving around the plates, putting them back on the tray, a restless nervousness about her. She went over to open the window to the low terrace, to let the fresh air in. The action seemed to imply her ex was stinking the room out.

They all said hello to me in turn and Dad asked if I had my hearing aids in.

Then the door opened. It looked like Drew was playing Cluedo now as he didn't smile at me when he saw me. He merely nodded at us all and told us to take a seat. Deborah went to excuse herself, he said he'd like a fresh pot of coffee in ten minutes.

So it wasn't going to take long.

We were all gathered in one room, the duck egg blue drawing room, with the big bay windows. The settees were the same but had been recovered, it looked so different from the day I had climbed off the sofa with Oodie, blown out my candles and trotted off down the Long Drive after Papa.

That memory was clearing now. Why I had my lacy dress on, why I had that feeling of the wet lace clinging to my bare legs like a thousand little beasties. How young I had been to see something so awful. I'm glad the real horror has not come back yet, I hope it never does.

Papa dancing on a rope.

And a hand . . . giving him a push.

And I had fallen in the pool.

Dad had to get me out.

Melissa chasing me.

Everything was so different then, so many people had gone and those that were left were gathered here in this room. The bit players.

There were some murmurings as Drew sat down and placed the file he had been carrying in his lap. I knew him well enough now to notice the tension in him. I looked out the window and noticed that even the weather had given up. There was no wind, the sky had drifted to a translucent grey. No rain. No sunshine. Nothing.

My dad sat on the settee. On the table sat a big pot of coffee, a pot of tea, eight mugs, and a plate of biscuits ready. The coffee pot looked big enough to me, maybe it was going to be a long meeting after all. They had already helped themselves to the sandwiches. I wonder what my dad had been doing before he came to get me. Heather was sitting on the end of the big sofa beside me, folding and refolding the pleats of her linen skirt, brushing away non-existent crumbs. I thought she might have been scowling slightly at Tom or even at me, maybe we were keeping her from her game of bridge.

Dr Scobie sat on the other single chair, the one nearest the fire, listening to Tom McEwan, Carla's dad, talk to Dad in the simplest most mundane of conversations, about the farms, the eagles, the damage to the banks after the surge of the tide and if the powan had survived. Tom had aged well, thinner, healthier, relaxed even. He was nodding in agreement as if the man beside him was not the man who had put him in jail. They seemed close. I knew that Tom had walked out of jail and into a job. Had Dad paid him off? Guaranteed him a position elsewhere? Of course he had.

I had a feeling, looking at them all, that the carousel was spinning again, round and round. The rooks coming home to roost.

Drew was dressed in a suit, his jacket open. Tie clipped back. There had been police all over the Benbrae yesterday, and all over the Tentor Wood today. I had seen the lights up in the wood overnight, figures in overalls walking around but from the talk round the house, the idea of the sewers being breached had stuck. Even Debs was saying it was as if the house was truly cursed.

'Thank you for coming along,' said Drew, softening it with, 'but you appreciate that you know you didn't have any option.'

Dr Scobie opened his mouth to say something, but Drew silenced him by lifting one finger. 'I am here to update you with regard to the disappearance of Elizabeth Rose Nicolette Melvick.'

I looked round, wondering why everyone was in this room with us. This should have been Dad and I, and DS Drew Murray. Unless . . .

'We discovered a body on the estate yesterday. We have now carried out a post-mortem, established a likely cause of death.'

I looked at him but he avoided my eyes. Why was he doing this so publicly?

'The injuries are not consistent with an accident, nor does it appear that she took her own life. Her mobile phone has not been located.'

Heather moved to say something but then thought the better of it.

'I've read all the statements including Deborah Sullivan's who met Beth out at the lay-by. Then Heather Kincaid, you drove past her twice.'

'And I only spoke to her once, I had money to hand in, from the church. So yes, I said a few words to her out the car window and on the way back, I waved. It's quite simple and straightforward.'

'Alistair Connolly saw her in-between as he was leaving this house, and Ivan, you said you were up at the house.'

'I was. I was in the study.'

'And Deborah is a witness to that.'

'We went through all this before. Deborah and Alistair, then Heather then Deborah all saw me here.'

'But that alibi really depended on where Beth was going and when she was intending on coming back. Or when she actually disappeared. So Tom, you had been released from jail the year before. You were on holiday from work.'

'I wasn't here though.'

'But you were in the area, visiting your mother? Six-mile drive from here, three of them on a road that's very rarely used.'

Tom nodded. Everybody in the room looked at him. 'When I said here, I meant the house. I didn't come near here.'

'And Heather? That morning you had no alibi either, you went' – he made quotation marks with his forefingers – 'for a drive, after you left the Italian House.'

'Beth was seen after I saw her.'

'After the time you said you saw her.'

'If you insist.'

'And you spoke to Beth.'

'Yes, as I said, then we waved and she texted me later. Much later. More than once. I told Ivan she had made contact.'

'And we all stopped looking for her.'

'She did text and say she was fine.'

'I doubt that.'

'She did,' argued Heather.

'No, I doubt it was her texting. That's what I mean, and that itself is interesting, that a message was to you, not her husband or her daughters. How much did that hurt? How much did that diminish her in the eyes of those that loved her? It also reinforced the message that she had rejected them for another. Cruel. And untrue, as we suspected then, and as we now know.'

'They were from her, she called the girls Mel and Megs, she . . . Well, they were from her.'

'Or from somebody that read the rest of her messages and copied her style. Not rocket science.'

'She kept her phone locked,' I said.

'And do you know her pin number?'

I nodded.

'I rest my case.'

Heather's face fell.

'So we are looking for somebody that knew her really well. As all of you in this room did.'

I was watching Heather's face, she was looking worried now.

'How exactly was my wife killed?' asked my dad.

'Dad!'

'Cover your ears, Megan, if you don't want to know. You shouldn't find that too hard.'

I glared at him, the bastard.

'We think she was strangled after having suffered a blunt force trauma to the head. I presume she was on her own, her assailant had the element of surprise. So a female could have done it. There's an interesting piece of local knowledge. The boathouse was being rebuilt at that time, the mosaic was under construction, as was the pontoon. All on the inside of the ten-foot-high boundary wall, the gate controlled by a keypad. There had been workmen about, people wanting to see the eagles, so you, Ivan, were enforcing the gate control system much more in those days than you do now. You had just had it installed. Beth was last seen walking away from the house on the other side of the wall, a long way from the mosaic and the boathouse. But this was the twenty-seventh of May 2016.' He raised his eyebrows at my Dad. 'The lay-by was just finished, because the eagles had come back.'

'Yes, of course there had been cars everywhere, people waiting to see the birds so yes . . . we built the lay-by but I don't see the relevance. It was finished by the time she went missing. Was that near where Beth was attacked?'

'Deborah said that she had walked past that point, Heather, your statement, ten minutes later says she was back at the lay-by.' Drew nodded. 'She never got on a bus. Perhaps she stayed there knowing you would be driving back after a short word with her husband, maybe she didn't want you to see where she was going, or who she was with or who was waiting for her, but it's obvious that she either walked from the side of the road to the site of the mosaic, or she was killed and taken there. Remember that the timing is up for grabs if any of the three people who saw her on that quiet deserted road had killed her.'

Heather placed her hand on top of mine.

The room went quiet.

'You think it was one of us, don't you?' I asked.

'Megan? Yes I do. I've been watching your moods, your sleeping, your sleepwalking, the family think you are mad, but I think, Dr Scobie, even you must notice that she has got so much worse now she's here, at home.'

'Because of the stress of Melissa and . . .'

'Or because she was being drugged. I had her cup tested, interesting mix of uppers and downers as my uncle would have called them. Easy to buy on the street. So yes, Megan, somebody in this house wanted you to be unreliable, dependant on the family.

'Somebody who knew this place inside out, somebody who knew there was a new trolley in the boathouse. Somebody knew the number for the gate, somebody knew the clothes Beth would take, somebody knew exactly what to leave to hurt Ivan. The necklace and the wedding band.'

'But there always was, in my day, a pull-along low-loader in the boathouse,' said Tom.

'We replaced it after, after the fire,' added my father, his mind already painting the bigger picture.

'That could have been used to take the body from the site at the lay-by to the boat and then across the pond. Or maybe all the way round, who knows? They could have used Melissa's secret running path, it was still there, three years ago.'

'And nobody noticed?' Heather was dismissive, crossing her legs violently, looking at her watch. 'All that going on in broad daylight.'

Drew was unperturbed. 'We have some photographs. The grass was four feet high at the side of the road. There was a ditch next to the wall, sloped at the side, left for drainage. It's not there now, but it was there then. I have the pictures from my uncle's camera taken two weeks before Beth went. I was thinking how I'd do it. Broad daylight and a body to get rid of.'

'The police went through all this,' said Dad a tension in his throat.

'Until Beth supposedly texted and everybody stood down. You found her things in your bedroom, Ivan. We have been manipulated as much as you.

'So how would I do it?' Drew got up and started pacing. 'Let's say I've met Beth on that road, some altercation, I hit her,

she's unconscious. What do I do? Leave the body there where
it will be seen? Strangle her, that's quick, not difficult. Then I
have a body. I remember the trolley. So I need to hide her until
I can get the trolley. So I roll her to the side of the ditch, drag
her along a little so there's tall grass between her and the road,
not the flattened grass that I'd created by dragging her. Then
I'd take the wedding ring, the engagement ring, the necklace.
Her purse, a plan is forming. Maybe later, when it's dark, when
nobody is looking for her, I get the trolley, put it in the ditch
and roll her onto it. You can see from the pictures that the
ditch is sloped at the end, easy to drag the trolley back up. I
figured it would take somebody about seven minutes to get the
trolley loaded and through the gate, behind the wall. Once on
Melissa's path nobody has a chance of seeing you. Risky, but
it's a quiet road on a Thursday. They could leave the body there,
move it later, maybe after dark, and they return the wedding ring,
the necklace etc to the house, pick up her passport, a few clothes,
dispose of them. And you thought she had rejected you all. The
text messages, they were cruel. It was humiliating so, like a
true Melvick, it was brushed under the carpet and not spoken
about.'

'No, nobody could do that, spur of the moment.'

'Who said it was spur of the moment. There's a cunning mind
at work here. Look at the big picture. Look at Beth. Look at
Carla. The dog that had its throat cut . . .'

'Marcie,' I mumbled.

'Marcie, maybe one person was responsible for it all,' said
Drew quietly, looking at us all.

'Don't be daft,' said Heather. 'You've been watching too much
Agatha—'

'Maybe, but she always names the guilty party. Usually in a
room like this, I think,' Drew said.

'So why are we all here? Is somebody going to confess?'
asked Dr Scobie.

'I think you should confess that you all had your reasons:
Megan? Beth constantly chose Melissa over you. She was never
really in your corner; she sided with Melissa who was always
so much more . . .'

'Demanding,' I said.

'Appealing,' Drew retorted.

The door opened and Deborah came in, placing another pot of coffee on the table.

'Deborah, would you say Melissa was more appealing than Megan?' asked Drew.

'Nope,' said Deborah, shooting a look at my father. 'They were different. You can't choose one child over another.'

I thought it odd, the way she phrased it. I wondered if she and Drew were up to something, the way she had been sent in with the coffee.

'Tom? Beth had put you in jail for something that certainly was not your fault but something had to be done. Heather, had you started coveting your friend's life, her husband, her daughter?'

'I had not.'

'Yes, you had. It was right up your street for Beth to go away over the horizon and give you a shoe in. And Donald Scobie, the Melvicks asked for your help with Melissa and with Megan. Beth didn't share the friendship her husband had with you. She didn't like the way you had failed to help Melissa. She was the one who took them away from treatment and you were the one who bene-fitted, financially, when they came back. And Deborah, did you blame her for the death of your daughter? And then you suffered the indignity of them having the Melvicks help you out, all being lovely. But that must have hurt.'

'Or,' said Deborah, with a sigh, 'maybe I was grateful for the chance to live here, near where my daughter died, with people who knew her.' She shrugged. 'I like being here.'

'Yes, I know you do,' said Heather, a concise bite to her voice.

'I get paid to be here,' Deborah snapped, moving her fingers as if she was flicking ash from her jeans.

I noticed she didn't have her Ugg boots on.

'Look, Carla was my daughter too,' said Tom, hands out. 'I had no truck with the Melvicks, I know what they did. I was guilty of what I was found guilty of. If I had been looking after the petrol as closely as I should have done, then Carla would still be alive. If I had stored the gas canisters properly and locked the boathouse, the explosion would not have happened. Whoever did what they did, they succeeded in killing my daughter because I turned my back.'

'And now that you have had five years to think about it, who do you think tampered with the petrol that day? Who went into the boathouse?'

'I have thought it through, again and again. I don't know.'

Drew nodded as if this was the answer he expected. 'We did find a lighter?'

'Debs?' said Tom.

'Yes, it was mine, I was down there. The cops gave me it back.'

'Why?'

'Because it was not important.'

'No, why were you down there?'

It was Tom who answered. 'She had come down to say that Carla was fucking it up as a bridesmaid, and she was to behave. Debs thought she had the chance of a job here.'

'I never said that.'

'Norma said you did.'

'Your ex-wife? Yeah, like she hung about, did she?' I saw the side of Deborah's mouth twitch. 'The minute you were arrested, she was off.'

'Why was Carla a bridesmaid anyway, Ivan?'

He shrugged. 'It was one of those decisions.'

'To help,' said Heather, 'in case Megan struggled with her hearing.'

'So Megan has her friend foisted on her on her sister's big day, sharing the glory of the bridesmaid and then that bridesmaid dies. What persuaded you to do that? What put that into your head, Ivan?'

Dad didn't answer, his eyes were full of fury.

'Was it the moment Carla came in through the front door, her and Megan looking like twins? How awful that must have been for you?'

'Obviously Megan was top of the list of killing Carla. She'd outstayed her welcome, Melissa felt that also. She was driven away so quickly after the incident. It was a full week before she could be interviewed. You had no idea where your daughter was, either of them were. Did you, Ivan? It must have crossed your mind that one of them might be culpable?'

'No, it didn't, but we all know Megan suffers from mental health issues.'

'Well documented Dissociative Identity Disorder,' added Donald Scobie, crossing his legs ready to pontificate.

Nobody said a word, but I could feel my cheeks burn.

'I thought we were here to talk about the death of my wife. If not . . .' My father stood up, as did Heather, ready to walk out.

'Sit down,' said Drew, with quiet authority.

They did.

'We had many ways we could address any issues we had with Carla, we are not savages,' explained Dad.

'Melissa was smashing up her bedroom and threatening to call off the wedding, she had a temper,' Drew said.

I was getting angry now. I had just buried my sister and had found my mother dead. 'Drew, Deborah had hurt her ankle, she couldn't walk.'

'Megan, you have to stop believing what people say. She claimed she had hurt her ankle,' Drew corrected me.

I ignored him. 'I went and got ice and came back, I think we would have noticed Melissa in her big white dress swanning around.'

'But you don't seem aware that she had changed outfit by then, it was dark, and she reappeared at the time of the carousel. She was in white for the first few turns, after that, when the fireworks started, she was unaccounted for. She was driven away in a navy blue trouser suit.'

'God, I had forgotten that. You are right.' I nodded. 'There was no sending away of the bride, the explosion had happened by then.'

'Why would she harm Carla? She would be free of her. She was moving to London anyway.'

'Because Jago is a bed-hopping, faithless little man who likes his flesh young, younger than Melissa was on her wedding day. That is the kind of man you let marry into your family, Mr Melvick. If you hadn't been blinded by his money, you might have noticed. The question is, did Melissa know? Jago's not going to say, is he? And it was only by good fortune, if it was good fortune, that Deborah sent you away for ice, Megan, otherwise you may have been in that boat with Carla. Except . . .' He slid four photographs on the table, we all looked as he handed them out. To me, to Tom, to Dad and then to Deborah. It showed an old fat man, obviously dead, sitting up in bed, his glasses askew on his nose, a case number printed on the top right corner, the name Bernard Long handwritten in black capitals.

Heather gasped and pulled away, not able to look at it.

'Who is this?' asked my father. We all looked round.

Deborah didn't appear to move, it was an effortless glide up towards the door muttering something about having had enough and going for some fresh air.

Drew caught her by the wrist, and as quick as a flash she bit him, and he let go, squealing. She was out the open window and away. Both Ivan and Tom got up.

'Leave her.' Drew shook his head, shaking his hand. He held up a finger. We heard the barking of a dog, then some extreme language. Drew walked over and closed the window, silencing the commotion outside. 'We had a police dog on site. I hoped she would do that, I didn't want to tackle her in here, God she has sharp teeth. I'll need a tetanus on that. She'll have money and clothes stashed somewhere on the estate, no doubt. Mr Melvick, you invited more than one devil into your house, neither of them were Carla.'

'Sorry?' Dad shook his head. He got to his feet then Heather placed a hand on his knee, almost begging him to sit down.

'Megan, pour us some more coffee.'

'She was so good to me,' I said. 'I liked her.'

'Of course you did, she went out of her way to get you to like her.' Drew talked, we sipped the coffee and I looked at the photographs. 'Her mother, Aileen Sullivan died in rather odd circumstances, dead in the bath. She had fallen asleep and drowned, wee Deborah was downstairs at the time, the only other person in the house. It makes you think.'

'She's a black widow?' asked Heather, shivering.

'She's a something. We are opening the investigations into the death of her son, Paul. Of Andrew McColl a man she lived with until he was found with the back of his head smashed in.' He pointed to a photograph of a vanilla wall with a broad crimson smear tapering down to a slumped bloodied figure on the carpet. 'And of this poor man Bernard Long.' He tapped at the photograph of the old man, sitting up in bed. 'She did an angel of death job on him. There are others, other men she drew into her net, picked clean then disposed of. She got close to people then killed them. But she had to keep Carla alive because of you, Tom, you would notice if that particular little albatross around her neck suddenly turned up dead. Carla was only sacrificed because there was a greater prize on the table, namely Megan. Because Ivan Melvick would have nothing to do with Debs while Carla or Beth was on the scene. She must have thought all her Sundays were coming at once when Melissa removed herself from the picture. And Debs fancied the Melvick money, don't get me wrong. It was the money, and there was Megan. Her own little project.'

'That's total nonsense.' Dad looked as though he was keen to leave, but the right thing to do was to stay.

'Is it? Just think of all that she had here. Debs came here just as Carla was getting her foot in the door, and Deb's saw the way the wind was blowing. Carla was growing, she'd soon cease to be of financial benefit to her mother, or her father. Carla was easy to dispose of when Debs had the chance of getting her hands on all this, she only had to get rid of your wife. She knew Melissa was getting married and would move away. Then remember, Melissa came back, ill, and Deb moved in to nurse her, that was moving a fly onto the web. And then, the bonus of little Megan coming back, and there's Debs, all supportive, getting a job here, being meek and mild. Befriending Megan, I saw it with my own eyes. Tell me, Mr Melvick, she was an attractive woman, was your relationship with her always professional?'

Heather rolled her eyes.

And then I got a whiff of her perfume, the perfume that Deb stole, that hung around in the bedroom Dad slept in. Deborah.

'You should all hang your heads in shame, you were all so busy with your own importance, and you didn't see what was going on under your nose.' He held up a photograph for us all to see. I didn't recognize it at first. It was Carla, much younger, much thinner, lying in a hospital bed, covered in bruises, tubes going in and out.

'Bloody hell.' That was Tom.

'Yes, that's what I don't get. I bet that you all deluded your-selves about Carla, well I think it is more true that none of you had the compassion or the empathy to realize that this was going on. This wee kid who was in all your lives yet, you all missed the abuse, the bruises, the broken arms, the fact she was dragged out the hospital with pneumonia, with a severe head injury. She was abused by her mother's boyfriends. Her behaviour was appalling, and you didn't question why. None of you. Even the professional here. You must have seen her, heard the story. You've been a friend of the family, did Beth never mention Megan's strange little friend.' He looked at Dr Scobie. 'And why was that, because she wasn't worth your time or your attention? Too busy pampering the privileged offspring of a rich man to have any humanitarian concern for a kid who was really vulnerable? Shame on you, shame on you all.

'So I will leave you with that. You deserve all that's coming to you.'

And with that, he walked out.

The drawing room door slammed behind him, then the louder bang of the front door. There were voices raised outside.

'Oh dear,' said my dad. 'There is truth in what he says.'

'I'll pour us that coffee,' said Heather, her smile rather fragile.

Carla

There were no young men around for me to mess about with, the cops knew where to find me at the weekend that last winter, pissed on Thunderbird and cider, if I was lucky some vodka. I had a reputation as a cheap tart and an easy screw, but I always made them pay for it and I put the money away for a rainy day that never came as I never realized how much it was pissing down on me all the time. What I really should have been saving for was my day when the sun shone.

In the summer something changed. I was in trouble again, this time they were talking about a residential care order and Dad had taken me to the Italian House where he was working. We had driven up north, I was nursing a huge hangover and was in my bed all day. But the next day, he had to pop into work and then I saw the gates, the garden, the lake, the trees that dipped their leaves in the water like fingers off a rowing boat. I had never seen anything so beautiful, or smelled air so clear. My dad let me climb on the wall at the gate and pointed.

That was the first time I saw the Italian House. I think I had heard about it and the folk that live there with their good manners and good morals.

Ivan, he was called Ivan Melvick, he was a handsome man, getting more handsome as he got greyer. I had seen him around, he was blond now going grey, hair slightly long, a romantic, and I thought he was a man who might save me.

But he couldn't.

I know who did it. I think Megan knows but, not only does she not hear what she doesn't want to hear, she also does not see what she doesn't want to see. Everybody forgets the hired help, they are invisible to the Melvicks, scuttling around under their feet, making dinners and doing the laundry. In the older original parts of the house there are tunnels running behind the living accommodation, narrow corridors for the servants to run backwards and forwards so they didn't need to walk into the family while they were carrying dirty laundry to the utility room. The house had changed as the family had changed, some symbiotic evolution but the attitudes don't change. There was still a divide between them and us. Megan was one of them, *and I was very much one of* us.

Megan

'Deborah's been taken away,' said Dad. 'Thank God, what a disturbed woman.' The words came out Dad's mouth but he didn't look like he understood what he was saying, he was trying to reconcile the Deborah he knew as the helpful carer with her as a killer. 'Thank you for your help on this, DS Murray, I realize now that your attentions have been part of some operation. I really thought you were here to look out for my wife, you knew about Deborah, didn't you? You took advantage of me.'

'We knew about her past. But I am not finished here. Can I have a quiet word? In the study? With you and Megan?'

And so the three of us walked to the library, Drew leading the way, carrying his file in his arm.

'That was harrowing,' I said, pulling my legs underneath me as I sat on the wing-backed chair. 'I really don't understand it.'

'You will go mad trying. So don't.'

'Go mad, or go madder?' asked my father.

'Inbreeding.' Drew seemed to pause until my father, my quiet acquiescent father, got himself comfortable in his chair on the other side of the fireplace. 'Have you been out to the Benbrae, all the way round?'

'Nope, I've never been down that way, that was more Melissa's thing. She told me she made a path round there with her constant running.'

Drew nodded. 'It's all overgrown now. That's what sparked the idea of Beth being moved, it's hidden. And the items she left were left in the house which pointed to somebody *in* the house. Have you ever been down to the tree? I know you saw it on Friday.'

My father said nothing.

'I think you should tell her, Ivan.'

I noticed the Ivan. My dad and Drew stared at each other for a long time.

It was my father who looked away first. 'Do you remember being a wee girl, Megan, me picking you up and taking you away from the old oak, down at the Tentor Wood?'

'Vaguely.' I had a flash of something, gone before it could register. 'I thought you were laughing.'

'I was crying. My father had just killed himself, Papa. On your fourth birthday.'

'I don't remember much, just that it was my birthday. I saw the tree swing, it made a creaking noise, and then . . . Then I saw Papa step forward. It was like he stepped forward to walk on the water. And then there was the awful noise.' I closed my eyes, thinking. 'I saw you there, Dad, you were there watching him. You didn't try and stop him, you let him kill himself. Or did you help him? You could have put your hand out and stopped it. Why didn't you?'

'Yes, why did you not do that, Mr Melvick?' asked Drew.

Ivan pursed his lips, getting his stiff upper lip ready. 'Why do you think? I did it because he was my father.'

'You were crying, Dad, I thought at the time that you were laughing because Papa was dancing. But you were crying.'

'Mr Murray, can I . . .'

'DS Murray, abetting suicide is a crime, Mr Melvick. I am sure you know that.'

'There's no evidence, no witness and you're not getting any help from me.'

'But Megan only has a vague memory of it.'

Both men looked at me, Drew's eyes were cool and blue, Dad's eyes pleading with me.

'With the lapse of time and Megan's struggles with her mental health in the past, nobody will believe her.' Dad was dismissive.

'I think they will when they realize that your actions and the cause of her mental health issues are one and the same. We believe it's the trauma of what she witnessed that led her to choose to isolate herself from the world. And then her elder sister, knowing the family's dark secret taunted her with it. It was cruel, Mr Melvick, cruel. And you didn't stop it.'

'I didn't know . . .'

'Is no defence in law.' Drew stood up. 'At the moment, I am taking the view that this is a family matter. So I will leave you and your daughter to discuss it.' He turned to me. 'I will be outside if you want me, Megan.' He then turned to Dad and bowed his head slightly. 'Sir.'

'No, DS Murray, Drew, please stay. You seem to have a clear head, and we could do with that right now.' Dad looked up at the Munnings.

'Dad, I don't I think I do have a memory of it all. Not all of it. I have bits here and there but mostly I have noises and then silence, an image of your arm reaching out. It could have been anybody's arm, there for any reason.'

Dad smiled. 'You were always my bright girl, Megan. You worried me so much more than Melissa. Her anxiety was worse but you were self-contained, quiet. You were very close to Papa and even at the age you were, you started to notice when he was struggling a little, confusing you and Melissa, confusing Melissa and your mother. Not just getting the names wrong but confusing them totally and then telling us that Gran was out with the girls at the flower arranging club.'

'She had died years before I was born?'

'Three years before you were born to be exact. Then he wouldn't eat his dinner because he was waiting for his mum to

come and pick him up, and he would get into trouble if he ate
before supper.'

'I thought he was funny. Dementia?'

'I suppose so. Looking back, it has been in the family for
many years. There is madness in this family.'

'But you are not mad, Ivan Melvick. I bet all kinds of things
have been happening to you, losing things, misplacing things.
Megan told me,' said Drew.

'I have been, I know I have been. No point in denying it.'

'You said so in the study that night but I doubt it. I wouldn't
take heed of anything that was reported by Deborah, anything
that could be engineered by Deborah. She was around the house
when the dog had its throat slit, just because she went out the
door and said goodbye, doesn't mean she left the premises.'

'But she discovered the pan burned out and put the gas off.'

'Only because she put the gas on herself. She's a highly
manipulative psychopath.'

'But she was so believable. I bought into that madness, from
years of inbreeding before. I don't doubt it exists. I thought I
had escaped it, I hoped that you and Melissa had escaped it as
well but then Melissa started to be a bit' – he searched for the
word – 'peculiar. And then you'd bang your head at loud noises,
punch yourself on the ears. Melissa went strange at fifteen or so;
you didn't even make it to five.' He dropped his head into his
hands, looking for some absolution. 'I cannot tell you how bad
I felt when the explosion happened at Melissa's wedding.'

'We all felt bad.'

'I know, Megan, I know. I was there, I heard it. Tom was very
upset by it, so was Beth but Deborah wasn't. Looking back.
Hindsight is always twenty twenty.' He sighed. 'I was worried
about the madness that lay within this family and I had no idea
of the sheer lunacy that walked in through the door. And I
welcomed it in.'

'She was a very clever woman, a survivor, don't forget that.'

'Maybe if she had lived a different life, had a different start,
she may have gone on to live a different, better life.'

Drew placed his fingertips on his chin, thinking. 'As Carla
would say, shite is shite by any other name. If you feel better
thinking that Deborah could have lived a different life then do

so, but she killed those closest to her; her mother, both her children, any man whose death could benefit her. And then she killed your wife. There's a lot of death in her wake.'

'But I must correct you on one thing, Drew. You see on that day I was trying to take my father down from the tree, take the pressure off from his neck in much the same way as you did for me. I was reaching for him, trying to pull him back to the bank and to safety when I heard a noise. I doubted that I heard it, my father was gurgling and wheezy, he had let out this awful yowl, but I did hear a splash out there through the grass and the trees. I saw a flash of white and blue, splashes. There was a grunt.' He closed his eyes. 'And I saw Megan in the faerie pool. We had left her with Melissa up at the house, yet here she was. The dog was barking. The stories of the pools are true, a man can't get out, never mind a four-year-old child. So I made a decision. I let my father go. I rescued my daughter.

'I made the right decision. I did the right thing.'

Carla

Ivan was doing his being brave impersonation. It was a lot to take in, a woman he had trusted and befriended was the killer of his wife. He had sacrificed his father for his daughter.

There were a lot of secrets still to come out.

I had never lost faith in Megan, not the way he had and now he felt awful. He was sitting at his desk, his fingers entwined round a cup of coffee, thinking about Beth, what had happened to her. What Deborah, my mother, had put him and his children through and maybe, I hoped a little, that he saved some of those memories for me, her only daughter, the cheeky one with the blue hair, the girl he used to pick up to help her finish her paper round, way back in the day when our families were connected merely by the fact that my dad worked for him, nothing more than that. And somehow we got sucked in, the cancer of my family spread through to his, killing as it went. The cancer was called Deborah and she hid in plain sight.

TWENTY-THREE
Tuesday

Megan

The sun was setting.

Drew was poking around the remains of the mosaic with the toe of his trainer, dressed in a white linen shirt that was open outside the belt of his old jeans. Whatever he was here for it wasn't work, but it was nice to see him, nice of him to come along when most of the villagers were probably too scared to come near the place in case the bad luck we had was catching. He bent down, picked up a piece of yellow tile, shattered jaggy edges at odds with the fine patterns of veining still present on the top surface. He looked up, still holding the yellow fragment, and he gazed out over the flat calm water of the Benbrae to the weeping willows and beyond, then back to the yellow tile in his hand.

'Please don't.'

He turned, looking at me with his huge blue eyes, alarmed at my tone.

'Sorry, I thought you were going to skim it, the way you were holding it and looking.'

He raised an eyebrow. 'It's part of Carla's memorial, I wouldn't throw it in the water.'

'It would be much worse than that. My dad holds the Melvick family record, seven bounces. He takes it very seriously. If you challenge him, he will ask you for a duel at dawn.'

He turned away and muttered something under his breath that might have been, Wouldn't bloody surprise me.

'Here, I think that bit you have fits in there' – I pointed to an indentation in the concrete – 'yes, then that bit and that bit.' I pointed to another.

He looked up at me from his position near the ground. 'You

really are good at getting other people to do stuff for you, aren't you? Do you have an inherited chromosome for that?'

'Probably. For them to be them, there always has to be an us.'

But he reached out and moved one piece of tile against another, a full yellow leaf of sunflower appeared, a sliver of brown centre. I looked around for any fragments that might hold the green of a stalk.

'Why are you here? It doesn't seem like you're at work, not dressed like that.'

'I like you, Megan, why should I not come here?'

'We are cursed.'

'Are you?' He stood up, playing with a small piece of tile, flicking it around the palm of his hand. 'I wanted to run something past you. Something that's been on my mind.'

'Oh God, not again.'

'Hear me out. Does it not strike you as odd? The parents don't notice, the doctor doesn't notice, the nurses don't, but at four years old, they realize there is a problem with your hearing. In the summer of 2003. And maybe nobody in your bloody family noticed that you couldn't hear because you could. Why do you have excellent language skills when, it's said, you were deaf right from birth? Because you weren't. Maybe you decided to be deaf because of what you heard that day in the Tentor Wood, and what you saw, your Papa. Maybe you have refused to listen to anything ever again unless you wanted to, it had to be your choice, none of this mandatory noise that goes on nowadays is of any interest to you.'

'Really?' I was almost laughing.

'You might not want to hear the rest.'

'You've started now.'

'You know how most people think, wrongly, that schizophrenia is multiple personalities living in one's head?'

'I am not schizophrenic, Dr Scobie says so. It's DID. That can come from childhood trauma. When you started talking there I thought that was what you were going to say, I got my DID in the Tentor Wood. Maybe my hysterical deafness as well. Who cares? It is what it is and it is in the past.'

Drew was not to be put off. 'Dr Donald Scobie? He's a good friend of your dad's. All he did was keep an eye on you and turn up at any time you got yourself into trouble. He played the mental illness diagnosis and you got a get out of jail free card. That was one of the perks of being a Melvick, but I'm not sure how much good that did you. Maybe your dad was worried that if Melissa had moved beyond all medical help then maybe keeping a close eye on you might work better. So no, you are not schizophrenic, schizoids suffer a breakdown of the solid state personality that one person should have, the default setting if you will.'

I found a piece of green stalk and handed it to him. 'I am following you so far.'

He laid the piece down, it didn't fit. 'The solid state hard drive is the normal state of being. The computer model is a useful way of explaining it, the hard drive runs off the most obvious and observable programme but sometimes . . .' He looked at me, then went back to the jigsaw on the ground. 'Sometimes there is another programme running in the background while the main programme, our personality, deals with the important issues of the day. The other is in the background, co-existing, often in a role that differs from that of the main personality, controlling certain aspects. But usually the main personality continues to do what it has always done, totally unaware of the other personality hobby horsing on it. But if that person lets their guard down or when the main programme is set to hibernate, the other person-ality comes out to play.' He placed a piece of stalk under the green, a tile of yellow and blue marked the start of the sky. He kept talking, his fingers working, feeling their way over the scattered remnants.

'Rogue personality, the second personality – the mosaic person-ality, if you will – has scattered actions, spots there and here, seemingly at random in such a way that the whole picture cannot be seen. It's only when the entire is seen from a distance that we see which personality is in control at any time, and that is why' – he tilted his head, taking a different view of the sunflower – 'that it is why it's called the mosaic personality disorder.'

'It kind of fits,' is all I could say, my eyes fixed on the sunflower jigsaw, how small the pieces were, how big the picture. 'We loved our sunflowers . . .'

'It fits exactly, you had one personality hidden in behind yours, and I think you can guess what that was. Whose that was?'

I thought of the night Jago had accused me of trying to

sleep with him, of the night Debs was scratched on the face.
'Carla?'

'Yes of course, Carla.' He waited a while for that to sink in.
'I have been reading that file. You and Carla were together for
some very difficult years. And she died. You witnessed that. She
was burned alive in front of you and at some point along the
way, some of that slipped into your psyche. You wanted to find
out who did it to her. She wanted you to find out who did that
to her. Yet you knew, you had been told often enough that she
might not have been the intended victim, it might have been you.
The guilt of that was not an easy burden to bear.'

I nodded, seeing a big piece of sky and a cloud. I handed it
to him, our fingers touched for a moment.

'I think it's fair to say that Carla was many things that you
are not.'

'That is true, so true.'

'So there can be a degree of unity, if you will, you know when
the two characters come together, each uses the strength of the
other.'

'It completes the picture.'

'Indeed.'

'Except I think I would have known if that was going on, I
was—'

'Oh you were totally aware of what you were doing in daylight
hours, but what about at night, or when you were overtired, or
drugged, or lying down during the day thinking about Melissa
or lying out here in the Benbrae. Those times you said to me
that you liked to relax and let time drift. Those times when you
nipped along to Jago's room, hitting Debs on the head, what was
all that about? All those times you were lying to yourself.' But
he was smiling. 'Well there's nothing like another voice in your
head for breeding a sense of paranoia.'

I pulled my cardigan round me, watching the *Curlew 2* on the
water, floating, tugging on her mooring, a trout jumped, a flash
of white and a splash, then nothing, gone before you saw it.
More than a chill hung in the air, I felt death crawl over my soul.
I felt Carla. 'She loved it here.'

'Why would anybody not love it here? She was born in a
shithouse over in Dunoon somewhere. Of course she loved it

here and she loved you, she made you strong and you made her
stable, I bet you have never really felt that she left you at all.'
    'Not until recently, very recently, I feel she has gone now.'
    'Dr Scobie said that when you came here you spoke of her in
the present tense. In your head, she is still very much alive.'
    'When I came back, it was as if I was coming home and that
Carla would still be here. And I was looking forward to it.'
    Drew dropped his voice. 'Yet you didn't feel that way about
Melissa?'
    'No. She was . . . well, Melissa was always somewhere else, so
there was no point in missing her when she was gone, was there?'
    'Dr Scobie thinks that if you go into a clinic, for a period of
time, away from us and this place, then you can have treatment.
You can get rid of Carla. He thinks that will make you well.
According to him, she has to go.'
    I smiled, holding the shard of tile in my hand. I felt the sharp
edge on the skin of my thumb, a sharp cutting edge.
    Drew suddenly stood up, facing me. 'Carla has to learn the world
is not against her.' He took the tile and placed it on the ground.
'She is still very much part of the picture. Don't let her forget that,
Megan. Never let her forget that.'

Carla

*My memories of this grand house and the people who live here
are as strong as the colour in the Munnings in the study. Even
though I was only ever a fleeting visitor, a voyeur on the Melvicks,
I can sense every aspect of those memories. Overall, good times,
the happiest and safest of my life and I am never going to leave.
I can scent the pine in the air, the breath of the breeze on my
cheek, the brackish water that I can still taste on my tongue. The
sweet smell of the ponies' coats, the hay, the constant pitter patter
of a dog two feet behind me. And the feel of the* Curlew *under
my back, her soft warm wood that smelled vaguely of varnish,
mahogany and sea water. And her movement, the gentle nudge
nudge of the waves on the Benbrae when the wind got up.
    I'm glad to be here.*

EPILOGUE

B y the following month the Benbrae had filled itself of water
and *Curlew 2* was back, bobbing around where and when
she pleased, nobody had bothered tethering her to the side
anymore as the boathouse and the pontoon had become totally
useless. Getting wet to go out and get a boat was neither here
nor there, so we left her as she was, free to float.

Deborah was held in custody awaiting trial. She was mounting
some kind of defence based on all the abuse she had suffered at
the hands of men. And I suppose some of that may be true but
as Carla had said, many a time, Deborah made her decisions and
she chose her men. How could one person create so much havoc
in one family, before easing her way into the house and the life
of a man of substance and morality? Was that what Deborah
really wanted all along? I had told Dad that the Melvicks were
going to stand up for their duty properly as the law dictated.

Dad looked at me as if I was a little mad. 'Do you not think
I know how to conduct myself in public?'

Deborah said that Dad was abusing her. Heather came to Dad's
defence on that one. Then Deborah had changed her story and
said that Dad had abused Melissa. She really was a first-class
liar with a scattergun approach, dirt doesn't stick though, not to
my father. I think he had no idea how other people wanted,
expected him, to behave and what we needed to do right now as
a family. And I think he was surprised that I did know.

There had been a change of responsibility. He was no longer
the man in the charge, the man with all the answers. He had
taken to asking me my opinion, and listening to my answers. He
had crumpled, and it had been very public. It was about to get
worse with the court case, Deborah had already said publicly
that she was going to reveal all about the goings on in the big
house, and that had caused a minor flurry of interest in the press,

but we had already been picked clean and there was nothing more to discover. I was Dad's rock now, and the Italian House was slowly closing its doors, building its wall around us. With this imprisonment, we had protection against the outside world and the circling wolves.

And Heather surprised me. I thought she would hang around, show my dad some of the friendship that she had shown my mother, but I was wrong. I should have trusted my first impressions. Heather dropped us like the proverbial hot stone and trotted off to her yoga class to tell her stories of her narrow escape from the hands of a serial killer while staying at the Italian House. She did turn up at the funeral, as my dad buried my mother, her best friend. Dad kissed her on the cheek, and gave her her place as the close family friend. He did the right thing. She had dabbed at her eye and made the most of her hostess duties at the funeral, in a very good suit and lots of make-up, then she quickly seems to have decided that my dad was too old for her and she buggered off to another gym class.

I could only think of how much Carla would have enjoyed smacking her right in the face.

After Mum's funeral, I sat on the front terrace with Drew, drinking a cup of tea and thinking about nothing. The house stood empty behind us, casting its shadow. But we had walked down to the Benbrae that morning, he had taken my hand and pointed out that the pond was filling up with water again. Some of the fish had survived, *Curlew 2* was a bit warped, the mosaic was being repaired, a monument to two people now. And the sun had focussed its rays on the far end of the Benbrae, the end under the Tentor Wood. It looked magical and inviting now.

I'd leave the faeries to their mischief.

And Carla is here.